Broken HEART

THE HEARTS OF SAWYERS BEND
BOOK SEVEN

IVY LAYNE

GINGER QUILL PRESS, LLC

Broken Heart

Editing by:
Samamntha Skal, samanthaskal.com
Julia Ganis, juliaedits.com
Olivia Zugay, storyflowsolutions.com

Find out more about the author and upcoming books online at www.ivylayne.com

Contents

Also by Ivy Layne

Don't Miss Out on New Releases, Exclusive Giveaways, and More!!

Join Ivy's Readers Group @ ivylayne.com/readers

THE HEARTS OF SAWYERS BEND

Stolen Heart

Sweet Heart

Scheming Heart

Rebel Heart

Wicked Heart

Wild Heart

Broken Heart

Reckless Heart

THE UNTANGLED SERIES

Unraveled

Undone

Uncovered

THE WINTERS SAGA

The Billionaire's Secret Heart (Novella)

The Billionaire's Secret Love (Novella)

The Billionaire's Pet

The Billionaire's Promise

The Rebel Billionaire

The Billionaire's Secret Kiss (Novella)

The Billionaire's Angel

Engaging the Billionaire

Compromising the Billionaire

The Counterfeit Billionaire

THE BILLIONAIRE CLUB

The Wedding Rescue

The Courtship Maneuver

The Temptation Trap

Chapter One

STERLING

"Give me the statue."

Forrest stared at me, his hazel eyes surprised, then carefully blank. "What?" he asked, shaking his head.

Of course, he was confused. After refusing to speak to him for over a year, I was standing on his doorstep just before midnight, demanding he hand over a priceless family heirloom.

"I need to see the statue," I clarified, impatient. "Let me in."

"What?"

Forrest still wasn't getting it. But why would he? He didn't know that the statue had been haunting me. Teasing me. Demanding I come here and see if I knew what I thought I knew.

For most of the last year, that ugly little statue of Emperor Vitellius had meant nothing to me. Nothing and everything. The statue was the reason for my broken heart. It was the reason Forrest Powell had come to

Sawyers Bend and taken a job at my family's inn. The reason he'd pursued me and made me think he loved me. The statue was the cause of all my heartbreak.

Except that it wasn't. Forrest Powell was the cause. He was the one who'd chosen to lie. He was the one who'd used me for his own ends. The statue of Vitellius was innocent. And while Forrest's secrets had broken me, the Vitellius held its own secrets. Secrets that might have the power to set me free.

Even after a year, the sting of his betrayal hadn't faded. I couldn't bring myself to look him in the eye. I stared carefully at his left ear and said, "I need to see the statue. Just let me in."

Without another word, Forrest stepped back to allow me through the door of his house. I'd never been here. He bought the place after I dumped him, putting down roots when I'd expected him to walk away. He had what he'd come for, after all.

It had been weird, not knowing where Forrest lived. Too many nights, I woke, dreaming of the statue of Vitellius, haunted by it. Until I'd hunted down Hawk, our head of security, and asked him for Forrest's address.

Hawk knew all; he had a file on Forrest. He gave it to me grudgingly and only after asking, "You sure you know what you're doing?"

"Nope," I'd answered. "But I need it anyway." Feeling the weight of his brotherly concern, I'd added, "It's about the statue. It's not personal. I promise."

He'd grunted and given me the address, saying only, "Be careful."

At the moment, I didn't care about careful; I just

wanted to see the statue. Following Forrest through the entry into the rest of the house, I had an impression of high ceilings, wood beams, and glass, but that was it. I didn't bother to look around. I couldn't risk letting my heart crack open even a little bit.

We came to a stop in his modern chrome and concrete kitchen, and I turned to face him, my eyes on the frayed collar of his T-shirt, ignoring the way it stretched over his broad shoulders. If I looked at him too closely, I'd be lost. Those dark, soft curls. Messy, as if he'd been running his hands through them. Cheekbones that would have made his face austere if not for his full lower lip and the golden warmth of his hazel eyes. I couldn't look at his face and not remember everything I wanted to forget.

"Why do you need to see the statue?" he asked.

"I can't explain until I look at it. I know it's late, but this is important." I could have waited for a better time. I could have come to see him in his office. But after months of that fucking statue teasing me, the answer had come to life the night before like a puzzle piece snapping into place. And I couldn't wait a second longer, no matter how much it hurt to be this close to him.

I could feel Forrest's eyes on my face, assessing me. "I'll get it," he finally agreed, turning to head for a hallway off the kitchen.

"Get a pad of paper and a pen. I forgot to grab one on the way out of the house," I said, yanking out a chair and sitting at the kitchen table, then popping back up, prowling around the room for the switch that would turn on the light above the table. "I need a light. Do you have a magnifying glass?" I called after him.

I sat back down, tapping my fingers on the table. I was so close to finding out if I was right. I needed to know, needed it enough to put myself through this pain. I'd lied when I said the sting hadn't faded. This wasn't a sting. Being this close to Forrest was fucking agony.

People say *time heals all wounds,* but it wasn't doing a fucking thing for this one. It was all my own fault, too. Not the breakup—that was one hundred percent Forrest's fault. His lies, and his stupid attempts to convince me that he'd made a mistake, that he cared about me. I wasn't falling for that bullshit again. Losing him the first time was bad enough, the ache in my chest a raw thing that never went away. Not that I could admit that. Like the perverse creature I could be, I'd convinced my brothers not to fire Forrest, setting myself up for the torture that was sharing the small town of Sawyers Bend with the man I never wanted to see again.

I took after my father, arrogance my failing. I was too proud to admit it was killing me, having Forrest this close. I could have changed my mind and asked my brothers to fire him. They would have done it gladly. I could have asked West, our police chief, to run Forrest out of town. West was notoriously by the book, but he might have done it for me if I'd asked.

But I wouldn't ask, couldn't ask. Everyone I loved had seen me at my worst; the whole goddamn town had seen me at my worst. Over and over. Now, I was clawing my way to my best, and I wasn't going to let a single person see my broken, bleeding heart. Especially not Forrest Powell.

I waited for him to come back with the statue, my heart speeding up in my chest. I needed to see it. I needed to know.

I hadn't thought about the statue at first. The shock of Forrest's lies had clouded everything. It had been hard enough just getting out of bed in the morning. I didn't have any room for wondering about the statue that had brought Forrest to me in the first place.

Later, after the worst of it became bearable, the statue began to invade my dreams. A rock crystal bust of Emperor Vitellius on a white marble base embellished with bronze medallions, the whole thing was only six inches tall. As a piece of art, it wasn't particularly valuable. More than that, the bust of Emperor Vitellius was straight-up ugly. The rock crystal carving was mostly transparent, giving him a ghostly look that wasn't enough to hide the petulant, whiny expression on his face.

As a child, Vitellius had reminded me of my father, Prentice. So much so that after my father had stolen the bust, I'd imagined he took it because the Vitellius reminded him of himself. Forrest's father had a kind smile, unlike Prentice. Back then, I hadn't known that my father hadn't just stolen the statue from Forrest's father, he'd taken his company as well. And Alan, distraught at the loss of everything he'd worked for, had taken his own life.

As a child, I'd only known that the Vitellius fascinated me. It was ugly. Graceless. But something about it had tugged at my mind. The Vitellius statue had secrets.

I'd hide behind the thick velvet drapes in my father's office to poke and prod at the statue, asking it in whispers to tell me its secrets. It hadn't.

Until one day, when the Vitellius had whispered back.

I didn't tell anyone what I'd learned—I knew what a secret was. And then the statue had disappeared. And, in the way of children, I'd forgotten about it. Until it had turned up a year ago, the linchpin of my failed romance.

Forrest had come to Sawyers Bend to find the statue and steal it back. He'd come to get revenge on the Sawyers for ruining his father's life. In the end, he hadn't done either. It hadn't taken Forrest long to figure out that my siblings and I were nothing like our father. And Forrest had ended up buying the little statue at auction, erasing the need to steal it back from my father. The Vitellius was his again.

I'd been the fallout.

Now, Forrest returned, setting the statue of Vitellius on the table in front of me, followed by a spiral-bound notebook open to a blank page. He placed a pen and a small magnifying glass beside it. "Are you going to tell me what you're doing here?" he asked.

I ignored him, picking up the Vitellius and turning it over so I could get a better look at the bottom of the marble base. I still couldn't see it, though Forrest had told us it was there. Picking up the small magnifying glass and turning on my phone's flashlight, I leaned in, squinting, willing my eyes to focus.

There they were: numbers and letters in a long string, engraved by laser. Neat, precise, and so tiny I'd never seen them before. The few people who knew about the string of numbers and letters thought it was an account number, but no one had been able to find the source of the account. According to Forrest, it was supposed to be stuffed full of cash. The promise of all that cash was the reason my father had stolen the Vitellius in the first place. And that cash was the reason I'd knocked on Forrest's door after all this time.

It was Forrest's money, but he couldn't find it without me. It wasn't an account number engraved on the bottom of the statue. It was a code. And I was the only one who knew how to break it.

Or at least I hoped that was the case. I could be completely off base. It wasn't like I was an expert, more like a closet math geek who had always loved the lore of secret codes. In high school, they'd fascinated me. By the time I was old enough to do something useful with that fascination, I'd been neck deep in rebellion, wasting my time drinking and chasing boys, my budding intellectual curiosity extinguished.

It had taken me years to come back to myself. Too many wasted years, leaving me in my mid-twenties with a college degree and a roof over my head but not much else. I was getting my shit together, piece by piece. I had a job. I thought I might have a plan for a career. But I was still pretty much a mess. And then I started dreaming of the Vitellius. I didn't know what it meant, thought it might be my broken heart dreaming of Forrest the only way it could bear.

But it turned out the dreams weren't about Forrest at all. They were my brain trying to remind me of the past and those stolen moments behind the heavy velvet curtains. The dreams were the Vitellius whispering the secret of the medallions to me one more time.

A few days ago, I woke in the middle of the night, my eyes flying open to stare at my ceiling, seeing everything at once. The numbers were a code, and I would have bet the little I had that I was the only one who knew the key.

Taking a deep breath, I let it out slowly, my mind racing. I'd needed to see those laser-engraved numbers and letters to know. And now that I had, I had a decision to make. A part of me wanted to trust Forrest, but... I'd done a lot of foolish things in my short life, far too many to count, but I wasn't a fool, and I wouldn't be one now.

Setting the Vitellius on its base, I leaned back in the chair and crossed my arms over my chest. "I know how to find the money," I said, steeling myself to meet his eyes. I expected to see greed or triumph, even disdain.

I wasn't expecting blank confusion. He looked like he hadn't even heard me.

"Forrest," I said, my tone sharp, snapping awareness back into his eyes. "I said I can find the money."

This time, he heard me. I expected him to laugh. Smarter people than myself had tried to find Alan Buckley's lost fortune. My own father had spent years trying to figure it out. An annoyingly familiar voice in my head asked, *Who am I to think I can do it?*

Instead, Forrest said, "I don't care about the money."

"Yeah?" I asked, raising an eyebrow. That had been his story when we found out why he was really in Sawyers Bend—he didn't care about the money, he just wanted me, blah blah blah. I hadn't bought it then, and I wasn't buying it now.

He'd already proven he was a liar. Forrest's father had hundreds of millions of dollars after he sold his first company, and he'd hidden it all. That could be over a billion by now.

I didn't care who you were—that was too much money to not care about. I'd grown up in a house that was practically a castle. These days, I was mostly broke, but after the way I grew up, I knew better than anyone that money couldn't buy happiness. Not even close. But it sure as hell didn't hurt.

Forrest leveled his hazel eyes on me, no trace of humor in his expression. "Chasing the money cost me enough. I don't care about it anymore."

"I do," I snapped.

No change in his expression.

I tried a different tack. "I'll find it for you. For a cut."

At that, he straightened, frozen for a second before the side of his mouth curled up, and he crossed his arms over his chest. "How big a cut?"

And there was the CFO my brothers had hired. After his dumb assertion that he didn't care about the money, I couldn't resist poking at him. "If you don't care about the money, how about I get all of it?"

The side of his mouth quirked higher, light sparking in his eyes. "I don't think so. You can't get the money without my statue, and technically, it's my inheritance."

"Well," I said, "since I'm pretty sure the inheritance my father left me is a big fat nothing, maybe the finder's fee on yours will make a nice nest egg. Fifty percent."

The grin disappeared from Forrest's face. "Ten." So much for not caring about the money.

"Forty-five," I countered.

"Fifteen."

I looked down at the Vitellius, then steeled myself for the impact and looked Forrest dead in the eye. My chest ached, a raw wound that stole my breath. Deep inside, I silently screamed, *Why? Why did you have to fuck everything up by being such an asshole?* And beneath that, the question I couldn't stop asking: *Why couldn't you love me?*

Fucking hell, it hurt to look at him. It took everything I had to hide my heart.

Maybe Forrest was right. Maybe the money wasn't worth what I'd lose chasing it. My self-respect. My sanity. I'd let this man bring me to my knees. I'd crawled out of a bottle after my father died and my oldest brother came home. I'd spent the last year getting my life together. Was I going to risk all that hard work just to fill my bank account?

The problem: it was only partly about the money. I had room and board covered, but not much more. I was working for my sister during the day and studying when I could, but that would take time to pay off. I was sure the trust my father had left me was empty. It would be five years before I'd find out, but knowing Prentice Sawyer as I had, I couldn't believe he'd left me a single penny. I wanted a nest egg. Security. I never wanted to ask anyone for anything ever again.

But more than the money, I wanted to solve the puzzle. I needed to solve it. For months, the Vitellius had been haunting me until I finally understood the secret of the statue and the dancing medallions. I could do this. I wanted to solve what no one else could. I wanted to beat my father and walk away laughing, my bank account stuffed full.

Would it be worth it? To be this close to Forrest, to feel this stabbing agony every time I was stupid enough to look him in the eyes? Definitely not for fifteen percent. But maybe...

I shoved my chair back from the kitchen table and stood. "Twenty-five. I have better things to do with my time than negotiate with you. Twenty-five percent, or I'm walking out the door."

Chapter Two

FORREST

I would have agreed to a hundred percent.

When I opened the door and saw Sterling standing there, I would have agreed to anything. In the year since I'd finally told her the truth about who I was and why I'd come to Sawyers Bend, she hadn't spoken a word to me. She wouldn't look at me, wouldn't acknowledge my existence. And now here she was, on my doorstep.

If she'd asked me straight out, I would have given her everything. But by the time she made it into my kitchen, I remembered this was Sterling Sawyer I was dealing with, and I had to be a lot smarter than just giving her whatever she asked for.

I'd tried throwing my heart at her feet. She'd kicked it back to me with a furious glare.

I got it. I did. I'd lied.

I'd lied a lot. Over and over.

Not about being in love with her. Not about how I felt or what I wanted. But I'd lied about who I was, why I was there, why I'd asked her out the first time. Those kinds of lies hadn't mattered when I'd first met her. I'd underestimated her, just like everyone else did. And by the time I realized how badly I'd fucked up, how much she meant to me, I was out of time.

I'd planned to tell her the truth. I was going to do it, I just... I was waiting for the right time. And then fucking Elliot Hall and the Learys had shown up, and I couldn't lie any longer.

I got the statue back, but I lost Sterling.

Now, I wasn't lying when I said I didn't care about the money.

I mean, yeah, I guess I was a little because it was money, and it really helped to do things like pay the bills and put a roof over my head. After my father died, my mother worked hard, but times were tough. My father's fortune would have come in handy. But those years were behind us. My mom was good. I was better than good. I'd worked my ass off, and while I wasn't the genius that my father had been, I'd inherited enough of his brains to land myself some pretty good opportunities.

I wasn't a billionaire, but I had enough in the bank to honestly say that if it was a contest between my father's mysterious fortune and Sterling, I'd pick Sterling any day.

The second I'd said I didn't care about the money, I saw the dismissal on her face. She wouldn't even look at me. It didn't matter if it was true—telling her I didn't care about the money was a waste of time. She didn't believe me. And why should she, when I'd told her so many lies already?

So, I did what I was born to do. I negotiated. Maybe someday I'd win her trust back, but I couldn't do that unless I could get her to spend time with me. When she shoved her chair back and stood, I thought for a minute that I'd pushed too far, that I'd lost before we had a chance to start again. But she hadn't walked out. She'd come at me with a reasonable solution. Twenty-five percent was the perfect compromise. Enough that Sterling felt she'd won something and low enough that she'd believe I cared about the money, which was the only thing she was willing to believe.

I didn't care about the money, but I was curious to know how Sterling was going to find it. Plenty of people had puzzled over those numbers, and so far, no one had found a damn thing. If Sterling said she knew the answer, I believed her. People had been underestimating Sterling Sawyer for her entire life. At first, I'd been one of them. I knew better now.

I paused as if I was considering her offer of twenty-five percent. I couldn't let her think I'd caved too easily. "Agreed," I said.

Sterling sat back down at the table, pulled the spiral-bound notebook and pen toward her, and began to write. I made out the date and the beginning of a sentence before she scribbled it out and started over on a fresh sheet. I waited, growing more curious by the second.

Finally, she said, "Read this. I'm not a lawyer, but it should be good enough. If I find the money, I get twenty-five percent of what's in the account. If it leads to multiple accounts, I get twenty-five percent of the total. If it leads to a combination of cash, securities, or other goods, I get twenty-five percent of the total value."

I read through what she had written up, signed, and pushed it back to her with the pen. Sterling signed and took a picture of the contract with her phone. Business concluded, she pushed her phone aside and picked up the little statue of Vitellius.

"You know the key to break the code," I guessed.

Her eyes flashed up to me, and for just a second, I caught the real Sterling through the guarded mask she wore. There she was, so alive, that sharp brain firing behind eyes so blue they made the summer sky seem faded. It was a Sterling I'd only caught sight of in our last days together a year ago, a Sterling I longed for.

A heartbeat later, the mask came down like blinds dropping, and her eyes flicked back to the statue. "Mhm," she said.

Confirmation? Denial? I couldn't tell.

She picked up the statue, turning it in her hands. Gently, she set it down on its base and pressed her thumbs to the edges of one of the brass medallions. I wasn't expecting to see it turn a quarter rotation and quietly click into a new position. I stared down at the statue. I'd handled that thing for more hours than I could count, wondering what the hell my father had been up to, what he wanted me to see, and I'd never felt the medallions move.

Sterling turned the statue, staring at it, lost in thought, reaching slowly before her fingers settled against the next brass medallion, and she turned it in the opposite direction. This time, it rotated halfway around before clicking into place. The third medallion turned almost all the way around before I heard the click. The final medallion didn't turn at all.

With a single press of Sterling's finger, that medallion sank several millimeters into the base before popping open like a tiny door. Sterling ignored my indrawn breath. I didn't know what I expected to see inside. A secret compartment, maybe? But the marble behind the medallion was indented only slightly, revealing more numbers and letters, these far bigger than those engraved on the base. The alphanumeric string was arranged above and below a line, like the longest fraction I'd ever seen.

Sterling grabbed the spiral-bound notebook and roughly turned from our signed contract to a fresh page. Picking up the pen, she copied the long fraction onto the top of the page. Once she had it, she closed the medallion, picked up the statue, and looked at me, her eyes on my shoulder, avoiding mine.

"Hold this up so I can see the base," she ordered.

I did, holding the statue under the light while she used the small magnifying glass and painstakingly copied the alphanumeric string onto the pad in front of her. Whatever she was looking for, I didn't see it. A massive fraction that couldn't be a fraction. A long string of numbers and letters that wasn't an account number. But Sterling very clearly knew exactly what it was.

I watched in fascination as her teeth bit into her perfectly curved pink lip, her eyes flicking back and forth, the pen moving up and down, drawing lines in the air above the paper. Tapping one number, then a letter. Matching. Scribbling something out. Shaking her head.

Crossing it out with slashes of dark blue ink and trying again. More scratching out.

Sterling let out a huff of breath, the pen bobbing up and down in her fingers as she stared at the mess of numbers and notes in front of her. What did she see that I didn't see?

I had no doubt that she was on to something. There was a lot more to Sterling than most people guessed. She was the most beautiful woman I'd ever met. It was the eyes that got me first. So alive, like blue flame. Every inch of her body was perfection, her hair long, golden waves, her soft skin glowing with warmth even in the winter. She had dazzled me at first sight so much that I'd missed the rest—how intelligent she was and funny, sometimes veering into brash. How deeply she loved. And I hadn't known until far too late that she was wounded and vulnerable and not nearly as guarded against a man like me as I'd assumed she would be.

According to Sterling, she'd partied her way through a handful of different colleges before finally graduating. But when she graduated, it had been with a math degree. That wasn't the only reason I believed she could unravel the mess on the page in front of her. Sterling wouldn't be here unless she was damn sure that being near me would be worth the payoff.

For over a year, she'd avoided me like the plague. I hadn't crowded her, but I'd been around. Working at the inn every day with her brothers. Sitting outside her hospital room when she had a head injury. Helping to board up the windows when her sister's business was broken into a few months ago. Through all of it, Sterling had acted like I didn't exist. If she was sitting at my kitchen table, it was because she was absolutely positive she was going to succeed.

I watched her study the page, trying to figure out what she was looking for. I knew my way around numbers. I was the Chief Financial Officer of the Inn at Sawyers Bend. Numbers were my job, but this was not the kind of math I knew, if it was math at all.

Sterling scratched out another set of scribbles and sat back, closing her eyes. She took a deep breath, letting it out in a gust as she lurched forward, dropping the pen. She flipped the notebook around so the giant fraction she'd transcribed from the secret panel was at the bottom of the page and the alphanumeric string from the base was at the middle of the page, both upside down.

Head to the side, eyes narrowed on the page, Sterling pulled her lip between her teeth, biting down so hard I wanted to protest. But Sterling's lip wasn't any of my business anymore, so I kept my mouth shut. A second later, she sucked in a sharp breath, bounced in her seat, and tore off the page. Flipping the notebook back around, she started again, this time transposing the fraction she'd found behind the secret panel so the bottom line was now on the top. She copied the alphanumeric string from the base below the rearranged fraction, her eyes popping back and forth.

It still didn't make sense to me, but Sterling snatched up the pen and began to write. "Holy fucking shit," she whispered to herself, the pen moving faster. She lifted her face to mine, her eyes bright and glowing with triumph. "Holy fucking shit, Forrest. Do you see this?"

I didn't. Not at first. She slashed out with the pen, dividing the long string of letters and numbers into sections, and I saw it: *East Eagle. 1523. KCUB. B42001.*

"Is that an address?" Sterling asked. "East Eagle? It sounds like a street name." She looked at me, expectant, and the words teased at the back of my brain.

East Eagle. She was right. It did sound like a street. And more than that, it sounded familiar.

My first instinct was to think of Sawyers Bend. And Boston, where I'd lived before I'd moved here. But this was my father's code. What did East Eagle mean to him? And then it snapped into place: Willow Springs. I'd grown up there, a sleepy little town too far west of Atlanta to qualify as a suburb, at least back then. Like many small towns, Willow Springs had a Main Street. And branching off Main Street, just past the town hall, was Eagle Street.

"East Eagle Street," I said slowly, my mind flying back in time. "In Willow Springs, Georgia."

Sterling grabbed her phone, tapping furiously at the screen. Her fingers curved in a tight grip as her eyes flashed to mine. "Do you know what's at 1523 East Eagle Street in Willow Springs, Georgia?"

I shook my head.

"A fucking bank!" Sterling let out a whoop, dropping her phone to drum her hands on the tabletop. "I knew it!" Picking her phone up again, she tapped the screen, her eyes flying over the page.

"What's the rest of it?" I asked, pointing to her notes. *KCUB. B42001.* "What does that part mean?"

Sterling shook her head, chewing on her lower lip as

she thought. "I don't know. It's too short to be an account number," she mused and lifted her phone again, tapping and scrolling until she found what she was looking for. She read aloud, "Willow Springs Community Bank, which has been in operation since the mid-sixties, offers safe deposit box rentals."

B42001. "Box 42001?" I asked. My mind raced—safe deposit boxes needed a key, and I didn't have a key. My father died when I was thirteen. Seventeen years had passed. If there had been a key, I had no clue where it was. My mother had gotten rid of most of his things. Anyway, we'd needed the cash back then. If she'd had a key to a safe deposit box, she sure as hell would have opened it.

Maybe she had. Either way, we were going to find out.

I leaned forward, picked up the small statue of Emperor Vitellius, and turned it in my hands before I set it down in front of Sterling. "I guess this means we're going to Willow Springs to see if we can talk our way inside a safe deposit box."

"I guess we are," Sterling said. "And we're going to come back with a big-ass pile of money."

She stuck out her hand, offering to touch me for the first time in a year. I took her hand in mine, savoring the brief contact. I hadn't lied—I didn't care about the money; I could always make more money. But there was only one Sterling, and I'd go to the ends of the earth to touch her again.

Willow Springs was just the beginning.

Chapter Three

FORREST

I wasn't invited to pick Sterling up at Heartstone Manor, the family estate she'd banned me from a year before. Instead, she knocked on my door at eight a.m. sharp, just as she'd told me she would. I opened it to find a Sterling I wasn't expecting.

She stood at my door in a navy linen sheath dress, her golden hair tamed into a sedate, gleaming twist, one sleek lock falling to curve around her cheek. Her makeup was artful and sophisticated, dramatic in a daytime-appropriate way, but the whole effect was not the Sterling I knew. This Sterling was polished, elegant, and bland. She was all image, her costume a wall between me and the woman I knew she hid inside.

"Ready?" she asked me, a challenge in her blue eyes.

I nodded. "I'm ready."

"You can drive," she said. "I don't want to pay for gas."

Most people wouldn't get it—the heiress to the Sawyer fortune worrying about paying for gas. But I did.

When her father had been alive, Sterling had a limitless credit card, the monthly bill covered by Prentice. Then Prentice was dead, and Sterling's oldest brother, Griffen, took over.

Unlike Prentice, Griffen Sawyer did not believe in parenting with a blank check. As far as I could tell, Griffen was the closest thing to a real parent Sterling had since her stepmother died when she was seven. Griffen had come back to Sawyers Bend to find his little sister at the bottom of a bottle. He'd given her an ultimatum: get your shit together or get out.

I didn't know Griffen Sawyer well, but I worked with his brothers, Royal and Tenn, and they talked about him often. I knew enough that I'd bet there was no way Griffen Sawyer would have thrown his baby sister out on the street. But Sterling hadn't known it, and between her two options, she chose to get her shit together.

Once she cut back on drinking, she got a job at the inn, taking over for an employee who was out on maternity leave. After my lies were exposed and Sterling dumped me, she hadn't wanted to see me at work every day. Understandable, though I'd felt her absence every day. Like someone had switched off half the lights, the inn was darker after she quit. She'd gone to work for her sister, Quinn, at Quinn's backcountry guide business, Sawyer Outdoor Adventures. According to town gossip, Sterling had revamped Quinn's website, organized her inventory system, started a summer camp program, and was doing some kind of outreach with local businesses to bring in more customers.

I wasn't surprised. When she'd been at the inn, she'd

taken to event planning as if she'd been doing it for years. I thought there wasn't much Sterling couldn't do if she put her mind to it. And now she was sitting beside me, headed to Willow Springs, Georgia, determined to get into a safe deposit box we didn't have the key for.

"Do you have a plan?" I asked.

"What do you mean?" Sterling kept her eyes pointed firmly out the window, locked on the deep blue sky, the trees a vibrant green under the bright July sun.

Monday morning traffic was light once we were clear of town. I didn't know what excuse Sterling had given Quinn for missing work. I doubted she'd told her sister she was with me. I'd told Tenn and Royal that I had a last-minute appointment and wouldn't be in. Not a lie. Just not the whole truth.

"Do you have a plan to open the box?" I asked. If it was even a box we were looking for. We'd assumed the number on my father's code referred to a safe deposit box, but we didn't know. We didn't *know* much of anything. Not really.

"Yep," she agreed.

"We don't have a key," I reminded her.

"Nope," she said, a little too quickly.

Was she lying? "Do we have a key?" I asked.

Her eyes flicked my way, bouncing off the second they hit my face as if looking at me scalded her eyeballs. My gut twisted. I hated it, fucking hated that she couldn't even look at me. If I thought apologizing would do any good, I'd be on my knees. But that was the problem with lying—if you did it enough, people didn't believe a fucking thing you said, including when you apologized.

I'd have to show her she could trust me and hope she was paying enough attention to see. That would be hard when she refused to meet my eyes

I swallowed my emotions and repeated, "Do we have a key?"

"We might," she said.

I resisted the urge to demand more. If she was willing to tell me what she knew, she would have already. It was driving me crazy. I was dying to know how she thought we were going to get into safe deposit box 42001 without a key.

I'll admit I was a little curious about what might be inside. Only a little, though. I knew that the second Sterling had her money, she'd walk away, and I'd never see her again. If I thought I could get away with it, I would have offered her a bigger cut just to spend time with me, to give me a second chance. But I had a feeling a move like that would only play into every misconception she had about me. Paying for her company wasn't the way to win her back. It might just be the way to drive her off for good.

My thoughts ran in circles as we drove. How were we going to get in the box? What had my father hidden there? What if the number didn't refer to a box? Then what?

And the thought most often on repeat: How could I keep Sterling with me long enough to prove I was worth another chance with her?

Getting her to look at me for longer than a second would be a start.

I didn't come up with any answers in the three hours

it took us to get to Willow Springs. I thought I'd recognize the town when we pulled in, but too much had changed since I'd lived there. We passed strip malls packed with chain stores, gas stations, and, finally, a supermarket. When I was a kid, we'd driven to the next town over for groceries and gas. Willow Springs had grown while I'd been away.

Nothing seemed familiar until we turned, and I saw the brick buildings lining Main Street, their black shutters and old-fashioned awnings exactly as I remembered. We drove by the big, square park at the center of town, a bronze statue of the town founder in the center. Bittersweet nostalgia struck at the flashes of memory. Going to the library across the square and picking out my own books. Getting ice cream at the shop by the park and eating it on the benches with my dad.

For just a second, I could taste the sweet, cold ice cream, and hear the rumble of my father's voice. Then I popped back to the present, to Sterling sitting beside me, trying to pretend I didn't exist. I let out a short sigh. I'd been living a good life until I decided to go chasing after my father's lost statue. Since then, it seemed like I'd made one bad decision after another. My job at the inn was the only thing that hadn't been a mistake. When it came to my personal life, I couldn't seem to get anything right.

I followed the GPS down Main Street to a left turn onto East Eagle Street. The bank was on the corner. It was go time.

I didn't remember the bank from my childhood, but it looked like every other small-town bank I'd ever seen. Brick, white columns, two stories. I pulled into a spot and turned to look at Sterling. Her teeth cut into her lower lip—her only outward sign of worry. Otherwise, she was cool perfection. Feeling my eyes on her, she straightened in her seat, her mouth relaxing, and her mask of perfection fell into place once again.

For a second, the Sterling beside me had reminded me of the woman I loved, and my heart ached. I loved all versions of Sterling, but the perfectly polished figure beside me wasn't the woman I missed. I missed who she'd become in those last days before it had all fallen apart when she'd trusted me, laughed with me, confided in me.

I'd done things in my life I wasn't proud of and made decisions I wished I could take back, but nothing came close to my regret at lying to Sterling.

"What are we going to do now?" I asked.

Sterling's head turned in my direction, her eyes skating my way, then sliding back without ever making contact. "Follow my lead," she said, picking up her purse from where she'd stashed it at her side and opening her door.

If I'd been here for the money, maybe the lack of information would have made me nervous. I wasn't completely disinterested in the money. According to my mother, there had been a lot of it before my father died. Hundreds of millions of dollars, stashed in an investment account, inaccessible without my father to tell us where to look. By now, it could be a fortune beyond my comprehension.

Could be. Or it could be gone. It might never have existed. I didn't know. The money wasn't real to me. It was a myth. A fairy tale. I couldn't get my head or my heart engaged in the idea of all that money when I was too distracted by the hope of winning back Sterling.

Unlike that money, Sterling was very real. I knew I could have a happy life without my father's fortune. I couldn't say the same about a life without Sterling Sawyer.

I left the car, locked it, and caught up to her, savoring the sound of her navy heels clicking on the sidewalk. I pushed open the door to the bank and stood back, allowing her to enter before me. I'd swear every head in the bank turned, the entire room holding its breath as she strode in, her golden hair shining under the lights, diamonds flashing at her ears and around her neck. I had a second to wonder about the jewelry—especially the ring on her finger—before she was approached by a handsome young banker in a suit.

"May I help you?" he asked, not sparing a glance for me, all his focus on Sterling. I didn't blame him. It was for the best, anyway, since I had no idea what the plan was.

"We have a safe deposit box," Sterling said, her voice smooth, cool, and filled with assurance.

"Oh, well, if you give me the number," he began.

"Box 42001," Sterling said, finishing with a slight curve of her lips.

The young man's eyes widened, I thought at Sterling's little smile. I soon realized I was wrong when he said, "Excuse me, I just need to check something. Why don't you have a seat?" He pointed to a love seat awkwardly set in the middle of the lobby beside a table holding a cut crystal candy bowl.

"Of course. Thank you," Sterling said, nudging me

with her elbow. She turned and made herself comfortable on the loveseat, helping herself to a butterscotch. The banker's response seemed to have confirmed something for her based on the slightly smug smile she wore.

"Were you expecting that?" I asked, wanting to know what was going on in that head of hers. She'd worked her way through my father's code with equal parts excitement and frustration. Watching her face as she sucked on the butterscotch and smiled to herself, I wondered if she knew that she herself was a code, and I'd give anything for the key.

Sterling didn't answer my question, but I thought I was right. She hadn't expected to be led straight to the box, though she'd been expecting something. Maybe not the banker's exact response, but something out of the ordinary. I was growing more curious by the second, but given her reaction to my questions earlier, I thought I'd get further if I kept my mouth shut for now.

We waited, the minutes ticking by. The young banker didn't return, and no one approached. Finally, a woman appeared before us wearing a gray suit with a pink flower tucked in the pocket, her white hair in a precise bob, reading glasses perched on her nose.

Chapter Four

FORREST

"You're here inquiring after box number 42001?" she asked.

Sterling stood. "We are," she confirmed.

I shifted my gaze from Sterling to the woman in front of me and held out my hand. "Forrest Powell," I said, and to my surprise, her eyes lit up, her fingers closing around mine in a tight squeeze.

"I should have known," she said. "You have the look of your father, except for that hair. That you got from your mother. I'm Madelyn Grady."

I smiled back at her, searching my memory for her face. "I'm sorry, I don't—"

"Oh, no, the last time you saw me, you were in short pants. But I knew your parents well. It's wonderful to see you all grown up. Alan said one day you'd come for the box." Her smile faded as her gaze shifted to Sterling. "Unfortunately," she continued, "we can't go any farther. Alan stipulated that only family is permitted, I'm afraid."

But it was my day for surprises. Sterling turned to me,

her left hand raising to rest on my shoulder. I took in the diamond flashing on her ring finger and had only a second to wonder what the hell she was up to before she gave Madelyn Grady a blinding smile and said, "I'm his fiancée, Sterling Sawyer."

Sterling leaned back to hold out her right hand, startling Mrs. Grady into a friendly handshake. Then she turned back to me, rose up on her toes, and pressed a lingering kiss to the side of my jaw. My brain froze. It was as if every dream I had came true in an explosion of congratulations and happy smiles and the fresh memory of Sterling's kiss.

Reality slammed back into me a second later, the dream slipping away as Sterling slid from my arms. I realized at once I could play a part as well as she could. Turning my head, I brushed my lips over hers, my arm winding around her waist, holding her against me, drawing in her surprised gasp.

She melted against me, her lips so soft under mine. For a moment, I forgot entirely where we were and what was at stake. For those few seconds, she was my girl again, and I had everything I wanted.

Then Sterling stepped back and turned a perfectly composed smile to Mrs. Grady. "I'm so sorry," she said. "Sometimes we get a little carried away."

Mrs. Grady's eyes were misty, an affectionate smile on her face. "Oh, how wonderful. I think a fiancée counts as family."

Sterling flashed the same smug smile she'd had earlier my way before we turned to follow Mrs. Grady to a door at the far end of the bank lobby. My brain was stuck on that kiss and the ring on her finger. Had she known we'd need to pretend to be engaged? Was that why she wore a diamond on her ring finger? She didn't usually wear diamond rings at all, much less on that specific finger.

We followed Mrs. Grady up a wide, carpeted staircase with a polished oak banister. "I'm afraid I can't personally give you access to the box," she said. "But Mr. Webber, the bank president, can help you."

Behind Mrs. Grady's back, I raised an eyebrow at Sterling. That smug curl of her lips didn't change. If she hadn't been expecting a meeting with the bank president, it wasn't a surprise either. I hadn't been positive she'd get us this far. But as much as I wasn't sure I wanted to face what was in that box, my curiosity was almost rabid.

Mrs. Grady led us down a hall to a set of solid oak double doors. Knocking twice, she waited until a voice said, "Enter," before she swung the door open and waved us inside.

"Mr. Webber, I have Forrest Powell and his fiancée, Sterling Sawyer, to see you." She withdrew and closed the door, leaving us with a man who looked like he was the age my father would be if he were still alive.

He stood, coming around the side of the desk, his hand extended to me. Mr. Webber, first name unknown, had a stocky build, broad-shouldered, seeming taller than he was. His iron-dark hair was threaded liberally with silver. His sharp eyes narrowed as he scanned me for a beat before his face broke out into a smile.

I wasn't surprised to hear him say as he crossed the room, "I knew your father well. He was a good man. It's a shame what happened." He took my hand and gave it a vigorous shake. "I've been looking forward to this day. Alan always thought he'd be here with you, but instead..." He released my hand. His expression chilled as he looked at Sterling. "Sterling Sawyer?" he asked, with the raise of an eyebrow.

She held out her hand as she nodded. "Yes, I'm Sterling Sawyer. It's good to meet you, Mr. Webber."

"Prentice Sawyer's daughter?" he asked, releasing her hand.

"Unfortunately," she answered, lifting her chin, her eyes level on his. "You knew my father?"

"I did. I'm also aware of how Alan Buckley knew your father."

With that, I understood everything. This man knew what had happened, how Prentice Sawyer had stolen my father's business and the statue, driving my father to take his own life. To anyone who knew the truth, the idea of Alan Buckley's son marrying a Sawyer was incomprehensible.

Before I could jump in to defend Sterling, she shook her head, her eyebrows drawn together. She could play a part, but the regret in her eyes wasn't an act. "I only recently learned the extent of Prentice's relationship with Forrest's father. I'm sorry to say I wasn't surprised to learn the full truth." She sighed. "My father was not a good man."

"No, he wasn't," Mr. Webber agreed. "So, how did this happen?" He looked between the two of us, his gaze landing on me.

I'd messed up my life enough with lies. Except for Sterling's fake engagement story, I wasn't going to lie to

Mr. Webber. "I went to Sawyers Bend looking for revenge," I said. "Instead, I found Sterling, and I learned that Prentice's children are nothing like their father."

Mr. Webber gave a gruff nod. "Can't say I know many people who miss Prentice Sawyer, but the things I've heard about his son, Griffen... He seems to be the apple that fell very far from the tree."

As well as I had come to know Tenn and Royal, I was glad to hear that the Sawyers' reputations were changing. Sometimes, death wasn't enough to clean the slate, but in the short year and a half since Prentice had died, Griffen had begun to show the world a different kind of Sawyer.

Stepping back, Mr. Webber gestured to the chairs opposite his desk. We followed his cue and sat, Sterling setting her navy purse on her knees, the ring on her finger bright against the dark fabric. Where had she gotten it? Did she borrow it from one of her sisters? I didn't think so. It wasn't a small stone, but it was plain. Boring. Not a ring I would have bought her.

It didn't matter. We weren't engaged. This was all an act, and I was getting distracted. I leaned back, resting my ankle on my knee, and continued where we'd left off. "I've been the CFO for the Inn at Sawyers Bend for the last year. I work with Royal and Tenn Sawyer every day, and I can tell you they're nothing like Prentice. And if he were still alive, I know my father would love Sterling as much as I do."

"You and your mother went back to her maiden name after she left town?" Mr. Webber probed.

I nodded. Clearing my throat, I said, "She wanted a fresh start. I thought about changing it back after I turned eighteen, but—" I searched for the words that might explain why I hadn't been able to bring myself to do it. "My mother has been through a lot. She's happy now. Finally remarried to a nice guy. I don't want to bring back painful memories."

Mr. Webber seemed to understand, giving a slow nod as he sat back, ruminating. Sterling reached out to take my hand in hers. It was part of the act, though I wanted to think it wasn't. I wanted to think she hadn't even realized she'd reached out to me.

Mr. Webber didn't miss the gesture. Maybe it was that, or maybe he'd come to his own conclusion. "Alan said you'd come for the box, and when you did, I should ask you for the key."

His language threw me. Not *Do you have your key?* But *I should ask you for the key.*

I didn't understand.

Sterling did.

Her fingers closed tight around mine in a quick squeeze. Leaning forward, she said, "The key is Buck."

The sound of my childhood nickname sliced through me. My father, far more traditional than my slightly hippie mother, had hated the name Forrest. Sometimes, I thought they must have been a bad match from the start, though I remembered lots of laughter along with the arguments. My father had refused to call me Forrest and instead called me Buck, a shortened version of his last name my grandfather had also used.

Mr. Webber gave Sterling a wide smile. "Well done," he said with a nod. "Excuse me, I'll be back." He rose from his chair and pushed open a door hidden in the paneling beside his desk.

"How did you—" I started to ask, and then I remembered the deciphered code she'd shown me the night before. KCUB. Buck spelled backward.

Sterling shrugged a shoulder. "I wouldn't have gotten it so easily, except I had to reverse the key to break the code. It made sense that he might have reversed something in the answer itself."

"How did you know about Buck?"

Her eyes went ice-cold, the vibrant blue shade suddenly glacial. "You told us last year when we found out who you really are."

I wished I hadn't asked. I hated thinking about that day. Seeing the pain on her face as I'd explained my lies had been agonizing. Until then, I'd held out hope that I could talk my way out of it. That day at Heartstone, I'd realized I hadn't just made a mistake. I'd royally fucked up the best thing that had ever happened to me.

"Clever," I said, glad to see the cold melt from her gaze at the praise.

"I wasn't sure," she admitted in a low voice, "But I thought it was worth a try."

"I'd say," I agreed.

The panel door swung open, and Sterling straightened, electricity running through her body, her eyes glued to the rectangular metal box Mr. Webber held in his hands.

My heart sank.

This was it. She'd cracked the code, and now we had the box. Our time together was going to end.

The box was too small to hold much cash, but my father wouldn't have kept the money in cash anyway. Would it be an account number with passwords? Stock certificates? I was finally going to recover my father's mythical lost fortune, and I was going to lose Sterling all over again. She'd get her twenty-five percent, and she'd walk.

At that moment, I knew I'd been telling the truth when I said I didn't care about the money. Sitting there, watching Sterling track the progress of that metal box across the room, knowing she hoped it was the answer to her empty bank account... All I felt was loss.

I'd had her back, talking to me, smiling at me, touching me, for less than twenty-four hours. I couldn't let her go. Not a second time.

I didn't want the money. If I thought it would keep her with me, I'd give her every penny.

But I couldn't buy love. Especially not Sterling's.

With every step Mr. Webber took, the box drew closer. Sterling's anticipation rose right along with my dread. I wasn't ready to let her walk away, and I couldn't stop her. I needed more time. Time for her to remember what we'd had, to see that everything we were together was still there. If she could just forgive me...

But it had been a year, and she still hadn't forgiven me. She probably never would.

Letting out a breath, I watched as Mr. Webber set the box down on the edge of his desk and opened the lid. Steeling my heart, I looked inside. There was nothing but a single index card, like the kind I'd used to make flash-cards in grade school.

The lined side of the card was facing up. In my father's precise, printed writing, I saw the phrase, *A mockingbird on my shoulder, singing with my strings in the Poplars.*

Beneath was another long alphanumeric code.

"What?" Sterling breathed, reaching out to pick up the card. She flipped it back and forth, then leaned forward to check the box for anything else. There was nothing. Squinting down at the card, she said, "It's another code."

Mr. Webber's hand came down on my shoulder. He squeezed, then gave a fatherly pat and said, "Good luck, Forrest. If that's what I think it is, you're going to need all the luck you can get."

Chapter Five

STERLING

"Your father imagined you'd go on this journey together," Mr. Webber said to Forrest, "but it does my heart good to see you with your beautiful future wife beside you. You can't do this with your father, but it means something that you can do it with someone you love."

Forrest looked poleaxed. I didn't think he'd expected this trip down memory lane. Neither had I. I'd only been thinking about the box and how to talk our way into opening it without a key. And now here we were.

Except there wasn't a pot of gold at the end of the rainbow. Just another code to break. Well, really, this time, it was a clue and a code. At least I hoped *A mockingbird on my shoulder, singing with my strings in the Poplars,* was a clue. I had no idea.

"I'm assuming we can take this with us," Forrest said, plucking the index card from my hands.

"Of course," Mr. Webber said. "Guard it carefully."

"I will." Forrest tucked the index card into the inside pocket of his suit coat.

My head was spinning, torn between elation and consternation. I'd done it. I'd cracked the code, found the bank, and bullshitted my way into Alan Buckley's safe deposit box only to find another fucking code.

I slid into the comfortable social niceties I could perform without much conscious thought, saying goodbye to Mr. Webber with a handshake and a half hug, thanking Mrs. Grady for her help, and following Forrest out of the bank, the whole time trying to figure out what the clue meant. Did it lead somewhere? Was it the key to decode the letters and numbers beneath? How could it be?

I'd done something no one else had been able to do—I'd gotten us this far. But damn it, I thought that would be it. We'd find the box, get our payday, and I could sail off into the sunset, loaded down with cash.

I buckled myself into the passenger seat of Forrest's car, trying to figure out what was next. The part of me that loved cracking Alan Buckley's code shouted that the next step was obvious. I'd just have to decipher the clue about mockingbirds and strings and hope that led me to the key I needed to decipher the code. My fingers tingled with the desire to act, to solve the puzzle and decode those letters and numbers into the next step in our quest.

The rest of me wasn't so sure that twenty-five percent of Alan's money was worth the risk.

I wanted the money. It wasn't that I didn't want to work. I did. I'd been studying and mapping out a new career. I wanted to do more with my life than sleep late, drink, and party. I'd wasted too many years on that already. But I'd also learned money wasn't just for buying things or showing off. Money was safety. If I could pay my own way, no one could tell me what to do. I could take care of myself on my own terms.

My father and I always had an uneasy relationship. Most of the time, he'd ignored me. According to Miss Martha, our family housekeeper, I'd thrown some memorable tantrums when I was a toddler. I'd come to Heartstone at four years old, probably terrified and alone after my mother died, and I'd screamed out all that fear and grief, pounding my little fists into Darcy, my stepmother.

I didn't remember my mother, Trina. From everything I'd heard, she'd been happy to be Prentice's mistress, not as thrilled about raising a child. Then she was gone, and there was Darcy, who loved me with everything she had despite my being a constant reminder of her husband's infidelity. Darcy had absorbed my tantrums, returning my screams with love, and eventually, I'd settled. It took too long for Prentice. He wrote me off as a hellion and a disaster before I made it to kindergarten.

My father had seen his children as vehicles to further profit, bartering us and arranging marriages to suit his purposes. As I'd grown, my sisters tried to protect me from Prentice's machinations. Their efforts were a waste of time. Prentice continued to ignore me, too afraid to try to set me up with one of his associates in case I embarrassed him. Which I most certainly would have, completely on purpose.

The best way to keep Prentice at a distance was to be

the hellion he expected, a loose cannon he couldn't trust. It worked to protect me from my father's actions, but I couldn't escape his words. When we crossed paths, he took every opportunity to remind me what a useless disappointment I was. I was born to be a party girl, beautiful but brainless. *What makes you think you're anything special?*

Well, fuck him. He was dead, and I was still here. And more than that, I'd solved the riddle he'd been chasing for most of my life. I didn't have the money, but I was a step closer than Prentice Sawyer would ever be. How could I stop now? My father might be dead, but I still wanted to prove him wrong. I needed to. I wanted the money and the triumph. I couldn't walk away.

That was my ambition talking. I had a lot more ambition than anyone around me realized. Maybe too much, because chasing after Alan Buckley's fortune was going to be a hell of a lot more painful than I'd thought. I'd planned to ignore Forrest, focus on the money, and walk away. I was fooling myself. I was playing with fire with every second I spent with him, risking my ability to walk away whole. He'd taken enough of my heart as it was. I didn't need to hand him the rest.

Forrest sat beside me in silence, smoothly navigating the road back to Sawyers Bend. Everything would be so much simpler if I was over him. I didn't want to care about the way he'd frozen when Mrs. Grady said he looked like his father. The way he'd gone still when he'd learned the key was his own name: Buck.

He'd come to Sawyers Bend to get revenge for the father he'd loved. I understood revenge. Solving the code and finding Alan's fortune would be my own revenge, and I wanted it so badly I could taste it. I wanted to stand over my father's grave and gloat.

So, I was a hypocrite. I was still furious with Forrest, but I understood why he'd come to Sawyers Bend. I snuck a glance at his profile. Why did he have to be so fucking good-looking? It wasn't just the cheekbones and the strong line of his jaw or the way his hair twisted into soft curls at the top of his head, where he let it get a little longer.

I'd loved running my fingers through the short bristles at the back of his head, then sinking them into those luscious brown curls. And his hazel eyes, punctuated by flecks of green and gold at the center, his lashes so long I was torn between admiration and envy. I needed four coats of mascara for my lashes to look like that.

I'd tried, but I couldn't forget what he looked like under that suit. Forrest wasn't a fitness nut, but he ran and lifted weights most days. And God, did it show. Forrest Powell had stamina. I'd never had sex like that in my life. I'd had plenty of mediocre sex, some pretty bad sex, and some that was good enough. But getting naked with Forrest was like nothing I'd ever known. I'd shut off that part of myself in the year since he'd shattered my heart, not remotely ready to let anyone close enough to touch.

My broken heart wasn't healed. Scabbed over, maybe, but all that raw pain was right under the surface. Now, to get the things I wanted most—the money, revenge on my father—I was stuck with Forrest Powell.

I glanced at his jacket pocket. "Can I see the card?"

After a pause, he pulled it out. I took it, examining it for anything I'd missed on my short initial viewing. There was nothing new. I lifted my phone and got a great shot of Forrest's hand.

"No pictures," he said. Tucking the card back in his pocket, he glanced at me, his eyes impenetrable. "You want to look at it? You do it with me."

I huffed out a breath. "Fine."

I tried to think. Mr. Webber hadn't said anything concrete, but I could tell he knew we were in pursuit of something big. If it was my father's wild-goose chase, I would have bet that any account at the end of the rainbow would be empty. But this was Alan Buckley we were talking about, and from what Mr. Webber had said, this was an adventure he'd planned to go on with his son. He wouldn't stiff his own kid.

I set my phone on the center console, screen down. Forrest handed me back the card.

"Does the clue mean anything to you?" he asked.

"No," I admitted. "I have no idea what it means."

"Well, what's the plan?"

"I don't know. It took me a while to figure out the first one."

Forrest cleared his throat, his eyes fixed on the road. "I meant what I said. That card is worth a lot. If you want to look at it, you do it with me. No pictures, no copies."

"You think I'm going to steal it?" I asked, incredulous. For once, I met his gaze without a flinch, pissed off at him all over again.

Forrest's eyes were guarded as they met mine before

moving back to the road ahead. "I don't know," he said. "I know you hate me. You've made that clear."

"I don't—" I started to say, though I didn't know why. I *did* hate him.

"Yeah. You do," he said, his voice heavy. I wanted to think it was with regret. "I get it. I lied. I hurt you. And I can tell you all day how sorry I am, but I know you don't believe me. I deserve that. If I'd stopped and thought about what I was doing, what was at risk, I would have done everything differently. But it's too late."

My chest felt like it was caving in, my eyes hot and stinging. He'd apologized last year when he came clean to all of us, but I'd been too angry and hurt to listen to anything he'd said. He was a liar, and I was done with him. End of story. But now—

I was still hurt. Still furious. But this time, I heard his apology, every word of it. He didn't make excuses. I believed that he was sorry. And still, I couldn't bring myself to let him off the hook.

The silence stretched, and Forrest cleared his throat. "Right. So, we've established that you hate me," he said. "And we're both aware that index card is worth a lot of money. Potentially."

"Agreed." Though, I thought he was wrong about the *potentially* part. I was very sure that card was worth a lot of money.

"Then you understand why I say no pictures, no copies. And if you want to see it, you do it with me."

I let out a sigh. I couldn't argue. If our situations were reversed, I'd say the same thing. "Fine," I agreed. I could do this. I'd solved the first code. Surely, that meant I could solve the next. It was just going to take time. And I realized, with a rush of relief, not all of that time had to be spent with Forrest.

I looked back at the card. The words would point me to the key. And once I figured out what the key was, then I could go back to Forrest and decode the numbers and letters below. I didn't need the card. I didn't need the code. I just needed to figure out what the clue meant.

I stared down at the card in my hand, reading the clue over and over, committing it to memory.

A mockingbird on my shoulder, singing with my strings in the Poplars.

I'd let the words rattle around in my brain for a while. They didn't mean anything. Not yet. But they would.

Handing the card back to Forrest without looking at him, I said, "I'll let you know when I need to see it again."

That was the last thing I said to Forrest Powell for seven days.

Chapter Six

STERLING

Five days had passed since my trip to Willow Springs, and I was no closer to figuring out the clue than I had been when I first laid eyes on it.

A mockingbird on my shoulder, singing with my strings in the Poplars.

It was nonsense. But I knew it wasn't nonsense. It made a very specific kind of sense to Forrest's father. I just hadn't discovered what that was. I drifted through the days, going through the motions, my brain turning the clue over and over, inside out and upside down. Still nothing.

It had taken me months to figure out the key to crack the code on the Vitellius. What made me think I'd solve this one any faster? Ugh, I pushed that thought away. Because I could solve it, that was why. I just had to keep trying.

I'd researched everything I could find about mocking-birds and strings and poplar trees. Separately, together, misspellings, literary references. Nothing. I was missing something; I just had no idea what.

Maybe I needed to see the card again. Maybe if...

No. That was the traitorous side of my brain. Or, more accurately, my body. My brain was fixated on solving the clue, but all my body cared about was Forrest Powell.

I'd woken twice in the nights since I'd last seen him, Forrest filling my senses. That trip to Willow Springs was my downfall. I hadn't spent that much time with him since I'd dumped him. I'd thought I was immune. Didn't my body remember the heartbreak? The constant ache in my chest, the hollow prickle of tears, the dull pain between my temples—sometimes it had hurt so badly I couldn't get air in my lungs. I'd thought he was my forever, and he turned out to be another liar. Living with my father, I'd thought I knew all about liars, but Forrest Powell had proven I wasn't as smart as I thought I was.

All it had taken was a few hours in the car with him, and my body didn't care about any of that. I'd wanted to ignore him, but sitting that close, his arm beside mine on the console, I'd been far too aware of him. He radiated heat. Or maybe it was just me, feeling him every time he was close.

It had been like that back then. I'd feel a tingle go down my spine, and there he'd be, across the crowded lobby of the inn. We'd share a smile, a second of eye contact, and it felt like he'd kissed me from a hundred feet away.

Sitting beside him in the car had been too much. My

body didn't care that he was a liar, and I hated him. My body remembered the orgasms. So many orgasms.

No man had ever kissed me like Forrest. When that bastard laid one on me at the bank, he'd known exactly what he was doing. I'd started it, making up the story about being his fiancée and kissing his jaw. I shouldn't have done it—the kiss, not the story.

Once I figured out that the key was Buck, I'd known the code was personal for Forrest's father. I'd had a feeling there might be a stipulation about family, so I'd grabbed the diamond solitaire from my jewelry box. It was bad luck, but it was the only ring I had that could pass as an engagement ring. My father had given it to my mother when she'd pressured him for marriage after she got pregnant with me. Prentice had no intention of leaving Darcy, but he'd bought my mother the ostentatiously boring diamond to shut her up. Forrest would never have chosen such a generic ring, but no one in Willow Springs knew that.

So, the fiancée story was a good idea. But the kiss on his jaw was not. I'd forgotten. I didn't know how. It felt like every moment of our short relationship was engraved on my heart, but I'd forgotten the warmth of his skin, the way he smelled. And then he'd kissed me back.

It was only a press of his lips, barely more than a peck. For an endless moment, I'd lost myself, leaning into him, feeling instead of thinking. No more than a moment, but it had been enough to remind my body of everything I was missing.

I hadn't had sex in a year. At first, I'd been too hurt, too angry to want anything to do with any man. And then

I'd looked around and hadn't seen anyone who seemed worth the effort. I'd met handsome men. Charming men. I organized things for Quinn's guide business. Plenty of hot guys came through there. Rugged, outdoorsy men. Polished executives who loved to fish. Whatever I thought my type was, I had my pick. Nice men. Funny men.

None of them had sparked the tiniest bit of interest. I'd started to wonder if that part of me had shut down, had broken. And then I'd shaken Forrest's hand to seal our deal. The second his skin touched mine, I knew that while my heart was still thoroughly broken, my body was very much in working order.

I'd woken the night before from a dream of Forrest, of the two of us stretched out on a blanket in the summer grass. I was draped over his chest, looking up at a mockingbird perched on his shoulder. Stupid brain.

Meow. I looked down to see my black cat, Shadow, sitting at my feet.

"Are you ready for breakfast, baby?" I asked, putting my toothbrush away and leaning down to scoop her up. Shadow belonged to me and my sister Parker equally, but she spent most of her time at my side when I was home. Parker and I had briefly shared a kitten as young children. We'd discovered her lost on the Manor grounds and hidden her from Prentice. When he found out, he gave the kitten to Parker in an attempt to drive a wedge between us.

Prentice had never liked when his children bonded. He wanted us to live in fear—of himself and each other.

Sometimes, his scheming worked. It had certainly driven Ford and Griffen apart, but it hadn't worked on Parker or me. Parker snuck the kitten into my room every night until one day, the kitten was gone. In the end, Prentice always got his way. After our father died, Parker took me to the shelter, and we came home with Shadow. This kitten wasn't going anywhere.

Shadow had grown out of her kittenhood, but she was still small. Sweet-natured, she rarely meowed except when her belly was empty.

"I don't have any food up here, sweetheart," I said, nuzzling the top of her head as I walked to the door of my room. I usually kept a stash of her canned food in my room, but the day before, I'd used the last one. "We'll have to go down to the kitchen to find you some breakfast."

She let out another *meow*.

Silly kitten. Midway down the steps, she squirmed in my arms. I set her down so she could walk beside me, and she ran ahead. I expected her to continue down the stairs to the lower level to the massive pantry where Finn kept the overflow cans of cat food. Instead, she darted into the library.

"Shadow," I called after her, "I have things to do. I'm not waiting all day. Come on, let's get you some breakfast."

When she didn't immediately return to my side, I changed course and followed her into the library. Only a few feet into the room, I froze. My half-brother Brax stood in the middle of the library, Shadow in his arms. A chill went down my spine. Brax and I had been sworn enemies since I was born, three days after him. You'd think a three-day-old baby would be too young to have enemies, but if you thought that, you hadn't met Brax. Technically, all my siblings were halves, but Brax was the only one I thought of that way.

Braxton Reginald Sawyer was supposed to be the youngest Sawyer, the crown prince of the Sawyer clan. For a few short years, he had been. The dirty little secret of my existence hadn't been revealed until my mother's death when we were four. Prentice had taken pride in producing so many children when his ancestors had managed only one or two offspring per generation. My father might not have liked me, but there had never been a question that I had a place at Heartstone Manor as Prentice's daughter.

Suddenly, Brax had to share the spotlight with my adorable self. We looked so much alike that we might have been twins. Golden hair and skin, my father's electric blue eyes, excellent bone structure. And Brax had the one thing I didn't. Height. He towered over me, my sweet little ball of fluff in his arms, a familiar sneer twisting his lips.

"Put my cat down," I said.

"She's fine," he replied.

Shadow didn't look fine. She squirmed in his arms, and his hands tightened.

"Put my cat down," I repeated, tamping down the fear in my voice. If he knew I was scared, he'd never let her go. We had enough years of sibling torment between us. I didn't trust Brax as far as I could throw him, and given that he was a foot taller and a hundred pounds heavier than me, I couldn't throw him far.

"What are you doing here?" I asked, striding forward.

I grabbed Shadow and tried to yank her out of his arms, hoping he wouldn't fight back. At the touch of my hand, Shadow squirmed, sinking her teeth into Brax's wrist. He let go in surprise, and I gathered her to my chest. She nestled against my neck, the rumble of her purr low and unhappy.

"Why are you here?" I demanded.

Brax lived here. We all did. According to my father's will, we had to live in Heartstone Manor for five years after his death, or we'd lose not only our inheritance—amount unknown—but also access to any Sawyer-owned property. Since all of us worked for family-owned enterprises, it was either toe the line or lose our jobs.

Brax handled the family's commercial real estate business. Though he managed properties all over the country, his office was based in the nearby city of Asheville. Until Prentice's will, he'd lived in a condo there and rarely came home to Heartstone Manor. These days, to comply with the will, he slept at the Manor, but that was it. He rarely attended meals. Until recently, I couldn't remember the last time I saw him in person. He'd come to Tenn and Scarlett's wedding, and it was the first time he'd met my newborn niece, Griffen and Hope's daughter. I'd seen him again at Savannah and Finn's Valentine's Day wedding. That was it.

Months of Brax slipping in and out of the house, here

only long enough to satisfy the terms of the will, until the last few weeks. Suddenly, it felt like he was everywhere. Was it because Ford was home? I thought back. Ford had finally been released from prison in the middle of May. I hadn't started bumping into Brax everywhere until the middle of June. I didn't know if that meant anything.

I should have known Brax wouldn't give me a useful answer.

"It's my house, too," he said in a snarl, rubbing at the bite mark on his hand.

"It's Griffen's house." I couldn't resist poking at him. Probably not smart, but I didn't give a crap.

"Yeah, well," he said, "maybe it's Griffen's house, but I have a right to live here, just like you. More of a right since I'm not the bastard daughter of the town slut."

There was nothing I wanted to say to that. It had taken me far too long to learn that I wasn't my mother. I knew better than to try to defend myself to Brax. He liked hating me too much to listen. I watched him stride away, heading for the very stairs I'd planned to take to the lower level. Change of plans. I'd use the stairs behind the dining room. They were closer to the kitchens and the pantry anyway.

I turned to my right, using what had once been the billiards room as a shortcut. I stopped abruptly, noticing the fire burning in the fireplace. No one used this room. My eyes were slow to see my brother Ford in an armchair by the fire, a book in his hand. He was so quiet that I almost missed him. Was this why Brax had been home more lately? My mind flashed back to when I'd seen him in the library, holding Shadow. Had Brax come out of the billiards room?

Curious, I asked Ford, "What did Brax want?"

Ford shook his head in answer. I wasn't sure what that meant, but he hadn't denied that Brax had been in here.

"You're in here reading?" I asked.

Stupid question. Of course, he was in here reading; he was holding an open book. I tried to think of something else to say.

I'd never been particularly close to my brother Ford. When I'd been young, it had always been Griffen who paid attention to us kids. Ford was the one who rolled his eyes and called us childish and a waste of his time. Then Griffen had been gone, exiled by my father when Ford double-crossed him.

For years, I'd seen Ford as a distant parental figure, not as cruel as my father but not anyone who particularly cared about me. Like I treated most adults back then, I tried to stay out of his way. A few years before my father died, Ford had changed. Of course, he didn't explain himself to me, his youngest sister, or to anyone at all. The best we'd been able to figure out, Ford and Prentice fell out, and it had been so bad Ford had moved into a suite at the inn.

After that, Ford had tried to look out for the rest of us, but—except with Quinn and maybe Avery—it was too little, too late. The Ford who had gone to prison for my father's murder had been powerful, connected, seemingly invulnerable.

We'd known he hadn't killed Prentice, but whoever

framed him did a good job of it, and he'd sat in prison for almost a year until a few months ago when new evidence had mysteriously appeared. The judge had taken his time, but eventually, Ford had been set free. He'd come home, but nothing was the same. This was Griffen's house now, and while Griffen had enough compassion to welcome home the brother who'd had him exiled, the relationship they'd had was gone. Once they'd been closer than brothers, the best of friends. Now everything was just fucking awkward.

Ford was a shadow of himself, thinner, paler, and so quiet I wasn't sure what to make of him. I didn't know what to say. He lifted the book in an affirmative gesture, acknowledging my question with a silent nod.

"What did Brax do?" he asked, his voice scratchy as if he hadn't spoken in a long time.

"Nothing, really," I admitted. "I just— I didn't like the way he was holding Shadow. I was afraid he—" I couldn't think of how to explain my unease. Brax hadn't done anything. "Was Brax bothering you?" I asked.

"Don't worry about Brax," Ford said. "There's still breakfast if you want some."

"I'm not hungry." At my words, Shadow let out another yowl and butted my chin with the top of her head. "But Shadow is."

"You'd better go feed her, then."

At that, I knew Ford was done talking. "I'll see you later," I said as I left.

It was so weird not to know what to say to someone I'd known my whole life. But he wasn't the same Ford. I hadn't been close to the old Ford, but I'd known how to deal with him. The same as with my father—limited contact. Talk back just enough to be annoying but not enough to get into trouble. They'd leave, and I'd be free to go my own way. I wasn't sure I wanted to drive away this new Ford. But I didn't know that I wanted to be friends either.

Chapter Seven

STERLING

Brax was nowhere in sight when I got to the lower level. I gave Finn a wave as I passed the kitchen, grabbed enough cat food to restock my supply upstairs, and fed Shadow.

"You're going to give yourself a stomachache," I told her as she gulped down her food. As always, she ignored me.

Her stomach satisfied, the two of us headed back up the stairs. My feet hit the hallway, and I heard Griffen call my name from his office. How he'd known it was me, I wasn't sure. Maybe it was his background in security, but I'd swear he could identify all of us by our footsteps. He was never wrong.

"Coming," I called down the hall.

Shadow stayed by my side as I changed direction for Griffen's office. I used to hate that room. When my father had been alive, his office was the scene of too many humiliations. I'd sit in one of the chairs in front of Prentice's desk, eyes on my feet as he reminded me of all the ways I was a miserable disappointment.

The day he'd been murdered, I'd found him there, in his throne of a desk chair, a neat red hole in the center of his forehead. I'd screamed for help, but I'd been the only one home. In a fog, I'd called emergency services, wondering if it was all just a bad dream. The indomitable Prentice Sawyer couldn't be dead. But he was. Relief tainted by guilt still overshadowed my grief.

For weeks after, the memory of my father's body, so still and cold, had given me nightmares. Until Griffen came home, I would have sworn I'd never set foot in the office again. In those first few months after his return, we'd helped him redecorate by way of a bonfire in the yard, disposing of Prentice's heavy, dark curtains, his hunting trophies, and that hated throne of a desk chair.

Now, the office bore little resemblance to the forbidding room it had been before. The tall windows filled it with light, and more often than not, the sound of laughter drifted down the hall. I pushed the door open to find Griffen behind his desk, as usual, his dark blond hair falling in his eyes, papers spread out in front of him. He usually worked with his wife, Hope, and our brother, Royal, but this morning it was just him. My heart warmed at the smile he gave me when I walked into the room.

Griffen and I had come a long way. Our adult relationship had started with me throwing up all over his wife. Though Griffen could be a hard-ass, he was also patient. And like Darcy, he'd met my belligerence with love until I didn't want to fight him anymore.

I'd like to think I would have gotten myself on my feet on my own. And maybe, probably, I would have. Eventually. Griffen had sped up the process with a combination of his "take no bullshit" attitude and big brother hugs.

"What was that a little while ago?" he asked, leaving me confused until he clarified. "I could hear you in the library. Problem with Ford?"

"No, no," I was quick to reassure. "Brax. He—" I stopped and mentally ran through the encounter. I debated what to share; Griffen didn't need to hear me whine about my asshole of a half-brother. He knew what Brax was like. "He picked up Shadow and wouldn't give her back. I think he came out of the billiards room. I think he was talking to Ford." I sat in the chair opposite Griffen's desk, scratching under Shadow's chin, thinking out loud. "He's been home a lot more since Ford got back. That's weird. Isn't that weird?"

Griffen shrugged. "I don't know. I was gone a long time. I'm not sure I know what counts as weird around here anymore, but Brax always idolized Ford. You know he and I were never close. Maybe he feels more welcome now that Ford's back."

"Maybe," I said. That didn't feel right to me.

Griffen's eyes softened. "Sterling," he said gently, "I'm not sure you're rational on the subject of Brax."

I couldn't argue his point. I most definitely was not rational about Brax, and we both knew it. But that didn't mean I was wrong. I let it go anyway.

"Have you talked to Ford?" I inquired. I wasn't the only one with brother hang-ups.

"About what?" Griffen asked flatly.

I decided to let that go too. It wasn't for me to broker a peace between my two oldest brothers. The only one who could do that was Ford, and we didn't have the kind of relationship that left me comfortable enough to interfere.

"Are you going to tell me about your trip to Willow Springs with Powell?" Griffen asked, interrupting my thoughts.

My eyebrows drew together, and I glared at my oldest brother. "How do you know I went to Willow Springs with Forrest? Do you and Hawk have a tracking device on me?"

"No comment," was Griffen's answer. That meant yes.

"That's weird," I said. "You guys are weird. You know that, right?"

"Not weird," Griffen said. "Careful. And I think you'll agree we've got reason for it."

I couldn't argue with that either. My father had been murdered, and his killer was still out there. And Prentice wasn't the only one. Griffen's former fiancée, Vanessa, who'd also been Ford's ex-wife, had been murdered. Shot in the forehead, just like Prentice. Aside from those two murders, there had been plenty else going on. Someone had tried to kill Griffen twice. There'd been sabotage at the inn. JT, Royal's girlfriend's BFF, had been stabbed. The drama over the stolen Vitellius had involved everyone from the Irish mob to my cousin Bryce.

Then, my sister Parker's husband had tried to murder her. Our housekeeper, Savannah, who was now married to Finn, had a former mother-in-law try to kidnap her son, Nicky. Just a few months ago, my sister Quinn had been kidnapped. I still hadn't gotten the full story of why her kidnapper wasn't in prison where he belonged. She and Hawk claimed he'd gotten away. I had a feeling Griffen knew the truth. So far, he was the only one.

But I had to wonder—how were they tracking me? I'd driven with Forrest, so it couldn't be in my car. My purse? No, I sighed to myself. It was obvious. My phone. I always had my phone by my side, and it would be child's play for them to track me that way. I found I didn't mind that they had an eye on me. If anything, I was glad. With all the danger and drama, my brother and Hawk could be a little careful. As long as it didn't mean I had to answer questions about Forrest Powell.

Griffen waited, his sea-green eyes patient and kind. I hated telling Griffen no, not when he was always so damn reasonable. And if I was being honest, I wanted to brag just a little.

"It's nothing you have to worry about," I said. "Actually, I cracked the code on the Vitellius."

Griffen immediately knew what I was talking about. He sat back in his chair, arms crossed over his chest, a wide smile spreading across his face. "No shit? Really? How?"

I explained about the hidden panel and the key. "I made a deal with Forrest. Twenty-five percent of whatever we find."

Griffen's smile was proud and completely genuine. I liked seeing it. He and the rest of my family rarely saw me for anything other than the pretty sorority girl I once was. Of everyone, Griffen was the most apt to expect me to be more than that, but even he underestimated me. It was by design. I didn't want to let any of them down, ever again. If they didn't expect much, it was harder to be a disappointment.

"That's my girl. I didn't know you knew anything about code-breaking."

I swallowed, feeling suddenly tongue-tied. "It's not a big deal. I had a math teacher in high school who was into ciphers, and I thought they were cool. I guess I remembered more than I thought I did." I was leaving out a lot, but I wasn't ready to completely come clean about my closet math nerd status.

"So, you're a wealthy woman now?" Griffen teased with a raised eyebrow.

"I wish." I explained about the bank in Willow Springs and where the code on the Vitellius had led us. As I told him the story—meeting Mrs. Grady and Mr. Webber, knowing the key to open the box—I watched Griffen's proud smile turn into a grin.

"Sterling, nice job. That took some balls," he said with admiration.

I shrugged. "I was so curious to find out if I was right, I wasn't as nervous as I thought I'd be."

"What was in the box?" he asked.

I sighed dramatically. "Another code, along with a clue to the key."

"How close are you to cracking that one?" Griffen inquired.

"Not close at all," I admitted, slouching back in the chair as Shadow jumped off my lap. "Forrest wouldn't let me keep it, but I memorized the clue. I'm pretty sure the clue leads to the key. And once I have the key, I can crack the code and figure out where we need to go next."

"What was the clue?" Griffen wanted to know.

I told him, and he shook his head. "*A mockingbird on my shoulder, singing with my strings in the Poplars.* That doesn't make any sense."

"Tell me about it," I complained. "I've researched every angle I can think of, and nothing."

Griffen repeated the clue to himself and shook his head once more. "If it sparks any ideas, I'll let you know, but it doesn't mean anything to me either."

"Well, it only took me a year to figure out the Vitellius. So, you know—" I rolled my eyes. "I really thought that box was going to be it."

Griffen crossed his arms over his chest, the grin fading. "How are things with Powell?" he asked, the flat tone of his voice heavy with disapproval.

"He's a means to an end," I said. "That's all."

"Royal and Tenn trust him," Griffen said, "even though they're still pissed about how things worked out with the two of you. They think he's a good guy."

"What do you think?" I asked.

Griffen's mouth turned up in a half smile. "He was a huge, enormous jerk to my baby sister. I'm honor bound to hate him until you tell me otherwise."

I grinned as I stood and crossed the room to give him a hug. "That's why you're my favorite older brother. I have to head into town to get some things done for Sawyer Outdoor Adventures. I'll keep you posted."

"Sterling," Griffen said as I left the room, his voice stopping me in my tracks. "I'm really proud of you."

"Thanks, Griffen," I said, my throat tight with emotion. "I'm proud of me, too."

I'd be prouder if I could figure out the mockingbird clue. It had only been five days, but I wanted the answer to the clue now.

I started back down the hall, wondering if I needed to grab anything from my room before heading into work. I heard my name again, this time in a low voice, from the opposite direction as last time.

Ford, I realized, turning around and heading for the billiards room.

"I overheard your conversation," he said bluntly. Not a surprise. Griffen's office door had been open, and we hadn't been whispering. "Will you tell me what the clue was?"

I stared at Ford for a long moment. Could I trust him? I knew he hadn't killed our father. He was far too clever to have left such clumsy evidence behind—stashing the gun in his own closet and leaving the shoes that matched the footprints at the end of his bed. No, if Ford had killed Prentice, he wouldn't have been caught. But that didn't mean I could trust him.

On the other hand, even if he knew what the clue meant, he didn't have the code that went with it. Only Forrest had that, and knowing Forrest, it was locked away somewhere safe.

I could use all the help I could get. I repeated the clue. Ford said it aloud slowly, twice, his eyes closed. "I don't know anything about ciphers or code-breaking," he said. "Less than nothing, really. But...is there any way your code could have something to do with Thomas Jefferson?"

"What do you mean?" I asked, intrigued.

"It's just that...Jefferson had a mockingbird that sat on his shoulder. And the bird would sing when he played the violin," Ford said, a hint of curiosity in his voice.

I squinted at Ford. "That's the most random information I've ever heard. Why do you know that?"

Ford gave a shrug and held up the book in his hands. "I like biographies," he explained. "They had a decent library in prison, and I did a lot of reading. Jefferson named the bird Dick, and it sat on his shoulder and sang along with the violin. And more than that," Ford continued, leaning forward, his eyes suddenly bright. "Jefferson had a retreat he called Poplar Forest."

"No shit," I muttered, pieces falling into place in my brain. I sank into the armchair opposite Ford's and did a quick search on my phone using the words *Thomas Jefferson cipher*. It felt like a stab in the dark, but I hit pay dirt.

I held my breath, scrolling through one web page, then another. When I'd learned what I needed to know, I looked at my brother. "Thank you. Thank you. It would have taken me a million years to put that together."

To Ford's obvious surprise, I threw my arms around him in a quick hug and dashed out the door. I was going to see Forrest sooner than I'd thought. But first, I'd have to go shopping.

Chapter Eight

FORREST

“Sterling Sawyer is here to see you.” Penny, the assistant I shared with Royal and Tenn, didn’t give any indication that Sterling’s visit was significant.

I knew better. Sawyers Bend was a small town, and Penny kept her ear to the ground.

“Send her in, please,” I said in the most neutral tone I could manage with adrenaline spiking my heart rate. I hadn’t heard a word from Sterling in seven days, and playing it cool was killing me. I’d picked up my phone to call her at least a thousand times, and every time, I’d put it back down. Excuses to talk to her filled my head. We could brainstorm on the clue. I could hold her magnifying glass. Mostly, I just wanted to see her, to be near her again.

I resisted the urge to play on our shared quest as a reason to see her. I’d been an idiot so far when it came to Sterling, but I was finished making stupid decisions where she was concerned. If I wanted her back, I had to be smart. Pushing for more was not the way to go. She knew I wanted her, knew my feelings hadn't changed. And I was the one with the code. The second she figured out the clue to the key, she'd come straight to me. For now, I'd just have to wait.

I could be patient, and I had been, but every day of the past week had been an eternity. And now she was here.

I stood as she strode in, a small brown shipping box in her hands, her blue eyes bright with excitement. "Do you have it with you?" she asked the second the door closed behind Penny.

I pulled the index card out of my top desk drawer and set it in front of her on the far side of my desk. Sterling sat in the chair, perched on the edge, practically vibrating with tension. She snatched up the index card, her eyes flashing over my father's writing, then set it back down and pried open the box in her hands.

"You just have it in your desk," she muttered as she pulled at the tape. "Anyone could walk in and take it."

"It hasn't left my side," I assured her.

She let out a short grunt deep in her throat, but that was the only acknowledgment I got until the shipping box was opened, and she pulled out a smaller, clear plastic box from within. Inside was what looked like a wooden rolling pin.

I drew on my diminishing store of patience and waited until she'd opened the second box and removed what was inside. I shook my head, staring at it, still not sure exactly what it was. A cylinder of wood, about seven inches long and three inches in diameter, with handles on either end. Sterling held the ends, twisted her fingers, and the wooden barrel shifted.

I gave in to my curiosity. "What is that?"

Sterling's eyes lit with triumph as she grinned across the desk at me. "A Jefferson cipher wheel," she said. She held up the device, showing me that what I'd taken for a solid wooden cylinder between the handles was actually a series of discs with what looked like letters around the outside edge.

"How does it work?" I asked, fascinated as much by her excitement as by the cipher wheel itself.

"Each of these twelve discs has twenty-six letters. You turn the wheels to line up the letters in your message. Then you pick another line from the wheels, and that's your code."

"And whoever gets the code matches it on the wheel and then turns the wheel until they find a line that makes sense," I finished, understanding.

"That's the idea," Sterling said. "I wouldn't have figured it out, but my brother Ford read a biography of Jefferson, and look—" She turned the index card around so I could read it and explained what the references in the clue meant.

"My dad always did like biographies," I said. "So, you're going to use the wheel to break the code."

"I hope so," she said. "I guess we're going to find out. I need a pen and something to write on."

I handed her a legal pad and pen, watching as she painstakingly worked her way down the cipher wheel, letter by letter, fighting with the tight fit of the wooden discs. A thought occurred to me. "How do you know all the cipher wheels are the same? I mean, back when Jefferson was using them, they would have been. But now?"

Sterling's fingers froze, and she looked at me, abject horror flooding her eyes. "I don't. I don't know." She shook it off, lifting her chin and straightening her shoulders before going back to work on the next disc on the wheel. "This is the cipher wheel they carry in the Monticello gift shop. I paid extra for overnight shipping. It's supposed to be an exact replica of the original. Your dad strikes me as the kind of guy who would have used the original."

She was right—he was exactly that kind of guy. I nodded in agreement, keeping my mouth shut, my eyes locked on the wheel as she matched the code, one letter at a time. It took two full passes down the wheel to decipher the code.

Sterling stared down at the legal pad, her eyes flicking back and forth before she reached out and made four slashes, dividing the line of letters into five words.

Sweet treat under the trees.

Sterling looked up at me. "Sweet treat under the trees. Please tell me you have some idea what that means."

"Sweet treat under the trees," I said to myself, thinking.

"Maybe I need to read a Jefferson biography," she said, staring down at the words on the paper.

A memory shimmered to the surface of my mind. "We have to go back to Willow Springs. He's talking about the park. We used to have ice cream there after we went to the library."

Sterling sat back, her shoulders slumped in defeat. "So we go back to the park, and then what? He couldn't have hidden anything at the park."

"We won't know until we go check it out. He got us this far. Anyway, do you have any other ideas?"

"No," she said, dejected. "I guess we're going back to Willow Springs."

I glanced at the clock. "We can't go today. It'll be too dark by the time we get there." I gave my calendar a quick look. Clear. "First thing tomorrow," I said.

"Fine. I'll meet you at your house," Sterling said. She gathered up the cipher wheel, sent a dirty look at the index card sitting on my desk, gave me a short nod, and stalked out of my office.

I picked up the index card and sat back in my chair, my eyes lingering on my father's precise printing. None of this was what I'd expected when I finally got my hands on my father's statue of Vitellius. Like everyone, I'd figured the numbers were an account we hadn't been able to find. Then, when Sterling had determined it was a code, I'd thought that would be it. We'd go to the bank and get the money. Simple and straightforward.

My father hadn't been a whimsical man. He'd been gruff. Loving, sure. I'd never had a doubt he loved me or my mom. But a scavenger hunt using codes? I wouldn't have thought— Then it hit me, and wet heat coated my eyes. I'd lost him too young to know if this was like him. Maybe he'd been into codes and ciphers. Maybe he had been whimsical, but I hadn't had the chance to see that side of him yet.

When we were at the bank, Mr. Webber had said that my father intended for us to solve the codes together. Twin waves of grief and anger hit me at once. Grief for the time I'd lost with my dad, and anger, a furious, pointless rage.

Why would my father have set something like this up and then left us? I couldn't understand. Why give up? He'd lost his business and the Vitellius. But, surely, he hadn't needed the statue to unravel the code. Losing the Vitellius wouldn't have meant he lost everything.

Had he been so humiliated at losing the company that he hadn't been able to see a way forward? Had there been more going on than I'd known?

I let out a bitter laugh. Of course, there'd been more going on than I'd known. I was thirteen. I hadn't known jack shit about anything.

I couldn't solve my father's puzzles at his side as he'd planned. But maybe, as Mr. Webber had said, if I couldn't do this with my dad, at least I could do it with someone I loved. And if I managed not to fuck things up again, maybe it would help me get back the person I wanted most. Sterling.

Chapter Nine

FORREST

She was at my door not long after the sun crested the mountains, this time looking far more like herself in skinny jeans and a fitted T-shirt, her hair loose and flowing over her shoulders, a travel mug of coffee in her hand.

We were on the road minutes later. "Did you bring the cipher wheel?" I asked as we passed through town.

"Yep. And this time, I remembered a notebook and a pen."

If I'd hoped the car ride would give us a chance to talk, those hopes were dashed. Sterling sipped her coffee and stared out the window. At first, the silence between us felt odd, like a sweater that was too tight. Finding things to talk about had never been a problem when we'd been together. We could talk all night about everything and nothing. I'd told her more about myself than I'd ever told anyone.

We were past that now. I'd killed the ease between us with my lies, and I couldn't bring it back with force. I couldn't make Sterling talk to me. The only way I could rebuild trust was to show her she could trust me, and badgering her into conversation wouldn't get us there. Patience had never been a problem for me until Sterling. And where she was concerned, patience was all I had. Patience and hope.

A few hours later, we pulled into a space beside the park in Willow Springs, the town bustling on this sunny summer morning. The park itself wasn't deserted, but there were a few people lingering, everyone on their way somewhere, at least for the moment.

Sterling got out of the car ahead of me, following the sidewalk to the brick pathway that crisscrossed the park. In the center was a statue of the town's founder. We went there first, Sterling examining every inch of the concrete base and the brass plaque affixed to the front.

"Nothing," she said in disgust.

"It's not here," I said with absolute assurance, feeling off-balance but knowing I was right. Sterling was the expert in code-breaking. I was just along for the ride. But though the statue dominated the center of the park, it wasn't what we were looking for. I must have walked by it a hundred times with my mom or dad when I was a kid, and I couldn't remember either of them ever mentioning it. "It's not here," I repeated and walked around the statue to the brick path on the other side, following it to stop in front of a bench beneath an oak tree.

I stared down at the painted wooden slats, falling back in time to when I sat here and my feet swung, toes barely scraping the brick as I licked a strawberry ice cream cone. I could still hear my dad's voice in my ear.

"You've got a runner on the side, Buck," and I'd turn the cone to lick up the drip of ice cream before it could hit my fingers.

"Why the bench?" Sterling asked.

I cleared my throat, my words coming out rough and low. "My dad used to take me to the library on Fridays after school. After, we'd get ice cream over there." I pointed across the park to the ice cream shop that had been beside the library as long as I'd been alive. "We'd bring our cones over here and eat them on this bench. He always made me promise to eat every bite of my dinner so my mom wouldn't know we'd had dessert first. I always thought she knew, though."

I swallowed hard. It was so easy to remember the times they fought and how hard things were after he left us. Maybe easier than remembering the softness in her eyes when we'd come home, ice cream all over my shirt and a canvas bag stuffed with books. She'd smile at him and rest her head on his shoulder. There had been love, too. So much love. And then he'd been gone, and everything had fallen apart.

Sterling's hand closed around mine in a tight squeeze that was over almost before I registered her touch. "This has to be it, then," she said, dropping to a crouch in front of the bench and studying it. Shaking her head, she stood and walked around to the other side. "Hey, there's a plaque. Holy shit! Forrest!"

I joined her on the other side of the bench and saw it immediately. A small rectangular plaque.

This bench was donated by Alan Buckley in honor of his son, Buck.

Beneath those words was another code. This one read, KVOZAVREV.

My heart pounding against my ribs, I asked, "What does it say?"

Sterling already had the cipher wheel in her hands. "Give me a sec," she muttered, squinting down at the small letters on the wooden discs, turning them one by one until she had them all, then scanning the cipher wheel for a line that was more than random letters and numbers.

With a gasp, she surged to her feet, holding the cipher wheel above her head. "Boathouse!" she shouted in triumph, throwing her arms around me.

Her mouth landed on mine, and all thoughts of the clue evaporated. I wound my arms around Sterling, pulling her in tight, the feel of her spiking joy through my heart. I forgot all about my father, the money, the code, the pot of gold at the end of the rainbow, and just kissed her. Her mouth moved under mine, open and eager, as if she'd forgotten how much she hated me, as if we'd never been apart.

"You two done yet?" The man's voice came from behind me, gruffly amused.

My head spinning, I pulled my mouth from Sterling's. The second I caught sight of him, I shoved her behind me. He was a few inches shorter than me, with dark hair and steely gray eyes, wearing a well-tailored black suit that didn't hide the muscled bulk of his frame. Another man stood beside him wearing an identical suit, his eyes just as hard.

I didn't know either of them. Shielding Sterling had

been instinct, but I knew I'd been right. The one who'd interrupted our kiss lifted his chin at Sterling and said, "You cracked it?"

Sterling stepped out from behind me, her eyes impenetrable. "I don't know what you're talking about. I'm just here to get some ice cream with my boyfriend, and we were looking at the bench."

"Don't bullshit me, girl." The faint northeastern cadence of his voice hit me, and I had a sinking feeling in my gut that I knew exactly who we were dealing with.

"Don't talk to her," I said, mind racing, trying to figure out how to get Sterling out of here. We were in a public park in broad daylight, but if these men were who I thought they were, that didn't make us safe.

His eyes never shifted to me, all his focus on Sterling. "You cracked the code on the statue," he said. "You're a smart one, aren't you?"

Sterling didn't respond.

"It wasn't an account number, was it? It was a code. And you cracked it."

Sterling's eyes burned, but she kept her mouth shut.

The man didn't seem bothered by her silence. He tipped his head to the side, studying her. "I have to ask myself, what are you doing with this guy?" His eyes landed on me for a long second before shifting back to Sterling. "He used you. He lied to you. What did he promise you to get your help? A cut of the money?"

Something must have shown in Sterling's face because the man leaned in like a hound on the scent of his prey. "Do you know who I am?" he asked.

Sterling gave an abrupt shake of her head.

"Callum Leary."

Fuck. That was all he needed to say. I'd been right. Being in the middle of the town square in broad daylight couldn't keep us safe from these men.

Callum Leary finally acknowledged me with a point of his finger. "We've been waiting for this one to make a move. I was starting to think maybe the whole account number on the statue thing was bullshit. Especially since we heard about it from Elliott Hall."

Elliott Hall was Scarlett Sawyer's ex-husband, a low-grade fuckup of a criminal who'd stolen the statue from me after I bought it at auction. Before it made its way from Elliott to the Learys, Sterling's cousin Bryce had stolen it from Elliott. The Learys knew about the money. Hawk had been keeping an eye on them, and since no one made a move to come for it, I'd forgotten about them. Apparently, the Learys hadn't forgotten about the Vitellius.

Sterling nodded in recognition. "I know who you are."

"Good," Callum Leary said. "Saves me time. I have to ask you again—what are you doing with this guy? It's been a year, so I figure Powell can't solve it himself. What did he offer you?"

"Twenty-five percent," Sterling said, taking a step away from me.

I had to resist the urge to yank her behind me. Every cell in my body told me to drag her to the car, to get her away from Callum Leary and his partner by any means necessary. But I stayed put. Better to find out exactly what their plan was. I didn't like where this was going. I hated hearing him lay it out like that, reducing what I was to Sterling to percentages and all the reasons I didn't deserve her.

"You don't need the statue anymore, do you?" Callum asked.

Slowly, Sterling shook her head. Fear spiked down my spine, turning to ice in my gut. "Sterling," I said under my breath. She ignored me.

"So, you don't need him either," Callum said, nodding at me. "You're the code breaker. He's just dead weight. And we'll cut you in for a hell of a lot more than twenty-five percent. I like to have smart people on my team."

"That's why you hired Elliott Hall?" I asked, staring down into Callum's sharp gray eyes. I wanted to keep him talking so I could figure out an angle to get him away from Sterling.

He shook his head. "Elliott Hall was a mistake. I don't know who he's working for now, but it sure as hell isn't us. But you?" He nodded approvingly at Sterling. "You, we could make use of."

Sterling didn't say a word.

"Think about it," Callum Leary said. "We could make you a rich woman." He held out a black business card with silver print. I reached for it, and he jerked it away. "This conversation isn't about you, friend."

This time, I kept my hand at my side, the ice in my gut spreading as Sterling took the card, looked it over, and shoved it in her back pocket.

"We'll be in touch," Leary said.

Sterling's eyes were serious as they met Callum's, and

she gave a slow nod. It seemed to be enough for him. He turned and strode out of the park, his partner beside him.

Sterling and I watched them go, their dark figures shrinking as they crossed the street and disappeared from view. I heard her draw in a long breath and hold it. She let it out in a rush and gave me a tight smile.

"I think I'm in the mood for ice cream."

I stared down at her, frozen in indecision. I wanted to grab her shoulders and shake her, to demand she give me that business card so I could tear it into tiny pieces and light them on fire.

And she wanted ice cream?

"Fine," I muttered. Yelling at her wasn't the answer. Sterling wasn't going to give me that business card unless I wrestled her for it.

I followed her across the street, my eyes scanning everywhere for a glimpse of the Learys. Nothing. They were gone as abruptly as they'd appeared.

As much as I hated the idea, my first instinct was to head straight to Heartstone Manor. Between Griffen and Hawk—both former Rangers who used to be in elite security—and the crew they'd assembled for the Heartstone security team, we had ample resources to keep Sterling safe. And Hawk knew all about the Learys.

But I also wanted to follow my father's scavenger hunt. And Sterling wanted her cut of the money. The problem was, things had changed. The business card in her pocket meant the stakes had just gone up. Way up. We were in over our heads.

I ordered my strawberry ice cream and followed Sterling back to the park, my eyes still scanning every inch of the square and coming up with nothing but a normal weekday morning in Willow Springs, Georgia. She led me to the bench and sat on the side I'd always sat on.

I took my place where my father used to sit, and we ate our ice cream in silence until I finally broke. "Are you going to use that card in your pocket?" I demanded.

Sterling looked up at me, her eyes narrowed with scorn. "Do I look like an idiot? I know about the Learys. They almost shot my brother and kidnapped Scarlett and Thatcher. They threatened to torture them. If Griffen hadn't sent someone after them, God only knows what would have happened. I don't care how much money they promised me." She shook her head and snorted in disgust. "I can't believe you think I'd be that stupid."

"Oh, come on, I know you're not stupid, but I also know you don't want anything to do with me."

Sterling gave another snort. "I'm thinking you're the only idiot here," she said. "First of all, yes, I'm pissed at you. You're a liar and a user, and you broke my heart. But that doesn't put you in the same category as the fucking Learys. I'm fairly certain you're not going to shoot me, for one thing."

"That's a good bet," I agreed, relieved that she saw Callum Leary for what he was. I knew she wasn't close to ready to forgive me, but at least she didn't hate me enough to hook up with a criminal just to get back at me.

"Second," she said, giving me an appraising look, "I think it's pretty clear I need you to solve this. *Boathouse* isn't exactly a street address. But you know what it means, don't you?"

I didn't answer. I didn't have to. I took a lick of the

strawberry ice cream, letting it melt across my tongue, bringing me back to the past. To sitting under this very tree, on this exact bench, with my dad.

I knew exactly what *boathouse* meant. And I knew that whatever my father had in mind all those years ago, getting to the next clue wasn't going to be as easy as he'd planned.

Chapter Ten

STERLING

I should have been worried about the Learys. I should have been calling my brother or Hawk to let them know things had just gotten more complicated. I was more interested in the look on Forrest's face.

"Does the clue refer to an actual boathouse?" I asked, my eyes roaming the square as I ate my salted caramel cone, making sure the Learys didn't pop back up.

Forrest took another slow lick of his ice cream. The delay felt like a tease. Or maybe he just liked knowing something I didn't. Or he was pissed off that I hadn't shut down Callum Leary. He'd have to live with it.

I wasn't sure Forrest could understand the danger of saying a flat *no* to Callum Leary. I'd learned the hard way that there was a certain type of man who didn't like women telling them *no*. Callum Leary felt like one of those men to me. Refusing to take his card could have been an act of war. I wasn't sure I wanted it in my pocket, but taking it had been simpler than refusing. I'd figure out what to do with it and Callum Leary later.

"So?" I prompted, tired of waiting.

"It's a place," Forrest said. "But this isn't going to be easy."

"Where is it, and why not?" I asked, ready to catapult off the bench and onto the next clue.

I wanted the money. Of course, I did. But it wasn't just about the cash. Not anymore. I was chasing the win, the rush of elation when I worked the clue and the cipher, when I finally put the pieces in place, and the answer revealed itself. It was like my programming classes and the sense of satisfaction I got when I finished a new project, hit *run*, and my code worked. Except solving Forrest's father's clues was like that times a hundred. I wanted more, even if it meant torturing myself by spending time with Forrest.

"Well," Forrest said, after taking a last lick of his cone, "the boathouse is at the lake house. And my mother sold the lake house after my father died."

"Oh." I sank back into the bench. I hadn't thought about that. Alan Buckley had put this whole scavenger hunt together years ago, and I was starting to wonder if he'd intended to be at Forrest's side as he tackled the clues. Maybe Alan had planned to pass down his interest in ciphers. We'd never know.

"Where is it?" I wasn't going to give up just because somebody else owned the boathouse.

"On a small, private man-made lake about three hours from here. To the west. Not quite headed back to Sawyer's Bend but in that general direction."

"And what kind of lake house are we talking about?"

I pressed. "A cottage with a little boathouse or a mini-mansion packed with security?"

"Cottage-ish with a boathouse," he said. "Not packed with security when we lived there. Probably not now. As best as I can remember, it wasn't that kind of town. Wasn't much of a town at all."

I stood, brushing the crumbs of the cone off the front of my jeans and tossing my hair back over my shoulder. It was a beautiful summer day. Sunny and warm, but not miserably hot. A good day for a car ride.

"We've come this far. Let's go," I said. The sooner we cracked the next clue, the sooner I could retreat and get some space from Forrest. No reason to put it off if we knew where we were going. Maybe the boathouse would be the end. At this point, I was afraid to hope.

"You want to go to the boathouse? Even though we can't get in?" Forrest's eyes were distant, filled with doubt.

Annoyance prickling in my chest, I realized I wanted him to be as excited as I was about this crazy quest we were on. As soon as that thought registered, reality hit me. It had to hurt him to be here without his father. Adding in that Forrest had only been thirteen when he'd lost Alan and that Alan had chosen to leave his family—

I knew all about love and grief and betrayal. On top of that, the Vitellius and the code that had started our hunt was the thing that had broken us apart in the first place. Forrest probably had a lot of sticky, ugly, complicated feelings about all of this.

He had made it clear then and clear now that he

didn't care about the money. Maybe it was time I believed him.

I kept forgetting that I hated him, that I didn't want anything to do with him. Staring down at him, my hands propped on my hips, my eyebrow raised in irritation, I had to admit there was a part of me that wanted to forget about everything that had gone wrong. There was a part of me that wanted to do this together. As a team.

But that part of me needed to shut the hell up. We didn't need to be a team. I could solve Alan Buckley's clues with minimal input from Forrest. I'd get my payday and walk away. If he'd lied to me once, he'd lie again. I'd told myself that about a million times. But lately, a little voice had been asking, *Would he? Would he really?*

I'd made so many mistakes I couldn't count them, and I was getting a second chance. Didn't Forrest deserve the same?

I couldn't answer that. I didn't want to. If I did, I might have to forgive him, and I wasn't ready for that. I was ready to solve this thing, and I wasn't walking away because things were getting complicated. I was tougher than that.

"Don't you want to find the next clue?" I demanded.

"We don't even know what we're looking for," he shot back. "All it said was *boathouse*."

His tone made it clear he was more than a little ticked at me. I didn't care. "Then let's go to the boathouse and see if we can find anything."

Forrest crossed his arms over his chest, seeming to take root on the bench. "So, we're breaking and entering now?"

His obstinance was making me crazy. Did he want to give up? Now? I wanted to throw something at him, but my ice cream cone was gone. "I don't know how we're going to get in. We'll figure it out when we get there."

He sighed and looked around, evidently deciding that I had a point. "At least it'll be hard for them to follow us on the country roads," Forrest said, standing and balling his napkin in one fist. "Let's go."

He stalked across the park to the car, his eyes moving from right to left. I did the same, but all I saw was a normal summer day in a small town. No Learys in sight. That didn't mean they weren't out there, or that they didn't make me a little nervous. I knew what they were capable of, and despite his assurances, I didn't trust Callum Leary. Still, I figured we were safe in the meantime—Callum needed me to solve the clue, and I needed Forrest. We all had the same goal: solve the puzzle. Taking us out, or whatever hit men did, didn't help further that goal. Still, I didn't love the idea that we were relatively safe right up until we found Alan Buckley's money. I wanted the cash, but the second it was within reach, Forrest and I would have targets on our backs.

Forrest put the car in gear, and we headed out of Willow Springs. The drive to the lake house was quiet. Blue skies and green trees whipped by the windows, the bright summer sun beating down on the car. By noon, we had the AC at full blast.

On the way to Willow Springs, I'd been the one with her mouth glued shut. This time, it was Forrest, and I found myself wanting to know what he was thinking.

Was he grieving his father? Was he working on a strategy to break into the boathouse? Was he thinking about me?

Stop it, I ordered myself. *I don't want him thinking about me. We're over because I hate him, remember?*

I did. I remembered.

And still, I wanted to know—how much of the sadness in his eyes was about his father and how much was about me?

Oh my God, Sterling, my inner voice chided in exasperation. *Are you competing with his dead father for who hurt him more? Grow up. It's been a year since you dumped him. Get over it.*

I snuck a glance at Forrest, who had one hand on the wheel, his eyes haunted as he watched the road ahead. My questions were immediately answered. *Fuck.* None of this was about me. I was being a self-centered asshole. My broken heart wasn't at the center of the universe. I let out a sigh and leaned my head against the window.

It was mid-afternoon by the time we pulled off the state road onto a nondescript, winding country road. Long miles later, we popped out from beneath the trees to see a small lake, the shoreline dotted with cottages. The road turned, and we disappeared into the trees again, winding our way around the lake.

"Do you know where you're going?" I had to ask. I didn't think Forrest had been here since he was thirteen.

"Mostly," he said, keeping his eyes on the road.

"There's only one way around the lake. I just have to follow it until I find the right house number."

The somber look had left his eyes. A thread of energy ran through him, charging up with every turn around the shoreline. I didn't have to wonder if he truly recognized our surroundings.

I fell quiet, watching out the window. Based on the houses we passed, I thought Forrest was right about security. The cottages I saw weren't tiny or shabby, but they weren't the kind of mini-mansions I'd expect to be wired the way Heartstone Manor was. These places probably had basic out-of-the-box security systems, if anything. I'd be able to spot any sensors on the windows, and maybe they wouldn't have bothered with the boathouse.

I'd find out soon enough. My palms tingled with anticipation. What kind of code would it be this time? What kind of clue? And where would it take us when we found it?

Chapter Eleven

STERLING

Forrest slowed as we rounded a bend, almost coming to a stop before making a right into the gravel drive of a small cottage. White siding. Green trim. Green window boxes overflowing with flowers, the lake sparkling beyond the house. At its edge stood a matching white and green boathouse.

Forrest stopped the car, staring at what had been his family's lake house, his face blank, eyes shuttered. The moment stretched. I had to fight the urge to ask what he was thinking, what he was feeling. He had to feel something, being back in a place he'd shared with his father, but he didn't give a hint of what was going on in his head. Then, he abruptly put the car in reverse and backed out of the driveway.

"What are you doing?" I asked. "Is this the wrong place?"

"No," he said, "this is it, but we can't park in front of the house."

"Why not?" I asked, impatient to find a way into that boathouse.

"Think for a second, Sterling," Forrest said, his eyes glued to the right side of the road as we crawled forward. "Whoever is watering those window boxes isn't just coming up on the weekend. It's too hot this time of year. Someone is watering them every day. Maybe they ran into town for groceries. Maybe they're out visiting friends. But they will come back, and we don't want them to find our car there."

"I didn't think about that," I admitted, annoyed at myself. I was so focused on getting to the next clue, I was forgetting the most basic thing—the people who lived there.

Forrest pulled the car off the side of the road into some bushes. As we moved, the hood of the car pushed aside the greenery. I realized that we were on a driveway of sorts, but one that clearly hadn't been used in a very long time. Branches slid back into place behind us. When Forrest stopped, we were surrounded by the woods. It was a short trip through the trees and a quick dash across the lawn of the cottage next door to get to the boathouse. There was still no car in the driveway.

"Come on," I said, "let's go before somebody gets home. It might take us a while to search."

I dashed across the short expanse of lawn between the edge of the woods and the boathouse, hand closing over the knob, only to come up short as it refused to turn. Locked. Of course, it was locked. I stepped back, looking for a fake rock with a hidden key. I checked a few, all the real thing. I felt above the door frame for a spare key. Nothing.

I moved to the closest window and peered inside. A pontoon boat rocked gently in the U-shaped dock. The interior was neat as a pin; life preservers hung on the wall, and towels folded on a bench. What I didn't see were window or door sensors. If they had an alarm on the lake house, they hadn't bothered to extend it over here. Just as the thought solidified in my head, I heard a thunk and turned to see Forrest pushing open the door.

"What did you do?" I asked.

"I broke the lock," he admitted, looking a little sheepish. His eyes scanned the inside of the boathouse. "Cleaner than when we lived here," he commented.

"Does it look familiar?" I asked. "Did they change anything?"

Forrest let out a long breath. "It looks exactly the same. Some of those cabinets might be new." His voice trailed off as he studied the wall on the opposite side of the boat. "I think we had cabinets there, but I don't remember so many."

He crossed the boathouse, opening the first cabinet he came to. I followed suit, and together, we searched for something, anything that might connect to Alan Buckley's clue. I found fishing lures and old bottles of sunscreen, but nothing that looked like it could be a clue.

"What if he wrote something, and they painted over it?" I asked.

"Then I guess we're out of luck," Forrest said, shutting yet another cabinet.

"That's it?" I stared at him, but he refused to meet my eyes. "That's all you have to say?"

He turned, his hazel eyes intense with emotion for a second before he blinked and looked away. "What do you want me to say, Sterling? I can't find what's not here."

I wanted to argue, but I couldn't. He wasn't wrong. If it wasn't here, it wasn't here. But we'd barely started to look. I wasn't ready to give up. I didn't think Forrest was either, but I had to remember to give him space. Alan's ciphers were sending us down a memory road Forrest probably hadn't been prepared for.

From that perspective, I couldn't quite imagine how hard this must be for him. I couldn't relate to losing a father I'd loved. At best, I'd been indifferent to Prentice. At my worst, I despised him. I didn't remember anything of my mother except a faint memory of sweet perfume and a high-pitched laugh. But I'd lost Darcy when I'd been only seven, and the pain of it could still steal my breath. If Darcy had left these clues behind for me? A wave of grief hit me at the thought, followed by the desperate wish that I could feel her love once more from beyond the grave. So, I had to give Forrest the room he needed to work through this.

"What about—?" I stopped at the crunch of tires on gravel. "Shit." A glance out the window told me Forrest had been wise not to park in the driveway.

A gray sedan pulled in, followed by a dark SUV. A woman with short, dark hair got out of the sedan, followed by a man on the other side. They both looked a few decades older than us. Another couple about the same age got out of the SUV carrying a bag that looked like it was from a grocery store. The neck of a wine bottle poked out from the top.

"I'll set up a picnic on the dock," I heard the first woman say, and my eyes flashed to Forrest in a panic. The dock was attached to the boathouse.

"Fuck, fuck, fuck. Come on, Forrest," I grabbed his arm and pushed him away from the window.

"This way," he said, pointing me to a wooden ladder built into the back wall that I hadn't noticed. I skidded to a stop and looked into a dark square above.

"What's up there?" I asked.

"Probably a lot of cobwebs and mice, but it's big enough for us to hide in until they go away. Unless you want to go out there and explain what we're doing here."

I did not. I climbed the ladder, trying not to flinch at the thought of cobwebs and mice. I wasn't a scaredy cat, but cobwebs and mice in a hot, dark attic did not sound like fun. Cobwebs meant spiders. I wasn't a big lake girl, but I knew about dock spiders. And we were in a boathouse. My skin crawled. How much did I really want to find Alan Buckley's treasure?

Enough that I was willing to face whatever lurked above. I climbed off the top of the ladder and crawled across the rough wooden planks that made up the floor. It wasn't much of an attic. I saw life preservers so old the orange had faded to white, two mostly deflated, donut-shaped floaties, and a stack of ancient fishing poles. I scooted enough to make room for Forrest. He squeezed beside me, his head almost touching mine. It was hot, but not nightmarishly hot. A blessing, given it was a summer afternoon in Georgia.

The attic space ran the full length of the boathouse. It was long but low, and we could only sit upright in the very center. There were cobwebs, as promised, and probably some mouse droppings if I went looking for them, which I wasn't going to. But otherwise, it wasn't as gross as I'd feared.

Forrest shuffled on his hands and knees to the far end and peered out the dusty window overlooking the lake and the dock below. A few minutes later, he crawled back. "They set up a picnic on the dock. Sandwiches, salad, wine. They'll be there a while. There's no way for us to get out of here."

"Then we might as well search up here while we're stuck," I said. And we did, spending a hot, sweaty hour searching every inch of the attic. The water lapping at the pontoon boat and the wind in the trees around us more than covered any noise we were making, and I grew less and less nervous as we searched. I found the promised mouse droppings, too many cobwebs, and two black, hairy spiders. I managed not to scream, always aware of the four people just below the window at the end of the boathouse, happily eating sandwiches and drinking chilled white wine. I'd peeked through that window myself. They were having a lovely afternoon. I wished I could say the same. I'd have killed for a whisper of the breeze ruffling the surface of the lake.

If there was any clue left by Alan for his son, it wasn't in the attic of the boathouse.

I let out a sigh and sat cross-legged in the center of the attic. "I give up," I said. "Whatever we're looking for, it's not here."

Forrest moved to sit a few feet away, also cross-legged, one elbow on his knee, his chin propped on his fist. He looked glum. I felt glum, but not like Forrest. He looked more than glum—he looked defeated. I wanted to tell him everything would be okay, but I couldn't. I didn't know what was going through his head. Was he angry I'd dragged him here? Were the memories making him sad? I couldn't fix it if I didn't know what was wrong. And why the hell did I want to fix anything for Forrest Powell?

But I found myself saying, "You said you know I want nothing to do with you. But it isn't that simple."

Forrest's hazel eyes showed a flicker of acknowledgment. He didn't say anything, and I kept talking. Maybe I just needed to get it out, like lancing an infected wound.

"I've never had good judgment. With men, with sex, with love, with any of it. I don't trust anyone. I never have." I sucked in a ragged breath, both surprised and not, to find my eyes stinging. "Everything was so different with you."

Tears hit my eyes, and I turned my face away. I didn't want him to see me cry. It felt too raw. Too intimate. Too much to share with the man who had shown me what I could have and then taken it away. My chest ached, but I pushed through. I needed him to understand that I wasn't just being petty and bitchy. His lies had broken something in me. For the first time in my entire life, I'd fallen so hard I couldn't help but trust. I couldn't help but believe. And the truth had shattered me. It had been so hard not to fall back into drinking, just to dull the pain a little. Some days, I'd felt like it was all I could do to get out of bed in the morning and not take a drink before I fell asleep.

"Everything was so good with you," I choked out. "I thought this time—" I sank my teeth into my lip, fighting back the well of tears and trying to swallow through my tight throat. "I don't know how to let it go," I said. "Sometimes I want to." I raised my eyebrows, lifting my chin and looking past him at the flash of late afternoon sunlight on the water through the dusty window. "Sometimes I want to forgive you and just live our lives together, but I can't go through that again. I can't be wrong again. Not like that."

As soon as the words left my mouth, I calmed. It was what I'd needed, to let this out, with him. The pain of the last year settled, not gone, but not quite as sharp.

"I know," Forrest said, his voice heavy with pain and regret. "And I don't know how to fix it."

"I don't understand," I said, needing an answer to this one thing. "Why did you stay? I know you weren't that desperate for a job. And I know my brothers aren't that amazing to work for. So why did you stay in Sawyers Bend?"

Chapter Twelve

STERLING

It had been plaguing me since I let my pride goad me into telling my brothers not to fire him. I wanted to pretend he hadn't hurt me that badly, that Forrest sticking around town was no big deal. But it was. It was a very big deal, and it had fucking sucked. If it hurt me, I knew it had to hurt him. So why?

He shifted, turning to face me, pulling his feet in and resting crossed arms on his upraised knees. In the dim light of the attic, I thought I could see all the way to his soul and the open wound inside.

"I wanted to see you."

I shook my head. It didn't make sense. He'd only seen me a handful of times in the year we'd been apart. It wasn't enough to stay in Sawyers Bend.

"I wanted to be there if you needed me."

If I needed him. It was a weird thing to say, but I knew what he meant. A month after I dumped him, I'd almost died in a fire when my sister's estranged husband had tried to kill her. When I came to, in the hospital,

Forrest had been sitting outside my room. He stayed there, almost around the clock, until I was discharged. He didn't bother me, he didn't get in the way of the nurses, but he was there. Looking after me. Protecting me.

And more recently, when my sister Quinn's guide business had been vandalized, Forrest had been there. I worked with Quinn, running the shop and answering the phones while she was leading hiking or fishing trips. Someone looking for evidence proving who had killed my father had destroyed the inside of the shop. At the first glimpse of the destruction, my heart had cracked. And Forrest had been there, bringing coffee and cookies, helping Hawk board up the windows. We hadn't exchanged a single word, but he'd been there.

"You can't just hang around Sawyers Bend, waiting to rescue me from my fuckups," I said.

A ghost of a smile touched his lips. "First of all, none of those things were your fuckups. And second, I can go anywhere I want to. You can't tell me where I can live."

"And what if I tried? What if I asked you to leave?"

Forrest let out a huff of air. "I don't know. I love you, Sterling. I think I love you more now than I did when we were together. I know more about you now."

A bitter gust of a laugh sprung from my chest. "If you know more, I'm surprised it didn't make you fall out of love."

He shook his head, his eyes sad. "The irony is that if you'd trusted me enough back then to show me the things I've learned since, I would have come clean a lot sooner."

"Way to make it my fault that you lied," I muttered.

He sat as straight as he could under the low ceiling.

"That's not what I meant. It's my fault. I was wrong. But it's also the truth. I didn't understand. I saw you that first day at the inn and—" He swallowed, staring at the rough beam above his head. "You dazzled me. You're so fucking beautiful. Funny and crazy smart. You were dazzling, and I didn't see. I didn't see how much my lies would hurt you. I didn't think I could hurt you at all. And then I was so in love, I couldn't do a decent risk/reward analysis because I couldn't tolerate the idea of losing you. And I didn't know how much you needed the truth."

He fell silent. So did I. I didn't have anything to say. I wanted to yell at him, *everybody needs the truth*, but I knew what he meant. I liked to act like I didn't have any vulnerabilities, like I didn't have a soft, mushy center. Sterling Sawyer was solid badass, all the way to my core.

But that was a fucking lie. I'd loved Forrest more than I'd ever loved anyone, except maybe Darcy and Parker and Quinn and Griffen. But I'd never let Forrest in enough to see my truth. To see how much need I held inside me. How much I needed him to love me. How much I needed his devotion, his loyalty. I needed it like water on parched soil. Like the sun after the winter.

I needed everything he had to give me so fucking badly, and I hadn't let him see it at all. I could give a thousand excuses—it was the way I was raised; we didn't show vulnerability in our house, not unless we wanted to be punished for it. And that was true. But it was also bullshit. Because I loved him. I loved Forrest. And if I loved him, didn't he deserve to see all of me? Shouldn't I have trusted him enough?

But I hadn't. And then, when he lied, I'd punished him for it as if he'd known everything all along.

I let out a long sigh, pulling my knees up to rest my forehead on them. "God, we fucked this up."

"Yeah, we did," Forrest said, and I realized I'd spoken aloud.

My lips parted, and I almost asked, "*Can we start again?*" But I clamped my mouth shut. It was the heat and the dark. I was tired. I needed a nap. I grasped for excuses.

It was too late for us. It had to be too late for us, didn't it?

The slam of a car door struck our ears. Slowly, Forrest uncoiled his long frame and shuffled to the small window at the end of the attic.

"They're leaving," he said.

"What do we do?" I asked when he came back.

"We go down and keep searching the boathouse. Maybe my father wrote something on one of the beams."

"Maybe," I said. "It's worth a look, I guess." I wasn't ready to accept that the boathouse was a dead end. We hadn't had a chance to search thoroughly before we fled to the attic. Maybe the next clue was waiting for us on the side of a beam or hidden underneath one of the benches. My heart started to pound in anticipation once more. "We have to find it."

After a peek through the hole in the attic floor, Forrest called, "All clear," and we climbed down the wooden ladder.

Forrest surveyed the inside of the boathouse. "Grab that step stool and check the beams on that side," he ordered. "I'm going to check out those built-in benches by the door. I think I remember that my father built them. The life jackets hung above them."

I watched him get on his back to examine the underside of the benches before I climbed up on the step stool to examine the beams running the width of the boathouse. They were old, weathered, draped in cobwebs in the corners, unadorned except by nature. Alan hadn't left his clue on the beams.

From the other side of the pontoon boat, I heard a low groan. I jumped off the step stool and made my way to Forrest. "What did you find?"

"Good news and bad news."

"Yeah? Give me the good news first," I said. I was usually a bad-news-first kind of girl, but I needed some good right now.

"The good news is I think this is where my father hid the clue," Forrest said. "The bad news is it's not here anymore."

I got down beside him, looked beneath the bench, and saw what he meant. Someone, likely his father, had built a wooden box into the underside of the seat. Maybe it once had a locked door. Maybe it had been self-contained. But now, half of it was missing, and the splintered wood where two of the sides had been pulled apart was dulled with age.

Whoever had removed Alan Buckley's clue from the box had done it a long time ago.

"What now?" I asked.

Forrest rolled to his feet and turned. Reaching out a hand, he pulled me up. When I stood, he didn't let go.

His fingers wrapped loosely around mine, and he squeezed. "I think now we go home, regroup, and figure out our next move."

"Our next move?" I was ready to decipher a code, not investigate a mystery. I was also finding the pressure of his fingers on mine distracting, and I had to stay focused.

"We need to trace property ownership," he said. "Whoever owns this place now may not be the same person who bought it from my mom. Maybe it was the prior owners who found the clue. Maybe my mom found it. We need to do some searching, ask some questions. But first, we need to get out of here. We're trespassing, in case you forgot."

"I didn't forget," I said. "I just wanted to find that clue."

"I know." He squeezed my fingers again. "We'll find it."

I swiped a glance around the boathouse. My heart felt tethered here. I didn't want to leave without what we came for. It wasn't here, and the boathouse was only a shell. But it didn't feel empty. It felt filled with memories.

"Do you remember being here with your dad and your mom?" I asked.

His fingers threaded with mine. "Yeah. My dad had an old Woody, one of those wooden speedboats that look like they're from the twenties. We'd come out on the weekends and drive around the lake." He cleared his throat, his eyes seeing through the pontoon boat into the past. "My mom loved it. They were always happy here. He taught me to fish."

Forrest gave a slow look around, then turned for the door.

I glanced through the window to see the SUV missing from the driveway, the front porch of the cottage, and the lawn empty. "I don't see anyone out there."

Forrest looked down at the handle he'd broken. "Hold on." Pulling his wallet from his back pocket, he fished out a bill and set it on the bench beside the door. At my look of surprise, he said, "I'm not a complete asshole. I broke their lock. The least I can do is leave money to cover the damage."

He wasn't a complete asshole. I was beginning to think he wasn't an asshole at all.

Watch yourself, Sterling, I lectured myself. *Of course, he's not a complete asshole. You wouldn't have fallen for him in the first place if that's all he was. It doesn't make him a nice guy. Doesn't make him worth the risk.*

I wasn't going to let anyone hurt me like that again. Especially not the man who'd done it the first time.

Forrest pushed the door open. I followed him out, blinking in the bright sun. My eyes focused, and I jerked to a halt in front of the man I'd seen earlier getting out of the gray sedan.

"Well...what do we have here?" he asked, his sharp eyes locked on Forrest's face. "Trespassers?"

Uh-oh. Busted.

Chapter Thirteen

FORREST

"Can I help you two?"

I looked into the smiling face of a man my height, about the age my dad would've been if he were still alive. Bushy white hair, white mustache, and wire-rimmed glasses around alert gray eyes. He was tanned, maybe from a summer boating on the lake, and something about him tugged at the back of my mind.

"I, uh," Sterling began. "We're sorry. We didn't mean any harm." She gestured to me and gave the man her most stunning smile. "Forrest's dad used to own this place. We were in the area, and the nostalgia got to him. We wanted to stop by—"

Sterling's voice cut off as the man's friendly but sharp eyes landed on her. Out of instinct, I reached out, winding my arm around her shoulders, feeling the need to protect her from this unknown threat, though I wasn't sure the smiling man in front of me constituted a threat. His gaze shifted to me, assessing.

"Buck Buckley?" he asked, leaning closer. "Is that you all grown up?"

"You know who I am?" I asked, taken aback. He was looking at me with a combination of joy and disbelief.

"If you're Buck Buckley, I do. Your daddy was one of my best friends."

I squinted at him, shaking my head even as I held out my hand. "I go by Forrest now. Forrest Powell. But I don't —" I started to say I didn't remember him, but that bushy mustache tickled the back of my mind, and I said, without thinking, "Your mustache used to be red."

He let out a guffaw, tipping his head back. "Damn right, it did. The red leaked out of my mustache and my hair a good ten years ago. Men in my family always go white early. Now, my Sugar Mae— Not a streak of white on that head, and it has nothing to do with her monthly trips to the beauty parlor." He winked at me, and I found myself grinning back.

"Sugar because she likes to bake," I said slowly, the fragment of memory floating to the surface.

"Mae she was born with, and Sugar for her cookies." The man took my hand and pumped it up and down with vigor. "She'll be so glad to see you."

He held out his hand to Sterling.

"Bob Murrell. I'm an old friend of Buck, uh, Forrest's. I knew him when he was a little tyke. Are you the fiancée? The Sawyer fiancée," he clarified. Sterling's back went stiff. Noticing, he added in explanation, "I ran into Jack Webber in town. He mentioned he'd seen you." Bob raised an eyebrow, but his smile remained friendly.

Sterling relaxed and smiled back, giving his hand a

firm shake. "Sterling Sawyer and I don't take after my daddy." She winked, and Bob tipped his head back and laughed.

"I sure as hell hope not. Come on up to the house. Sugar Mae won't forgive me if I let you get away."

"Yeah," I said, not sure where this was heading. "But we have a long drive, so we can't stay long."

Bob stopped and turned to face us. The gaze he pinned on me wasn't unfriendly, but it left no room for negotiation. "Y'all come back to the house."

"Sure," I agreed slowly, knowing I was missing something. I glanced down at Sterling and raised an eyebrow.

She shrugged a shoulder and said quietly, "Why not?"

"I parked down the road," I said. "If we're going to come in for a visit, I should move the car." Sterling's purse was in the car, and I didn't like not having transportation close by. Just in case.

"No problem," Bob said with a smile. "I'll introduce Sterling to Sugar Mae while you get the car."

That was a no-go. I wasn't leaving Sterling with a stranger, no matter that I remembered him a little from childhood. I crossed my arms over my chest and shook my head. "We'll both go."

"It will only take a few minutes," Sterling added, leaning into my side with the faintest pressure. She didn't want me to leave her alone with Bob. He watched us, eyes narrowing until he gave a nod.

"We'll all go," he said, pivoting to walk down the gravel drive.

"You really think we're going to take off?" Sterling

asked, falling into step beside Bob. "Forrest will want to see the house at least."

Bob flashed her a smile. "I'm not willing to take the chance. I haven't seen him in almost seventeen years. Mae would never forgive me if I let Alan's boy get away before she can put eyes on him."

I wanted to believe it was that simple, but my gut said Bob wasn't telling us everything. I didn't think we were in any danger, exactly, but I didn't like being in the dark. We fell silent on the short walk to the overgrown drive where I'd stashed the car. Another few minutes and we were parked in front of the cottage.

"Sugar Mae must be wondering where I disappeared to," he said to himself. Opening the car door, he got out, turning to us. "Come on. Bet you want to see the inside. We bought it from your mama when she moved out west. We haven't changed much. Upgraded the furniture. Redid the kitchen. That's about it."

I went through the front door to find a trim woman in the kitchen, stirring something in a bowl at the counter. Her brown eyes brightened as she turned to greet her husband, flaring wide with surprise at the two strangers behind him. Then, her mouth curved into a welcome grin.

"Oh, my lord," she said, her eyes locked on my face. "You are the image of your father. Jack Webber said you'd been in town, but I didn't dare to hope you'd show up over here."

She crossed the kitchen and pulled me into a hug. I hugged her back automatically, my head spinning. All I could think was that she smelled the same. Vanilla and sugar.

"You used to make the best cookies," I said. "With sprinkles."

"You remember!" Sugar Mae's smile was so wide I thought her cheeks would crack. "You were always such a good boy. I knew you liked my cookies. And now you're back, and you brought your fiancée. Hard to imagine little Buck all grown up and getting married, but time does go by, doesn't it?" She patted my arm, her eyes a little misty. "Let's get you a glass of wine. Is there any left in that bottle, Bob?"

"I'll open a new one," he said.

"Don't go to any trouble for us," Sterling cut in. "We have a long drive to get back to Sawyers Bend and—"

"One glass of wine won't hurt. You'll have plenty of time for it to wear off." Sugar Mae's smile dimmed a fraction, her eyes sliding across the kitchen to meet her husband's.

"You'll be hungry," Bob said. "Y'all must have been stuck in that boathouse half the afternoon."

I didn't bother to hide the truth. The heat of a flush on my cheeks, I nodded, feeling like I was thirteen again and in trouble for taking the boat out without permission.

"Yes, sir," I found myself saying.

"Then you'll stay for dinner," Mae said. "It may be instead of that wine, they could use some iced tea."

"Iced tea would be heavenly," Sterling said. "And again, we're so sorry for the trespassing. Forrest was remembering the lake and—"

"Young lady," Mae interrupted, "we know you're not here for nostalgia."

Sterling went still beside me. I wound my arm around her waist, pulling her closer.

"Why do you think we're here?" I asked.

Mae's eyes shifted to Bob again. He nodded. She shook her head and said, "I'll get the iced tea. We'll go out to the porch."

Bob nodded again. Sterling started to follow him. Her good manners got the better of her, and she stopped. "Can I help, Sugar Mae?"

"No, honey. You go make yourself comfortable on the porch, and I'll be out in a flash."

We followed Bob's tall frame through the cottage to the back porch overlooking the lake. I caught an impression of whitewashed walls and furniture in light colors with bright accents in the pillows and art. Overall, the place was cheerful, inviting, and oddly familiar.

We stepped onto the porch, and I stopped, the lake spread out before me, extending to the thick green trees on the opposite shore. The house hadn't tripped my memory, not completely, but this—I knew this view. How could I have forgotten this place?

"Just like I remember," I said. "Not the inside, but this view never changes, does it?"

Bob agreed. "Not so far. Especially not with the state park across the way. When your momma said she was going to move back to her people, we offered for this place. Thought we'd save her the real estate commission. We always loved this view when we'd come out here with your parents." He gestured us to a group of rocking chairs set up facing the water, loosely arranged around a low table.

The familiar mineral organic scent of the lake drifted into my nostrils. I loved that smell. I'd forgotten how much. The gentle slap of water against the shore was punctuated by shouts in the distance. I looked to see a family jumping off their boat to splash in the lake. Memories from my childhood came flooding back. We hadn't been here enough, but when we were, we were happy, the three of us.

And yet, my father had left me. Left us. It made no more sense to me now than it had then.

"I wish—" I let out a sigh and didn't finish the thought. It would have been too much to maintain the house from so far away. Of course, she'd sold it. Aloud, I said, "She needed the money."

"That she did." Bob nodded. "We lived here for about five years before we decided to do some work on the kitchen. While we were at it, we decided to add some more benches in the boathouse."

Suddenly, I knew exactly where Bob was going with all of this.

"Our carpenter found the compartment your father built under the bench," Bob said.

"What did you find inside?" Sterling asked, leaning forward. "What did you do with it?"

Bob looked from Sterling to me. "Don't see a ring on her finger to go with all those questions." He raised an eyebrow in my direction, his eyes genial, but the words had the slightest edge.

"We're getting the ring resized," Sterling said easily.

It should probably have bothered me to see how well she lied, especially considering she'd dumped me for the same offense. But even at my most defensive, I knew my lie had been different.

"What did you find in the compartment?" I asked Bob.

"I found something," Bob agreed. "I think it came from your father. Looked like something Alan would have left. And I think it's for you. I can't think of anyone else who should have it, at least."

"Can I see it?" I asked.

Bob shook his head. "I don't think so. Not yet."

"Why not?" Sterling asked, her brow furrowed. My girl wanted to lay eyes on the next clue, as did I. It had to be driving her crazy.

But as much as I loved watching her try to solve these things—the way she puzzled them out was fucking sexy—I was more interested in what Bob was hiding from us, and why.

Chapter Fourteen

FORREST

"What do you want for it?" I asked, mentally calculating what I was willing to pay for the next clue. I wasn't convinced there was a pot of gold at the end of this rainbow, but if we walked away, I wouldn't have an excuse to see Sterling.

Bob gave a snort of disgust, shaking his head. "You got me all wrong, boy." He looked up with a wide smile. "Ah, here she is." He hopped out of his chair to open the door behind me for Sugar Mae.

She came out holding a tray loaded with a pitcher of iced tea, four glasses filled with ice, and a plate of sugar cookies, covered in sprinkles.

"Now," Mae said as she sat, setting the tray on the low table, "tell me everything you've been up to. Where are you living? What are you doing? How's your mama? Are you in this neck of the woods for a visit, or have you come home? I want to know it all." Before I could answer, she went on. "You were always such a bright boy. So well behaved and sweet. Your parents were so proud of you. I thought we'd get to see you grow up, and then poof! Sometimes life just stabs you in the heart, doesn't it?"

I nodded, feeling an echo of that long-ago stab as I took in her familiar bright eyes. "Sometimes it does."

"Here's the deal," Bob said, leaning forward to pick up an iced tea and handing it to me. "You'll stay for dinner." He looked to his wife. "We have enough?"

"We do," she agreed with a nod. She continued where Bob left off. "You'll stay for dinner and catch us up on everything you've been up to since you left. You'll stay the night, and in the morning, we'll give you what your father left for you."

"Why not just give it to us now?" Sterling asked.

"We could," Mae said, her eyes sliding to Bob and then back to me. She reached out to pat my hand. "We could. Maybe we should. But it's been seventeen years—and I know you don't remember us the way we remember you—and the three of you were like family to us. In a million years, I never would have thought we'd lose your father that way. I would have said he didn't have it in him. Then he lost his company." Her eyes darted to Sterling, then back to mine. "And I guess he lost heart. I don't know. Sometimes, you don't know what people have inside them. We've missed him, and your mother, and you."

Mae handed me a cookie. I took it, a lump growing in my throat.

"Now, here you are," she said. "And I have a feeling if I hand you what you came for, you're going to disappear, and who knows when we'll see you again. So, you'll stay, you'll tell me everything we missed out on, get a good night's sleep. And you can head home in the morning with what you came for. Fair?"

I found myself nodding. It was a little weird. I wanted to say these people didn't know me... But they did. I just didn't remember. And if they wanted to let two strangers sleep in their house, who was I to argue?

"Sounds fair to me." Sterling flashed a blinding smile, picked up a cookie, and bit in. "I see why they call you Sugar," she said, a hint of a southern accent coloring her words. "These are delicious."

"I'll push dinner up a little early since you all have to be hungry," Mae said. "For now, tell me everything. How did you two meet? Seems an unlikely pairing."

"That's kind of a long story," Sterling said. She looked to me. "I'll let Forrest tell it. I'm curious to see what he'll say." She took another bite of cookie and sat back in her chair, a wicked grin on her face.

"We can start with that," I said. "But it's not going to paint me in a very good light."

Sterling let out a snort of laughter, but she didn't interrupt as I told the story of coming to Sawyers Bend for revenge and falling in love with her, the daughter of the man who'd ruined my father's life. By the end, Sterling had finished her cookie and taken my hand in hers. She didn't comment. Didn't condemn me. Didn't let me off the hook. She listened when, at Mae's urging, I went all the way back to the days after my father's death, when my mother decided she was done with Georgia. She'd wanted to go back to Oregon and her family. In a matter of weeks, she'd packed us up, sold the house, and driven us across the country to a new life, leaving Buck and my father's memory behind.

As we moved from the porch to the kitchen and Sugar Mae served up broccoli salad and roasted chicken, I remembered more. Seeing Bob and Sugar Mae here, at the lake house, hadn't jogged my memory because while they must have visited here at the lake, the Murrells were from Willow Springs.

As I talked and answered questions, memories came flooding back. Coming home from school and finding Mae and my mother at the kitchen table. My father, in his office, talking to Bob about who knew what, because I was a kid and I didn't pay that much attention to the grown-ups. I realized that my mother hadn't just moved us away from home, she'd excised a huge part of her life completely. For Bob and Mae, losing my father and then my mother and me so close together must have been like losing a part of themselves.

We talked into the night, Bob reminding me that my father had loved to fly-fish, something I'd forgotten, and Mae asking if my mother still devoured murder mysteries, then frowning at me when I told her I didn't know.

"I haven't seen my mother in almost a year," I told her. "Things weren't the same after Dad..." I trailed off. I didn't know how to explain the distance between us. I loved my mom. She'd always been my champion, my rock, ready with a hug or sage advice. But she'd also denied me my father, so bitter over his death that she refused to speak of him, refused to let me have my memories. It was like she'd been the perfect mom until it came to anything that had to do with my dad. Then she became a black hole, empty and cold. We should have grieved together, but instead, we'd grieved alone, and I was pretty sure both of us had done it wrong.

And on top of that, we'd fought bitterly when I told her why Sterling dumped me. Sterling wasn't the only woman I loved who I'd lied to. I'd never told my mom the exact name of my new employers, or Sterling's true identity. When the truth came out, I wasn't sure what my mother was more angry about: me lying about my job, that I'd lost the woman I loved, or that I'd reclaimed the Vitellius.

That fucking statue, as she called it. According to my mother, the Vitellius had ruined our lives once, and now I was letting it ruin my life all over again. *Leave your father in the past where he belongs*, she'd said and hung up on me. It had taken months to get on speaking terms again, and things were still distant between us.

My mother was right. I shouldn't have lied. Not to her, not to Sterling, not to anyone. But she was also wrong because I never would have met Sterling if I hadn't gone after the Vitellius. And the Vitellius was going to give me a shot at getting her back. And maybe a little bit of my father as well. But I couldn't tell my mom that. She'd never been able to see things clearly when it came to my dad.

Mae shook her head, sharing a long, heavy look with her husband. "She was so angry at Alan for leaving her. I'd hoped by now she would have forgiven him."

"She's remarried," I said, a faint smile coming to the surface at the thought of my stepfather. "Jerry's a good guy. I think she loves him. But I don't think she's forgiven my father." My throat tight, I said, "I'm not sure I have either."

Sterling made a rough sound in her throat and stroked her fingers over the back of my hand. I couldn't look at her. I hated admitting I was still angry at my father. And I knew instinctively that my anger was different from my mother's. Her loss was, in a way, a deeper betrayal. For all their arguments, they'd loved each other. And then he'd knowingly taken that away from her. From us.

"I still don't understand," I said. Bob knew what I meant. He patted my hand.

"Me either, son. But I've learned that in life, we rarely know the depth of another person's heart, even when we think we know them well. And Alan— Alan must have been struggling to have made the choices he did."

I nodded, my throat locked tight, anger and grief swirling in my chest.

"Well," Mae said, glancing at the clock, "I don't know about you two, but it's past my bedtime. Especially when I had wine in the afternoon." She reached across the table, taking my hand in a tight squeeze, her smile suddenly as dazzling as Sterling's. "I appreciate you indulging us with your time and your company. Nothing can bring back the past, but seeing you all grown up goes a long way." She let go of my hand and stood. "Let me show you to the guest room."

Chapter Fifteen

FORREST

Mae left us in the small guest room, closing the door behind herself. I turned at the sound of Sterling's giggle and saw a men's set of striped pajamas laid out on the bed beside a woman's embroidered nightgown.

"That was sweet of Mae," Sterling said, smiling down at the night clothes our hosts had left for us.

Sterling took her nightgown and disappeared into the bathroom with her purse. I heard the water turn on and looked back to the striped pj's. It was a nice gesture, but I wasn't sleeping in those pajamas. It would be like going to bed in a suit. And while the AC in the cottage was decent, it couldn't quite fight off the summer humidity.

I was lying on top of the covers when Sterling came out of the bathroom, her hair wet, the white nightgown so long it hid her feet. Sometimes, I forgot how small she was. The force of her personality took up far more space than her slight frame.

I changed places with her, taking a quick shower to

rinse off the leftover stickiness of the boathouse and sitting outside on a Southern summer night. Pulling my boxers back on, I crossed the dark room and slid beneath the covers.

Sterling eyed my bare shoulders. Drawing up the blanket, she slid her blue eyes my way. "Don't get any ideas. It would have been weird if I asked to sleep on the couch since they think we're engaged. Somehow, I don't think they'd buy that we're saving ourselves for marriage."

"Probably not," I agreed.

"Make sure you stay on your side of the bed."

"I can't promise that," I said honestly. "I have plenty of ideas, but I won't act on them."

"Hmm. See that you don't," she said in a crisp voice, turning out the light.

She rolled over and appeared to fall asleep. That was fine. I could keep my hands to myself. I lay there in the dark, letting the day wash over me. Strawberry ice cream. My father's message in the park. The Learys and Callum Leary's card in the back pocket of Sterling's jeans. I could slide out of bed while she was sleeping and steal the card, tear it up, and flush it down the toilet. I almost did it, my fingers itching to destroy the thing and cut off her connection to Callum.

But I stayed where I was. Destroying the card wouldn't remove the threat; it would only undermine her and piss her off, no matter how much I wanted to do it. Instead, I let myself drift, absorbing all the memories that had surfaced since Bob caught us leaving the boathouse.

Helping my mom and Sugar Mae at the hospital

fundraiser. Going fishing with my dad and Bob. So much I'd forgotten. In my grief and anger, I'd locked my childhood away, even from myself.

Sleep came, slowly pulling me under into dreams that smelled of the lake and sugar cookies. I woke hours later, the room silent but for the rattle of the AC down the hall. I opened my eyes to find Sterling's face inches from mine, one leg draped over me, her hand on my bare shoulder.

"This doesn't mean anything," she said as she shifted closer and touched her lips to mine. I took the invitation, drawing her lower lip between mine and sucking, nipping, tilting my head to drive my tongue into her mouth. God, the taste of her. It was home.

Sterling was where I wanted to be. She anchored me, gave me roots. This connection between us was everything. I kissed her again and again, my arms coming up to hold her. I found bare skin, the nightgown gone, and my mind short-circuited.

Sterling in my arms, her body against mine— This was all I wanted. She moved over me, straddling my waist, sitting up, and trapping my very hard cock beneath the heat of her. She leaned forward, her full breasts brushing my face. I turned my head to capture a nipple, sucking hard, loving her shocked gasp, the way her thighs tightened at the burst of pleasure. Sterling sat back up, a small dark square in her hand.

A condom. Had she been planning this? That was too much to hope for. But the idea that she was running around with condoms in her purse left me unsettled. Who was it meant for? Not me, that much I knew.

Let it go, I told myself. *All I've wanted for the last year is this. Sterling, naked in my arms. Now she's here. Stop fucking asking questions.*

That was my dick talking. But my dick was wrong. I wanted so much more than Sterling naked in my arms. I wanted her trust. I wanted her love. I wanted her at my side. I couldn't have any of that. But she was offering this. Her body, not her heart.

That would have to be good enough. For now.

I reached up to pluck the condom out of her hand. "Promise you won't hate me later," I said. "At least not more than you already do."

Sterling let out a sigh and leaned forward, brushing the tips of her breasts against my chest. "This doesn't mean anything," she said again, "but I promise if you make me come, I won't hate you for it later."

"That, I can do," I said, tucking the condom under the edge of my hip. Cradling her face in my palms, I pulled her down for a kiss, one hand on the back of her neck. Her mouth on mine, I let my hands roam, stroking down her spine, coming around to cover her breasts. Squeezing, tugging at her nipples, loving the way she squirmed against me. The heat of her branding me through my boxers.

I pushed at them with one hand, and she moved just enough to help me shove them down my legs and toss them on the floor.

"Where's that condom?" she demanded.

I handed it to her, and she tore it open, rolling it down, her fingers fumbling just a little. Impatient, I slid my hand up her thigh, dipping a finger inside her. So slick and so fucking hot. She was going to kill me, and I'd die happy.

A second later, she rose up above me, bracing her hands on my shoulders. I closed my hands over her hips, pulling her forward. Lifting her, positioning myself, and pulling her down. Propping up on my elbow just enough to fasten my mouth to her nipple and suck, hard.

I heard her gasp as she rocked her hips, taking me deep, grinding her clit into me, breathing my name. "Forrest. Oh, God. Forrest."

It had been a long year without her touch. I could have come ten seconds after she took me to the hilt, but I'd made a promise, and I wasn't going to break it.

Lying back, my hands tight on her hips, I rocked up into her in a familiar rhythm I knew would drive her out of her mind.

"Pinch your nipples," I ordered.

Sterling's eyes flared, her eyebrows pulling together as if she planned to argue. I rolled my hips again, grinding her clit between our bodies until her head tipped back, her hands rising to tug at her nipples, her hair falling around her, sliding over her skin like silk.

She was a goddess. My goddess, and I could have watched her move above me forever. But I intended to make good on my promise and then some, so I let go of one hip, sliding my hand to the apex of her thighs, and gently rolled her clit under my thumb. Sterling's body went stiff. She groaned low and long, not loud enough to be overheard by our hosts, but close.

Her pussy clamped on my cock in hard, hot pulses. I almost tipped over the edge with her. It felt so good, so right, so perfect—her coming around me, gasping my name. But not yet. Gritting my teeth, I held my breath, squeezing my eyes shut.

Not yet. I wasn't ready for it to be over.

Not yet.

Sterling collapsed, her body draped over mine, the thud of her heart a quick beat against my chest. Before she could catch her breath, I rolled her to her back and settled between her legs. Her eyes flew wide.

"You didn't—" she breathed against my ear.

My lips traced her jaw, answering the question she hadn't asked with a slow, sweet kiss. I nudged my hips into hers, grinding into her clit, filling her all the way, pushing her higher and higher until all she could do was sink her nails into my shoulders and hang on.

Her knees rose, and she tightened around me, whimpering my name. "Forrest. Oh, God, please."

This time, I came with her, spilling everything—my heart, my soul, my body—into her. I stayed where I was for a long moment, braced on my elbows, trying to catch my breath. When I rolled to my back, she didn't come with me.

Sterling lay frozen for a heartbeat. Then she sat up and was on her feet. "I'll be quick," she said and disappeared into the bathroom. True to her word, after a flush of the toilet and a minute of running water, she was back. I got up to deal with the condom. When I made it back to the bed, she was on her side, facing the wall, eyes closed, blanket wrapped around her shoulders as if nothing had happened.

Her words echoed in my head. *This doesn't mean anything.*

Maybe not to her. But deep down, my soul howled in fury. *This doesn't mean anything?* How could it not? How could what happened between us in this bed mean nothing? It had been perfect. You didn't get that passion, that sweetness, that connection without love.

It meant something, even if she was determined to pretend it didn't. I turned my pillow over and pressed my cheek to the cold cotton, waiting for sleep to find me.

It must have, eventually. I woke hours later, the sun stabbing my eyes, to find myself alone. Voices filtered through the closed door. After a shower, I used the unopened spare toothbrush Mae must have left for guests, seeing that Sterling had done the same with her own guest toothbrush. As ready for the day as I could be, I joined Bob, Sugar Mae, and Sterling in the kitchen.

Sterling smiled at me like nothing had changed between us. Maybe for her, it hadn't. That thought stabbed into my heart. I pushed it away. I hadn't given up in the year we'd been apart. I sure as hell wasn't giving up now.

We shared breakfast with Bob and Mae. On our way out the door, Bob handed me a small tin box, the same kind that once held the strong, chalky peppermints my father had loved. They'd made my eyes water, but when he'd held out the tin, I always took one.

"I don't know if you'll be able to make sense of what's inside," Bob said. "Lord knows I couldn't, but it wasn't meant for me. You stay in touch, you hear?"

"I will," I said, and I meant it.

Mae folded Sterling into a tight hug, a look of surprise flashing over Sterling's face before she returned it. I shook Bob's hand, thanked him, and hugged Mae. Minutes later, we were pulling out of the driveway, Sterling holding the mint tin in her lap. She hadn't opened it yet.

I was about to ask her to look inside when we turned onto the state road. There, parked in a turnaround on the other side, was a dark sedan, Callum Leary at the wheel. Sterling rolled the window down and gave him a wide grin as we passed, giving him a thumbs-up. He acknowledged it with a brief nod.

"What was that for?" I asked. "Please tell me you're not going to use that business card."

Sterling rolled her eyes. "Don't be an idiot. They obviously know where we were. They must be tracking us somehow. They won't go bother Bob and Sugar Mae if they think we got what we came for. They'll stay on us, right?"

That sharp brain was one of the many reasons I loved her. "Good point," I said. "Are you going to open it?"

"In a minute."

She waited until we had driven ten minutes without any sign of Callum Leary's sedan behind us. Then she pried open the lid of the mint tin to find another index card inside. She squinted down at it, turned it over, and then turned it back.

"Another code, right? A clue?" I asked, glancing down into her lap to see a string of letters and numbers written in my father's handwriting on an otherwise blank white business card.

"What the hell is that?" I asked. Sterling flipped over the card, but there was nothing on the other side. "Where's the key?"

"I have no fucking clue," Sterling said with a huff, clicking the lid back on the tin.

"What now?" I asked.

Sterling glanced behind us, looking again for Callum's black sedan. She shook her head and faced forward, her eyes flicking to me, then back to the road.

"Now we go back to Heartstone Manor and tell Griffen and Hawk about the Learys," she said. "I think we're officially in over our heads."

Chapter Sixteen

STERLING

We left Callum Leary behind us and made our way around the lake. I sat beside Forrest, eyes on the trees flashing by, my hands folded in my lap, mind reeling from the events of the past twenty-four hours. I didn't know what was up and what was down anymore.

I'd solved another clue and cracked the Jefferson cipher. I'd been feeling pretty full of myself when that mint tin had landed in my hands. Then I opened it and hit a brick wall. I'd seen alphanumeric codes before, but those had come with a key. Without a key, I didn't know where to start. I could write a program to decrypt a simple code. At least, I thought I could. I knew where to start, but it was really just a stab in the dark.

When I told Forrest we were in over our heads, I hadn't just meant the Learys. They were a problem all their own, but only one among many. I was lost when it came to this new cipher. And beyond that—

I glanced to my left to see Forrest, his eyes locked on the road ahead, a shadow of stubble on his cheeks, his curls mussed, and a tiny quirk to the side of his mouth, curving his full lower lip.

Fuck me. What had I been thinking? Talk about being in over our heads. Was I a glutton for punishment? Was I trying to make myself miserable? It was the only explanation for doing something so fucking self-destructive. This time, I couldn't blame Forrest. The night before, he'd stayed on his side of the bed just as he'd promised.

He'd said, "*I have plenty of ideas, but I won't act on them*," and I hadn't been able to stop wondering—exactly what kind of ideas? His words were a tease in my brain. What was he imagining doing to me? I knew what I'd had in my head, starting with pulling down that white sheet and seeing more than his bare, muscled shoulders.

Body and soul, no one had ever made me feel like Forrest. And it had been a year without him. Lying in bed beside him, I'd felt every one of those long, lonely days. He was right there, close enough to touch. I'd tried to sleep, tried to ignore him. Nothing worked. And then my body made the decision for me. It hadn't even occurred to me that he would turn me down, which on reflection, made me feel like kind of an asshole. I'd just assumed he wanted it, too. Why? Because all men wanted sex? Because he loved me? I was so wrapped up in all the ways he'd hurt me, I hadn't stopped to think about the ways I could hurt him.

At the time, I'd just wanted to touch, to feel, to go

back and bring a slice of memory to life. I'd promised him I wouldn't blame him later. My chest ached. He hadn't asked for sex. That was all me. All Forrest needed was the promise that I wouldn't hold it against him if he gave me what I wanted. I didn't know what I thought about that.

The sex was even better than before. Was that even possible? Maybe I was just sex starved. Forrest had always been deliciously bossy in bed.

Pinch your nipples.

The memory of the roughly growled order sent a shiver down my spine.

Forrest glanced over. "Are you cold? Should I turn down the AC?"

"I'm fine," I said quickly, turning my head to look out the window so he couldn't see the flush on my cheeks. It felt like my face was flaming red.

I'd lied to him. I told him it didn't mean anything; the truth was I didn't want it to mean anything. But if it didn't mean anything, I wouldn't be sitting here obsessing over it, would I?

In so many ways, I'd gotten my life together. I wasn't using alcohol to escape from life anymore. I had a job I liked. I was studying for a new career. I'd been keeping that part a secret, but still, I was making forward, positive progress in every aspect of my life. I was closer to my siblings than ever. I actually kept my room clean. And yet, I couldn't seem to get the slightest handle on my love life.

Forrest flicked on his blinker and looked over his

shoulder as he steered the car into a small gas station opposite the on-ramp to the interstate. I checked the dashboard. Half a tank. More than enough to get home.

"Why are we stopping?" I asked.

"The only thing you took from Callum Leary was his business card?" he stated, his raised eyebrow making it a question.

I wasn't following, but I nodded. "That's it. Just the business card. Why?"

He put the car in park next to the gas pump, unclipped his seat belt, and shifted to look at me. "Then how did they track us to the lake house? I know they're not tracking your phone. I'm pretty sure Hawk is the only one who can do that."

"What if they were tracking you?" I asked, turning the questions over in my head, a little surprised I hadn't thought of it first.

Forrest shook his head. "I doubt it. My phone probably isn't as locked down as yours, but it's company-issued, and my understanding is that those go through the same security process as the family's."

That threw me for a second, but then it made sense. Forrest worked closely with my older brothers, Royal and Tenn. A lot of their personal information, like schedules and contact numbers, would end up on Forrest's phone, as well as company information they'd want to keep secure.

"So, if it's not our phones..." I glanced around for Callum's dark sedan. It wasn't in sight, but now that Forrest had asked, I felt them watching us. I shivered again, this one far less pleasant.

"That's why we're getting gas," Forrest said. He got out, did the thing at the pump with his credit card, and started pumping the gas. Once it was set, he left it to fill the tank and walked around the car.

He circled the car once. On the second lap, he leaned over and disappeared from view. I'd been so distracted by second thoughts over my late-night seduction and looking for the Learys, it took me that long to realize what Forrest was doing. I unsnapped my seat belt and jumped out, going to my knees behind the front right tire, looking up into the undercarriage.

I had no idea what the undercarriage of a car was supposed to look like, which wasn't going to help me spot something that shouldn't be there. Regardless, I squinted up into the dark confusion of metal, rough asphalt biting into my knees as I crawled slowly backward. The gas pump clicked, indicating that the tank was full. We ignored it.

After a few minutes, I heard a satisfied "Got it," followed by the ding of metal on metal. I jumped to my feet and rounded the back of the car. "What does it look like?" I asked, holding out my hand.

Forrest showed me a small black box twice the size of a garage remote.

"Clever," I said. "What are we going to do with it?"

Forrest looked down at the device in his hand. "As I see it," he began, "we have four options. Option number one, we destroy it. Which would get them off our tail temporarily, but also let them know we found it and we don't want to be followed."

I nodded. That one was mostly downside, as far as I could tell.

"Option number two, we throw it out here," he said, gesturing to the trash cans beside the gas pumps.

"It would buy us some time," I said. "But eventually, they'd figure out that we weren't still at the gas station. What's option three?" I asked.

"We drive somewhere else and leave it there."

I mulled that over. "We could leave it at a hotel," I considered aloud. "Or in the next town, in a residential neighborhood. Or, I don't know, someplace we'd conceivably stop for longer than a few hours. Or..." I looked around the gas station, spotting an SUV with a packed bike rack, a plumber's van, and a state trooper. "We could put it on one of these cars. It might be fun for the Learys to chase down a state trooper."

Forrest grinned. "Only if we could catch it on camera. And I don't think we want to piss them off. I might not like it, but you're safer as long as Callum likes you."

"True," I said, "but he doesn't like me. He wants to use me. Not the same thing." I glanced again at the other vehicles getting gas and ditched that idea. I didn't want to bring trouble to anyone who hadn't asked for it.

"I'm voting for option four," Forrest said. "We put it back and drive home."

I grinned back, the benefits of option four immediately clear. "That's where they're expecting us to go, right? And if they think we're exactly where we're expected to be..."

"They won't know we found the tracker," Forrest finished.

"Then maybe they'll stop watching us as closely," I said. "At the very least," I added, "we could let Hawk and Griffen figure out what to do with it."

"I'll put it back." Forrest knelt, and I heard metal connect to metal with a satisfying magnetic click.

We hit the gas station shop for drinks and got back in the car. The rest of the ride home to Sawyers Bend was silent until we turned before town, heading toward Forrest's house.

"Aren't we going to go talk to Hawk and Griffen?" I asked.

"You left your car at my place. I thought you'd want it."

His simple, thoughtful words hit like a slap. I'd forgotten I left my car at Forrest's. Being with him like this had felt so natural, so right, despite the awkward silence between us. I'd forgotten we weren't together. I'd left my car at his house because I didn't want him to pick me up.

For the millionth time, I wondered if whatever was at the end of Alan Buckley's scavenger hunt was worth putting myself through this emotional torture. My body wanted what it wanted, but my heart was terrified. I could survive without the money. Did I need to prove my father wrong that much?

We pulled to a stop behind my car. I got out with a sigh, fumbling in my purse for my keys.

"I'll follow you to Heartstone," Forrest said, interrupting my thoughts and reminding me that this was about a lot more than Forrest and me and our failed relationship. Callum Leary was no joke. I needed my big brother, and I needed Hawk.

We were playing a dangerous game. It was time to get my head out of my ass and Forrest out of my heart. It wouldn't matter what was at the end of this scavenger hunt if I wasn't alive to enjoy it.

Chapter Seventeen

FORREST

I followed Sterling back through town, giving her space on the road but staying close. She'd been withdrawing from me all morning. My gut said she regretted her impulsive seduction the night before. I didn't want her to regret it. I wanted her to repeat it, preferably as soon as possible, but not if it was going to make her miserable the morning after.

It was hard sometimes to remember that we weren't together anymore. That conversation at the gas station about the tracker had reminded me of our past dynamic, the way we used to finish each other's sentences. It had always been like that with us, words and ideas flowing back and forth easily.

I'd screwed things up, and she'd dumped me, but it didn't make that connection go away. I'd never had that with anyone else. Neither had she—when things were good, she'd told me as much.

I was determined to fight for her. For us. But her quiet on the ride home made me wonder—what if fighting for us was hurting her? Everything in me recoiled at that thought. I loved Sterling so much that I didn't think I could find my way out of it. For the rest of my life, I'd love her.

I'd stayed in Sawyers Bend because I believed I could make her happier than she'd be without me. But what if I was wrong? She sure as hell didn't look happy now. I knew without asking that most of the darkness in her eyes was about me, not the looming threat of the Learys.

I had to decide what to do about that—even if that meant leaving—but not until we'd seen this through. Not until I knew she was safe.

Following Sterling's car, I passed through the gates of Heartstone Manor and down the long, winding road to the grand old house for the first time in a year. The asphalt of the drive was still cracked and crumbling at the edges, the result of Prentice Sawyer's lack of maintenance in the final years of his life.

But where before weeds had grown enthusiastically through those cracks, now there wasn't a weed in sight on the road itself, and those on the sides had been neatly trimmed. Heartstone no longer had the air of neglect I remembered from before. It was vaguely encouraging and unsettling at the same time. I hadn't quite imagined things changing in my absence, but of course, they had. It had been a year.

As I absorbed the changes—the trimmed bushes, the fresh sand someone had swept between the pavers in front of the house— it felt right. I hadn't liked Sterling living in Heartstone as it had been a reminder of her father's neglect.

I liked that she wasn't alone in a dusty heap of a house but surrounded by family in a home that was loved and cared for, even if all of it made me feel like everything we had together was so far in the past. She didn't look back at me as she parked and got out of the car, striding up the steps to the front doors.

I parked behind her and followed her inside.

"Griffen's probably in his office," she said as I shut the door behind us.

I stayed at her side through the entry and down the hall, trying not to remember the last time I'd walked this way, the day I'd confessed who I was. The day that had been the end between us.

Sterling reached the door, finding it half open. She dropped a brisk knock on the heavy wood.

At Griffen's call of "Come in," she pushed the door all the way open. His eyes lit as they landed on her and narrowed when they hit me. "What's wrong?" he said in a low voice, his eyes still on me, still narrowed.

I lifted my hands, palms out. "This time, it wasn't me," I said.

Sterling dropped into the chair opposite Griffen's desk. "I have good news and bad news and then some really bad news."

I sat in the chair beside her, waiting to see how she was going to spin this to her brother. Sterling wasn't reckless, but she didn't want to be told what to do, which meant she wouldn't want Griffen alarmed.

"Give me the really bad news first," Griffen said.

"The good news," she said, as if he hadn't spoken, "is that we found the next clue."

"And the bad news?" Griffen asked, resigned to doing things Sterling's way.

"The bad news is that I have no fucking clue what to do with it because there wasn't a key or a clue for where to find the key," she said with an annoyed roll of her eyes.

"Well, you figured out the first two, didn't you?" he asked.

"True," she said, flashing him a grin. "But I had an idea where to start with those."

Griffen sat back in his chair and crossed his arms over his chest. "You'll figure it out. It may take time, but you'll get it."

She smirked and tossed her hair over her shoulder. I couldn't help but smile. I'd hated seeing her sad. I loved her like this—saucy, vibrant, having fun teasing her older brother.

"So," Griffen asked, raising an eyebrow, "the really bad news?"

Sterling leaned forward and dug her hand in her back pocket. She pulled out Callum Leary's card and slapped it on Griffen's desk. "The bad news is that he showed up right after we found the second clue at the park in Willow Springs."

Griffen's eyes turned dark with a mix of shock and anger. He stabbed at his phone screen, and as whoever was on the other end picked up, he let out a terse, "My office." Stabbing at the screen again to hang up, he put the phone down. "When exactly did you see Callum Leary?" he asked, his voice dangerously calm.

Sterling's eyes flicked to me and back to Griffen. "Yesterday, late morning. And then..." Another glance at me and back to Griffen. "And then, um...again this morning. But we didn't talk. We just drove by."

"And she waved," I added, still irritated by her easy rapport with Callum Leary.

Sterling turned her head and scowled at me. "I didn't wave. I gave a thumbs-up," she retorted.

"Same difference," I said, and her eyes rolled to the ceiling.

"Why did you give Callum Leary a thumbs-up?" Griffen asked in that same deadly soft tone.

I wasn't afraid of Griffen Sawyer. Not exactly. But I knew enough of his background to know he could probably tear me into pieces without breaking much of a sweat. I was in shape, active, and athletic, but I had not been trained to kill with my bare hands. I knew my limits.

The door opened, and Hawk Bristol strode in, a broad figure with a glare that made me want to keep my mouth shut and follow orders. If I had any illusions about Griffen, I had none about Hawk. Hawk had been decent when I'd helped him board up the windows the day Quinn's guide shop had been trashed. But I knew where his loyalties lay, and they would never be with me. That was fine, especially considering it was Sterling he was here to protect.

In greeting, Griffen said to Hawk, "Callum Leary knows Sterling solved the first two clues. He approached them in a park in Willow Springs yesterday, and Sterling waved at him this morning."

"I didn't wave. I gave a thumbs-up," Sterling repeated.

Hawk's gaze bored a hole in Sterling's forehead. She

seemed oblivious. "Where were you this morning?" he demanded. "And how did Callum Leary find you?"

Sterling turned to me. "What was the name of the town?" she asked.

I told Hawk and added, "When I stopped for gas, I found a tracker on the car. We left it there. I thought it was smarter to let them see us go exactly where they were expecting us to go."

Hawk crossed his arms over his chest and gave me a slow nod. "Then we can leave it there, and they'll think you're staying put since that's exactly what you're going to do."

Sterling glanced at me, then back to Hawk, and finally to her brother. "No way," she said.

"The Learys almost killed Tenn," Griffen reminded her. "They were very clear about their intention to hurt Scarlett and Thatcher."

"I know," Sterling said, "But—"

"You think you do," Griffen said, glancing at Hawk and back to his youngest sister. "You think you know, but you don't. You don't know, and I pray that you never do."

Sterling's teeth sank into her lower lip, and she looked away.

At that moment, it was crystal clear—the two men in the room with us had lived a very different kind of life than the one Sterling or I had lived. My life hadn't always been easy. It definitely hadn't always been happy. But these two men had lived in a world outside the one I knew, a world I suspected the Learys would recognize.

"Sterling," I said, "maybe now..."

She clutched her purse, which I knew held the mint

tin. I hadn't taken it back. I should have. It was no less valuable than the first index card, the one I'd kept from her, saying I didn't trust her.

I could have argued that I let her keep the mint tin because the code inside was supposedly so much harder to break than those we'd seen so far. But that wasn't it. I just hadn't wanted to take it from her.

Something in my gut said that while money was a factor in Sterling's dedication to solving my father's clues, it wasn't everything. I felt the same way. The money would be nice, but there was so much more. Being near Sterling again, for one thing. And I was getting pieces of my father back, pieces of my childhood I'd lost.

Watching her since we'd started this, I thought that with every clue she solved, Sterling was discovering depths she didn't know she had. I wasn't going to be the one to hold her back.

"We're not giving up," I said.

"If it's about money—" Griffen said.

I shook my head and glanced at Sterling, who watched me, her brows pulled together.

"Maybe it's partly about the money," I said. "I promised Sterling twenty-five percent. If rumors are true, it could be twenty-five percent of a lot, or it could be nothing." Before they could interrupt, I pushed on, admitting, "The more I think about this quest and my father's intentions with the Vitellius and the first code... it's possible..." My gaze moved again to Sterling, wanting her to understand something I'd only just realized myself. "It's possible that this was just a game he wanted to play with me. A challenge or an exercise. It's possible there's no money at the end at all."

Sterling's eyes flared, and I thought she'd already figured that out. She set her jaw and shook her head. "It doesn't matter," she said finally. "Maybe there's money, maybe there's not. We'll never know until we see it through. And anyway..." She took in a harsh breath and blew it out. "Anyway, solving the last two clues brought us to Bob and Sugar Mae."

"Bob and Sugar Mae?" Griffen asked, and I explained our progress through the clues.

Griffen let out a sigh and shared a long, speaking glance with Hawk.

"I don't like this," Hawk said to Griffen.

Griffen shrugged. "I don't like it either."

"You can't stop us," Sterling said.

Griffen stared at her for a long moment, and I got the impression he'd like nothing more than to lock her in the dungeons of Heartstone Manor until he was sure she was safe. I didn't think Heartstone Manor had a dungeon, but I had no doubt Hawk and Griffen could build one with their bare hands if they wanted to.

They shared another long glance, and Griffen sat back. "You have to solve the latest clue before you leave Heartstone again?"

"I guess," Sterling said. "I don't know if I have to leave. I haven't gotten that far. I'm not sure where to start with this one."

"You don't go anywhere without checking in with Hawk or me, understand?" Griffen asked.

"For how long?" Sterling challenged, leaning forward in her seat.

"Hawk and I will let you know."

Sterling slouched back in her chair, glaring up at him, looking every bit the little sister she was. "You can't make me a prisoner."

"You're not a prisoner, Sterling. Just give us a few days to make some plans to keep you safe. You can do that, at least."

"She can," I promised, absorbing her sharp glance without a flinch. "I know you want to solve this," I said to her. "I do, too, but not if it means putting you in danger."

"Fine."

She didn't look like she was going to put up with being on lockdown for very long. I hoped she wouldn't have to. There had to be a way to keep her under the radar and out of the Learys' reach long enough for her to solve the remaining clues. If we couldn't—

I didn't want to think about what would happen if we couldn't.

Chapter Eighteen

STERLING

The meeting broke up, none of the men in the room looking happy with the outcome. *Tough luck.*

Hawk was the first to go. I followed him into the hall, leaving Griffen and Forrest behind.

"Hawk, hold on a second," I called after him.

He waited for me to catch up. With his arms at his sides and a welcoming light in his dark eyes, he wasn't the intimidating security chief from Griffen's office. He was my brother's best friend and my sister Quinn's partner. And after all we'd been through in the last year, I thought he was my friend, too.

"Are you okay?" His eyes darted to Griffen's door and back to me.

"I guess," I said, not sure how to answer.

Did he mean, was I okay about the Learys stalking me for my code-breaking brain? If I was being honest, I was fine with it, probably because it hadn't really sunk in yet. I was used to people wanting me because I was a

Sawyer, or because I was pretty, or because I had big boobs and a nice ass. People wanting me for what my brain could do didn't feel real.

Or was Hawk talking about Forrest? That was another thing I wasn't really dealing with. "Yeah, I'm fine," I said. "I wanted to ask—does this mean anything to you?" I pulled the mint tin out of my purse, still surprised Forrest had let me keep it. I opened it, handing Hawk the card inside.

Hawk studied it with his dark, serious eyes for at least a minute, turning the card over and flipping it upside down before handing it back. "I wish it did. You can't tell what kind of cipher it is?"

"Not so far," I said. "But there's something about it. I feel like the pieces are connected, but they won't fit together. Does that make sense?"

"Kind of," Hawk said. "But not enough to help." Changing the subject, he said, "Do you have a minute?"

"Sure." I hadn't planned to go to work today, and Forrest and I hadn't discussed what came next. If Hawk wanted some of my time, well, for him, I had all the time in the world.

"I want to show you something," he said, turning and heading for the front door of the Manor.

I fell into step beside him.

"You know," he said as we walked down the front steps, "I have a friend in Atlanta. He's working at Sinclair Security. Emmett Blake. You met him as Jay Reynolds."

"You mean the guy who kidnapped Quinn and then disappeared?" I asked, intrigued that Hawk was bringing up the mysterious Jay/Emmett. Quinn had asked me to let it go when I'd demanded to know why her kidnapper hadn't been arrested. I didn't know the whole story and doubted I ever would, but now that Hawk was bringing him up, I was dying of curiosity. On brand for Hawk, he didn't go into detail.

"It's a long story," he said, bypassing all the juicy stuff, "but Emmett is with Sinclair Security now, working for Lucas Jackson. Emmett knows a lot about ciphers and code-breaking. If you can't figure it out, let me know, and I'll connect you."

"Okay, sure." I hadn't thought about enlisting the brainiac spy types at Sinclair Security. For one thing, they were crazy expensive, and I didn't have much cash of my own. And for another, I wanted to do this myself.

I followed Hawk down the drive and then to the gravel path that led to the front door of the gatehouse. Once inside, we were greeted by a loud, demanding meep.

"Leo!" I called out to my sister Quinn's attack cat, a massive Maine Coon that looked like a bobcat but was very much a house cat. Leo came to his feet with a stretch, landed on the floor with a thud, and sauntered over to Hawk, rubbing against his legs but dodging Hawk's attempt to pick him up.

"Attitude," Hawk said with an amused curl of his lips. "I left him alone all morning, and now he's going to make me pay."

"Well, he is a cat," I said, scooping Leo up and draping him over my shoulder.

I was used to Shadow, who was a fraction of the size of Leo. The two cats had cohabitated at Heartstone while

Parker was redoing the gatehouse. I'd been afraid Leo would eat my baby Shadow, but instead, they'd become fast friends.

"You'll have to bring this guy over for a playdate," I said, and Hawk just shook his head.

"Not today. Soon. Stay there. I'll be right back," he ordered.

I watched him jog up the stairs to their bedroom on the second floor. Eventually, I suspected they'd let Parker renovate the other side of the gatehouse. But for now, this side—the one they actually lived in—was perfect.

When Hawk moved to Heartstone, the inside of the gatehouse had been stuck in the fifties, decorated with mouse droppings and cobwebs. Hawk had resisted Parker's efforts to renovate until Quinn moved in, and a busted pipe flooded the place. Hawk hadn't cared about a nice living space for himself, but he'd wanted it for Quinn.

I thought he was happy with the result. The renovated space looked as if it had grown from the woods surrounding the Manor. Shades of green adorned the walls, the furniture mostly wood, upholstered in soft fabrics in browns and grays with hints of sapphire, reminding me of the forest on a summer day. It fit Quinn to perfection.

Upstairs, Parker had turned two bedrooms and a tiny bath into a sumptuous suite complete with a walk-in closet I knew Hawk and Quinn would never fill. They were two peas in a pod when it came to that: ten thousand pairs of technical hiking pants, and I doubted they owned a set of formal wear between them.

Hawk came jogging back down the stairs, his hands empty. He came to a stop in front of me and said, "I'll trade you." Digging in his pocket, he pulled something out and shoved it in my hand as he lifted Leo from my arms.

I uncurled my fingers to find myself holding a deep blue velvet box. A jewelry box. A stab of excitement fired through me. My heart pounded as I looked up at Hawk, my eyes wide. "Are you—" I began, but he interrupted.

"Quinn and I talked about this, but it doesn't feel real without the ring. I saw this, and it said Quinn to me, but I want your opinion first," he said with an earnestness that brought tears to my eyes.

Hawk, who never asked for anything, wanted my input on something so important. My throat tightened as I flicked the box open to find a ring that proved this man knew my sister Quinn like no one ever had or would. It was delicate, white gold with leaves carved into the band, a diamond flanked by two small emeralds.

"It's absolutely beautiful and perfectly Quinn," I said, feeling a hot tear spill onto my cheek. "She's going to love it almost as much as she loves you."

Hawk's cheeks flushed, and he cleared his throat. "That's what I hoped you'd say."

"She'll love the ring," I assured him. "But I think you were set when you gave her Ginger."

Hawk's face cracked into a wide smile. He didn't smile much, but when he did, it was like the sun coming out from behind a cloud. "She does like her dog," he agreed.

Quinn had sworn up and down that she didn't

want a purebred dog, even a gorgeous Belgian Malinois. And she definitely didn't need an overpriced guard dog. But Ginger was not overpriced. She cost exactly as much as a perfectly trained animal would. She was sharp and protective and head over heels in love with Quinn.

"I'm a lot more relaxed about her leading hikes with strangers when she's got Ginger with her," Hawk admitted. "I know she agreed to Ginger to humor me, but it worked out pretty well."

Pretty well was an understatement. When Hawk's friend, Remy, had arrived with Ginger, Quinn had taken one look and fallen for her new dog.

I closed the box and handed Hawk back the ring. "When are you going to ask her? Do you have a date in mind for the wedding?"

He rolled his shoulders, resettling Leo after shoving the ring box in his pocket. "When I'm done building that arbor in the clearing where she used to sleep in her hammock. I want to marry her there. After I get the arbor built, at that point, it's up to Quinn. I don't need a lot of fuss. I just want her."

"I think she feels the same," I said. "But listen, I may have retired from the inn, but I am a pro at event planning. Seriously. You want any help? You just let me know."

"I'll have to talk to Quinn, but I'm pretty sure we're going to dump the whole thing in your lap," he said.

"I would love it if you did," I said, bouncing on my toes a little as I imagined it. Flowers in the trees, wispy tulle garlands, and fairy lights woven through the branches. "I could make the most perfect Quinn and Hawk wedding in the woods. I swear. You'll love it."

"I wouldn't ask if I didn't think I would," he said.

We shared a smile of perfect accord. If I could have custom ordered a man for my sister, I couldn't have done better than Hawk Bristol.

"I'm going to work on that code," I said, "and see what I can figure out. But if I can't crack it, I might ask you to put me in touch with Emmett. I'm assuming I can trust him."

Hawk just nodded.

It was a waste of a question. I already knew Hawk wouldn't connect me with anyone he didn't trust. He saw me not just as his friend but as a little sister, so I was surprised when he asked, "Are you back with Powell?" and didn't glower at me.

I shrugged, suddenly uncomfortable. Having relationship talks with anybody was unusual for me. Definitely not with Hawk. Sometimes with Quinn or Parker, a little with Hope, maybe, but not Hawk.

"No," I said firmly. "Definitely not." A flash of the night before seared my brain—Forrest's hot eyes, his growly voice. *Pinch your nipples.* I shook my head, half in denial and half trying to fling the mental image away. "Definitely not," I repeated.

"Why?" Hawk asked, and I stopped.

"Because he lied to me," I replied.

Hawk crossed his arms over his chest and nodded. "Yeah, he did. It was a massive fuckup, for sure."

"You think I should get back together with a man who lied to me about who he was? Who used me?" I trusted Hawk more than I trusted almost anyone on the planet. I thought he hated Forrest. I hadn't been expecting this.

Hawk shook his head slowly, then lifted one shoulder and dropped it in a half shrug. "Are you still in love with him?" he asked, surprising me again.

I tried to say no. I opened my mouth, and the word refused to come out. "Fuck," I muttered under my breath.

"Yeah," Hawk agreed. "Fuck." He shook his head. "It's been a year, Sterling."

"I know it's been a year," I said, not trying to hide my irritation. I didn't need Hawk to tell me how long it had been.

"Hey, don't get mad at me," he said. Leo shifted, restless, and Hawk put him down. "I'm just saying, the man loves you. He stayed in town, hoping that you'd give him another shot. He's been there every time you've needed someone. He hasn't pushed, but he's been here." He shrugged and lifted his hands up in question. "Is he going to lie to you again? My gut says no. But the truth is, it's always a risk. None of us are perfect, right?"

His words were cracking something open inside me, breaking the carefully constructed wall I'd put up around the idea of Forrest. I couldn't argue with what Hawk was saying. I was at the top of the list of people who weren't perfect.

"The only question here is, do you love him?"

I took a slow breath and let it out in a huff. "I don't want to love him," I admitted.

His mouth quirked into a half smile. "Maybe not," he

said softly. "Love isn't a choice... But at the same time, it is."

I couldn't help laughing. "Oh my God. Seriously, are you turning into Mountain Sage Guy with the wise advice? I don't even know what that means."

"Maybe that would be your sister's influence," he said with a flash of a smile. "But what I mean is we don't always choose who we love, but we can choose what we do about it. If you don't love him, that's one thing. You don't owe him a goddamn thing, especially after the way he lied. So, if you don't love him, fuck him."

I thought to myself, *I did* but didn't say it out loud. There was only so much Hawk needed to know.

"But if you do love him," he continued, "you might want to consider whether he's paid for what he did. Whether he deserves a second chance." He shifted, shoving his hands in his pockets. He rolled his shoulders back and met my eyes. "This is me paying it forward because I have a lot of fuckups under my belt, way more than your man, and I thought I didn't deserve anything good out of life. Your sister helped me understand that I can't undo the past. I can only make better choices going forward." Hawk crossed his arms over his chest. "I look at your man in there, and I see someone I understand. He fucked up good, no excuses. But he hasn't made any. He's only said he's sorry and waited. And I think you still love him. I can't see inside your head, but I know you pretty well, Sterling. I have to wonder, why aren't you back together with him?"

It was my turn to shift awkwardly, crossing my arms over my chest and then shoving them in my pockets in a mirror of Hawk's stance. "Because I'm scared, all right?" I confessed. "I don't know what to do."

"Follow your gut," Hawk advised.

"My gut is terrified," I spat out, hating to admit being scared, but it was true. "And my gut doesn't know what it wants. I can't go through that again."

Hawk nodded sagely. "I get that. It's okay to be scared, but you're braver than you know. You're brave enough to reach for what you want. So why not him?"

"That's a bunch of bullshit," I retorted. "I'm not brave."

"The hell you aren't," he countered. "What's with all those coding classes you're acing? Just for fun? Or are you reinventing yourself?"

I stared at Hawk, completely taken aback. "How did you know?" I demanded. "Are you spying on me? Dude, that's creepy."

Hawk laughed. "Not spying on you," he assured me. "I'd apologize for the invasion of privacy, but I didn't have a choice. Remember the night the security system went crazy?"

Who could forget? Alarms had been going off right and left as if an army had descended on Heartstone Manor. But every time they checked, no one had been out there. And then I understood. "You had to comb through everything going in and out of the servers to track down the problem?"

Hawk nodded in confirmation.

"And you saw all the traffic to and from the coding classes?"

"Yeah," he said with a grin. "I swear I wasn't spying

on you, but then I saw what you were up to, and I spied a little. You're really good. It's not my area. I know enough to get by, but you're speeding through the program. I'm assuming you're planning to do something with it."

"I'd like to," I admitted. "It feels right. It makes sense. I feel...powerful. I can do things, you know, not just throw a party or put together a cute outfit. I can make things happen, things other people don't know how to do."

That sunshine grin flashed across Hawk's face again. "That's what I mean. You're brave, Sterling. I'm not telling you to get back together with Powell; I'm just saying you deserve to be happy. I think he probably deserves it, too. Trust yourself. If he fucks up, your family will be here for you. Always."

I shook my head, not sure I agreed with Hawk about any of it. I didn't feel brave. And while I was probably still in love with Forrest, I wasn't sure I trusted either of us enough to do anything about it. "I'll think about it."

Hawk gave a solemn nod, then added, "If you can't crack that code, you should go to Atlanta. Talk to Emmett in person. And while you're there, Lucas Jackson."

"Why Lucas?" I asked, curious. I'd seen Lucas from a distance when he came to go over his system after the night everything had gone haywire, but I'd never talked to him.

"Because you're not just good at coding, you're good at code-breaking—two different things that aren't actually that far apart. And if you're interested in both, once you learn the things you need to know, Lucas will probably have some work for you. And between them, Lucas and

Emmett can tell you how to learn the things you don't know and can't learn in those online coding classes. You follow me?"

I thought I did, and the idea of not just knowing how to write programs—not just shaping the code to create my visions but getting into cybersecurity—sent a thrill through my heart. "You think I could do that?"

"Oh, yeah," he said. "Whenever you're ready, give me a heads-up."

"Thanks, Hawk."

"Anything for you, Sterling. Soon enough, you're going to be my little sister for real. And if your guy messes up again, let me know. I'd be more than happy to beat him up for you."

"You're the best," I said, leaning in to give him a tight hug.

He went stiff for a microsecond before those big arms came around me, and an awkward pat landed in the middle of my back.

I headed for the door and then turned. "Hey! You never said when you were going to ask her."

"Soon," Hawk said, his dark eyes lit from within. "Soon. Thanks for, you know." He patted his pocket where the ring lay safe until he was ready to give it to Quinn.

"Any time," I said. "You just let me know when I can get started with wedding planning."

"I'll keep you posted," he said, scooping up Leo once more and following me to the door.

I skipped down the steps of the gatehouse, my heart light, my head spinning with ideas. So many things I hadn't thought of. It hadn't occurred to me to ask Hawk to talk to the guys at Sinclair Security. It hadn't occurred to me that Hawk would speak up for Forrest.

It hadn't occurred to me that I was brave.

Hawk was one of the bravest people I knew. And if he thought I was, too, maybe it was time I did some reevaluating. Maybe it was time to take a risk and see how brave I really was.

Chapter Nineteen

STERLING

I wasn't usually the first one at dinner. Most often, that was Parker, accompanied by Nash unless he was out of town for business. But for the past few days, the lightness I'd felt immediately after talking to Hawk had faded. Now that the possibility that I could forgive Forrest had been introduced, I'd been restless, my mind shifting from my conversation with Hawk to the cipher in the peppermint tin to Forrest. Mostly to Forrest. I didn't want to think about Forrest. Hadn't I spent enough time thinking about him?

I couldn't settle. Instead, I ping-ponged around the house. My room felt too small. The family gathering room too big. The outdoors too hot and sunny. I'd helped Quinn with a canoeing trip that morning, finished up some paperwork at Sawyer Outdoor Adventures, and came home to stare at the cipher again. Not that this time was different than the other million times I'd studied it. I was missing something, and I didn't have the slightest idea what it was. I wasn't ready to ask for help yet. I would, if it came to that, but I was still stuck on the *stare at it and hope something makes sense* approach.

I ended up on the first floor, on my way to nowhere, and heard Savannah in the dining room setting the table. With nothing else to do, I stopped in to help her.

"Sterling, I've got it," she protested with a smile, her strawberry curls escaping her neat braid, welcome in her gray eyes.

I grabbed the silverware anyway. "I know," I said, "but I'm bored and annoyed with myself."

"Haven't cracked the code yet, huh?" she asked.

There were no secrets in Heartstone Manor, especially not from Savannah, our all-knowing, all-powerful housekeeper. She was only a few years older than me, but it felt like there was a lifetime between us. Savannah was one of the most capable people I knew. She made running Heartstone Manor look easy, but I'd grown up there. I understood how much it took to keep the place going, especially with a skeleton staff. Until we found my father's killer, we were living under high security. Too high to risk the kind of staff Savannah really needed. But even with all those restrictions, she made it look easy, and I was continually impressed with her. There wasn't much she couldn't do.

As suddenly as the thought came to life, I realized as capable as she was, she probably couldn't crack Alan Buckley's codes. I might not be as competent and capable as Savannah, but I wasn't useless either. I had skills. I was smart. I thought of my coding classes and Hawk calling me brave.

I watched Savannah lay the silverware on the table,

her brows furrowed as she adjusted the place setting just so. She'd married my brother Finn a few months before. Technically, we were sisters now. But before that, she'd been a widow and a single mother. I'd never seen her shy away from a challenge. In my mind, Savannah was one of the bravest women I knew.

"Should I give Forrest another chance?" I asked into the quiet room.

Savannah looked up from the place setting, her eyebrows raised and her gray eyes serious. "I don't know," she said. "Do you want to give Forrest another chance?"

I didn't know what I wanted. That was why I was asking Savannah. No, that wasn't true—I did know what I wanted. I was just afraid of it. And I realized it wasn't just that I was terrified of the pain of a broken heart. I also didn't want to be a fool, not again, not after I'd felt so stupid when Forrest had confessed he'd lied about who he was. With that realization settling into place, I rephrased my question.

"Would you think I was stupid if I gave Forrest another chance?" I asked, my stomach unsettled a little at my need for her approval. Savannah had never taken any shit from me, even when I was at my worst. But she'd been one of the first people to reach out a hand and help me up when I decided I wanted to be better.

"No," she answered immediately. "I wouldn't. And that's not me telling you what I think you should do," she said, turning to straighten the plate she'd set down. "I can't answer if you should give him another chance. That's something only you know."

"Why wouldn't you think I was stupid if I got back

together with him?" I pressed. "He lied to me. He lied to all of us."

Savannah nodded. "I know. And while I understand him lying to the rest of us, lying to you is harder to forgive. He betrayed your trust."

"I think I forgive him," I admitted, "but I'm afraid to trust him. I'm afraid to trust myself. I don't want to mess up again."

Savannah gave me a gentle smile and closed the space between us, pulling me into her arms for a tight hug. Slowly letting me go, she said, "Sterling, you need to give yourself more credit. You have a good heart and a sharp brain. Between the two, I know you'll figure out what you need."

Savannah's compliment filled my heart as that restless thing inside me finally settled. Other people might be nice to placate me, but not Savannah. She'd once handed me a spray bottle of tile cleaner and a rag after I'd gotten sick in my bathroom, telling me her staff didn't get paid to clean up after spoiled children who didn't know when enough was enough. Then she came back to check my work, armed with a fresh rag. With a shake of her head, she'd handed me the second rag and told me to try again. She'd pitied me, but she'd forced me to scrub every tile.

Not long after that, I'd stopped drinking. These days, I had a glass of wine with dinner occasionally, but that was it. I didn't want to be pitied, and scrubbing my puke got old fast. But Savannah didn't pity me now. She sounded like she admired me, and that felt pretty fucking good.

"What I need?" I echoed. "Don't you mean what I want?"

Savannah shook her head. "Maybe. But I don't think this is about what you want. I think you know what you want. I think you have to figure out what you need."

"I'm not sure I know the difference," I said slowly.

"I can't tell you what I think you should do because I don't know. I'm not you. But I can tell you that when I was falling in love with your brother, it turned me inside out," she said quietly, her voice pitched low so no one wandering by could overhear. "I didn't want to be in love with anybody, especially not Finn. He was complicated, and I felt like I'd just gotten my life together. I didn't want to take a risk again. I was scared."

"And?" I asked, setting out the silverware following her example, caught by the idea that Finn hadn't instantly won over Savannah. I'd seen them bicker often enough—the whole house had—but I'd assumed it was mostly foreplay. I'd only seen their courtship from the outside—the sparks and drama, then both of them blissfully happy. It had never occurred to me that Savannah might be scared of anything, much less Finn.

"I was flat-out terrified," she confessed, smiling at the memory.

"What changed your mind?" I asked.

"A lot of things," she replied. "Finn, being the easiest answer—just Finn. I knew there was no one who would take better care of my heart than him, that he would never give up or walk out on me. But it wasn't just about Finn. It was about how I felt when I was with him. I was safe enough to have an adventure. With Finn, I'm the

Savannah I want to be. The best version of myself. Does that make sense? I don't have to diminish my dreams to fit his. I don't have to be less for him to be more. And for me, that was what I needed. I don't know what you need, Sterling. Only you know that, and only you know if Forrest has it inside him."

I dropped my gaze to stare at the beautifully set table, letting Savannah's words settle. "And what if he does have what I need? Then what do I do with him?" I asked, thinking of the way Forrest had reacted to me breaking his father's code, intended for him. He hadn't been jealous or annoyed. He'd admired and encouraged me. Never once had Forrest made me feel less.

I jumped a little as Savannah's arm wrapped around my waist in a quick side hug.

"You'll figure it out," she said on her way out of the room.

Hawk and Savannah were a lot more confident in my emotional maturity than I was. Didn't they remember the mess I'd been when Prentice died and everyone came home? Unemployed, mooching off my father, drunk more than I was sober. That girl was me just as much as the person I was now. I'd fixed my life, mostly, and managed to maintain the improvements for over a year. I had a job, paid my bills, and was acing my classes. But *hot mess Sterling* was still inside me. How was I supposed to trust her with my future? With my heart? No way.

I sank into my chair at the table in the empty dining room, crossed my arms over my chest, and closed my eyes, letting my mind drift to that peppermint tin. As impossible as this new cipher was, it still made more sense than the emotional hurricane inside me. I pictured the patterns on the card inside the tin, the lines and shapes pulsing in my head, arranging and rearranging themselves. Nothing made sense. I was missing something.

I needed the key. So far, every cipher had a key or a clue to a key. Where was the key for this one? No matter how much I turned the code over in my head, I couldn't work it out. But it still felt more productive than continuing to obsess over Forrest Powell.

My family started to trickle into the dining room. I kept my eyes closed, pretending to nap. If the key wasn't in the peppermint tin, where was it? Had we missed some clue in the boathouse? Had the key been destroyed when the Murrells renovated? I couldn't figure it out. Probably because my head kept drifting back to Forrest. So far, the clues had been connected to his family, his father, and his childhood. To him. Did he have the code in some buried memory and didn't realize it? Or in something his father had given him?

Yeah, and maybe I just wanted to call Forrest and was looking for an excuse so I didn't have to admit to myself how much I wanted to see him. And how much that want had nothing to do with the cipher. I wanted to be with him. To talk to him. To watch a movie with him, to strip him naked and— *Damn it!*

I could just call him. Maybe we could go out and get a drink. Or an ice cream. Why was it so hard to admit to myself that I missed him? That I wanted to be with him?

Across the room, I heard my sister Avery shout, "Quinn! Oh my God! Quinn, let me see!"

I looked up to see Quinn holding out her hand, light

glinting off the diamond on her ring finger. Avery's dark eyes were wide with excitement. Hawk stood behind both of them, arms crossed, the tiniest hint of a smile on his face as he watched Quinn. His eyes were glowing with love. Damn, I liked seeing that. They both deserved this happiness so much.

I rose and rounded the table, sending Hawk a wink before grabbing Quinn's hand myself and admiring the ring. "Quinn, it's gorgeous," I whispered, pulling her into a tight hug and rocking her from side to side.

"Hawk said you'd do all the planning," she said, raising her eyebrows in question.

"If you want me to, absolutely," I said, and Quinn laughed, her dark hair sliding back off her shoulders, her face radiant.

"I want to be married to Hawk, and I want a beautiful wedding. But I don't want to have to figure out the wedding part."

"I've got you," I said, giving her another hug. "I already have ideas."

"I knew you would," Quinn said, her eyes falling to the diamond on her hand.

Then Hope was there with baby Stella in her arms. "Let me see," she insisted, and I slid out of the way, drifting back to my seat. Griffen called for champagne, dragging Savannah and Finn up from the kitchens to help celebrate Quinn's engagement.

I watched all the happy couples in the room and felt the absence at my side, not of a partner but of Forrest, specifically. He could have been here, celebrating with us, if I wasn't such a stubborn ass. I shook the thought away. Not that long ago, I hadn't even been speaking to him. One thing at a time. I was pretty sure Forrest was what I wanted. Now, I had to figure out if he was what I needed.

I let out a sigh, and my wandering gaze snagged on the two people who didn't look overwhelmed with joy for the newly engaged couple: Brax and Ford. They sat at the end of the table across from each other, neither of them smiling. Brax looked annoyed. Bitter, maybe? Hard to tell. I made a point of not knowing him, which meant I couldn't read his face well enough to tell if he was irritated by the delay of dinner, didn't like Hawk, or was pissed off about something else entirely. His eyes, so like my own and Quinn's, were brittle and squinty as he stared at Hawk, then Quinn. His gaze slid to meet mine, his mouth twisting in a cold smile that sent a chill down my spine. I gritted my teeth against a shiver. I was not going to give Brax the satisfaction of seeing he'd gotten under my skin. Even if he had.

Ford didn't notice Brax's creepy smile. He didn't seem to notice much of anything going on around him. He was right here, in the dining room with us, but he looked as if he was a thousand miles away, his expression blank, eyes shuttered. Whatever was going on in his head, he wasn't going to share with the rest of us.

We had champagne and toasted the happy couple. Sometime after dessert—a gorgeous cake that told me Hawk had tipped off Finn—Ford disappeared from the table. My eyes caught on Brax again. His jaw was set, his gaze dark as he glowered down at his cake, then raised a glance after Ford. He stood and slipped from the room.

Was he following Ford?

Chapter Twenty

STERLING

"What's that about?" a voice next to me asked. I looked over to see Avery sliding into the empty seat next to me, her eyes on the door closing behind Brax.

"I was just thinking the same thing," I said, wondering why Avery was sitting beside me in her Sawyers Bend Brewing polo shirt, her dark hair pulled back in a gleaming ponytail. Even sitting, she was taller than me, everything about her was larger than life—dark hair and eyes, strong brows, and a wide, expressive mouth. If she'd bothered with makeup or fashion, she would have knocked everyone dead. It was for the best that she rarely bothered with either. She was striking enough as she was. Five years older than me, we'd never had a close relationship, but we'd never had issues. As long as you didn't get between her and the brewery, Avery was a sweetheart.

"People are dropping like flies around here," she said, nodding toward Quinn and Hawk. "Another wedding soon, and now you're seeing Forrest again." I braced for her to weigh in, but Avery just shrugged. "He comes in sometimes to have a beer. He seems like a nice guy."

I didn't know what to say to that. Avery and I weren't BFFs. Aside from the age difference, for years, her brewery had been her first love and her baby, which meant she didn't have a lot of time or space for the rest of us. I didn't blame her. Until our father died, avoiding family seemed to be the safest way through life. And now, even with Griffen back and things so different in Heartstone Manor, Avery had been a little bit like Brax—buried in work, isolated even in the midst of our forced family reunion. But unlike Brax, Avery had always been cool, just busy with her own stuff.

"I was going to ask Quinn," she said, "but I don't want to bring all this up right now when she's so happy."

"Ask her what?" I said, curious.

"About the necklace she found in Prentice's hunting cabin. The one she brought to Harvey."

I knew what Avery was talking about. Quinn had taken over our father's hunting cabin and made it her own. While she was cleaning it up, she'd found a necklace we thought might be the key to the mystery woman our father had planned to marry. So far, the only information we had was that there was apparently going to be a new Mrs. Sawyer no one had met. Prentice had been fixing up his suite in the Manor for her. We had reasons to think she might have been pregnant.

Then the renovations stopped, and Prentice withdrew, leaving the estate less and less, trying to raise cash by selling art, though he'd had plenty of money in the bank. He'd stopped maintaining Heartstone Manor and become a hermit until the day someone had walked into Heartstone and shot him at his desk. We were no closer to figuring out who'd done it than we were the day he'd been killed. Ford had been arrested based on evidence so clumsy it had seemed clear to everyone that he was being framed. Video evidence recovered recently exonerated him, but he was only one name crossed off a very long list.

Trying to figure out who had killed my father was like grasping at straws. I didn't know a single human being with more enemies than Prentice Sawyer. In all the mysteries of the last years of my father's life, the missing fiancée was the one we hoped would point us to his killer. Put that way, the necklace Quinn had found didn't seem like much, but it was all we had.

"Since when are you looking into the necklace?" I asked.

Avery shifted, her eyes skipping to Griffen, then to Hawk. "I'm not looking into anything," she said.

I might not be BFFs with my sister, but I knew when she was lying. "You're trying to find out where it came from, aren't you?" I asked, knowing I was right when she looked away.

"Are you going to tell me to stop?" she demanded under her breath. "Because I've already heard that lecture, and I'm not interested."

I couldn't blame her. I understood the instinct to solve riddles and get to the bottom of things despite the danger. But my working on Alan Buckley's codes was a far cry from trying to uncover a secret that someone had killed to hide.

"I'm not going to tell you to stop," I said. "Not exactly. Have you talked to Ford? He thinks looking into things is how he got framed for Dad's murder in the first place."

"I know," she said. "I'm being careful."

I believed her. Avery was a brewer, part scientist, part artist. She'd banned me from the brewery and attached bar when I'd been drinking, but I'd been in recently. I'd seen how neat and orderly things were. She wasn't careless, and she wasn't stupid. Anyway, I was dodging the Irish mob and following a scavenger hunt of ciphers around the Carolinas. Who was I to talk about being careful? Sometimes, risks had to be taken.

"I don't have the necklace," I said. "As far as I know, Harvey still has it. I never asked Quinn if she got it back, but I have pictures of it."

Avery straightened, saying, "I didn't think to ask her about a picture."

"Are you done with your cake?" I asked. Avery nodded. "I left my phone in my room. Come up and I'll show you.

Avery was out of her seat before I finished talking. We left the dining room and went up the back stairs, coming out into the hall of the family wing to find the lights off and a familiar dark shadow only feet from my door.

Avery flipped on the hall light to reveal Brax, his hair golden in the soft light from the sconces, his blue eyes like ice. He wasn't touching my door, wasn't even within arm's reach, but something about the way he was standing left me feeling like he'd been doing more than just walking by. Had he been inside? Had he done something to Shadow?

"What are you doing here?" I demanded.

"Going to my room," he said, sneering down at me. "You keep forgetting I live here, too." Brax lifted his chin at Avery and strode past us down the hall. I waited for her to chastise me for being rude, but her attention was fixed on his back as he shoved open his door and disappeared inside.

"Going to his room?" Avery asked, pushing through the door into mine. "From where?"

I followed her, glancing back over my shoulder at the end of the hall and another closed door.

"Ford's room," I answered, not sure if I was right. But I had to be unless Brax had been hanging out in the stairwell. Or somewhere else. I grabbed Avery's arm and stopped her in the doorway. I swept my eyes over my room, taking in every detail. A soft meow sounded at my feet, and I bent over, scooping up Shadow and nuzzling her soft, dark fur. She seemed fine. Everything seemed fine.

"You think he was in here?" Avery asked.

"I don't know," I said, annoyed at myself. "I just...I don't trust him, and I hate that he's home so much lately." I bit my lip after the sudden outburst, surprised when Avery nodded.

"I know. He's never been my favorite brother, but he was easy to ignore. I work a lot, he works a lot—" She shrugged. "But now that Ford is home, he's around all the time."

"It's odd, right?" I asked.

Avery nodded. "I think..." She hesitated.

"What?" I asked, needing to know what she was thinking. I'd hated Brax for years. Forever. It never occurred to me that I wasn't the only one.

"I think," Avery said, "he wants something from Ford. I don't really get it. But I..." She hesitated again, drew in a quick breath, and said, in a rush, "I overheard a conversation they had in the library the other day. I was walking down the hall, and I heard Brax's voice raised, and I stopped. I was curious." She rolled her eyes, a clear assessment of her own nosiness. "Brax told Ford that he was the only one who didn't care that Ford had killed our father. That he was the only one who understood Ford, and they needed to stick together."

I didn't like the sound of that. We all knew Ford hadn't done it, so Brax was clearly up to something. Or knew something we didn't. I knew Brax liked to go after the weak, the unprotected. And while Ford could certainly protect himself, he was vulnerable and alone right now.

"Shit. Really?" I said. "Does he seriously think Ford killed Dad?"

"It sounded like it," Avery said, "but I mean, come on. There's no way."

"Definitely not," I agreed. "For one thing, if he had, there's no way Ford would have been caught so easily."

Avery laughed. "He's not at the top of my list of

favorite people, but I know he didn't kill Prentice. So, I don't know why Brax seems to think he did."

"What did Ford say?" I asked.

"He said..." Avery closed her eyes as if trying to see the memory clearly. "Ford said... 'I can't give you what you're looking for, Brax. I can't help you if you can't see.'"

"What? What did he mean?" Before Avery could answer, I asked, "Did Brax understand?"

Avery opened her eyes and shook her head. "I don't think so. Mostly because he said, 'What the fuck does that mean?' Ford didn't answer, and Brax stormed out."

"Did he see you?"

"No," she said. "The whole thing was weird."

"Everything about Brax these days is weird," I said, filing the conversation away to think about later. "Anyway, the necklace."

I grabbed my phone off the desk in my room and flipped through the photo album until I got to the pictures Quinn had texted me of the necklace. I dropped them to Avery's phone.

"Exactly what are you going to do with these?" I asked.

Avery shrugged. "Go around town asking questions. See if I can find anything similar. I don't know. I just... I'm tired of this, Sterling."

"Tired of what?" I asked, rubbing Shadow's soft ears until she relaxed into me, boneless and vibrating with purrs.

"Living like this. It's been almost a year and a half since Dad was shot, and we're still on lockdown with no idea who killed him. No one's come after any of us directly in a while, but that doesn't mean they won't. Especially now that Ford's home. I'm just tired of it. I want to know who killed Dad. I want to know who tried to frame Ford. I want us all to be safe. And I'm fucking frustrated as hell that nobody seems to be doing anything about it."

I thought Hawk, Griffen, and West, our police chief, might push back on the idea that no one was doing anything about it. But I got where Avery was coming from.

"We can't go on like this indefinitely," she continued, staring down at the pictures of the necklace, in the shape of a gold oak leaf, now on her phone.

No one had been able to trace the necklace to the original owner. But then again, no one had been able to figure out the code on the Vitellius statue until I'd done it. Maybe Avery could figure out who killed our father. "You're being careful, right?" I asked. "Someone tried to kill Ford before he got out of prison. Whoever did this, they're still out there."

Avery shrugged one shoulder, keeping her eyes on her phone. "Careful enough."

I wasn't sure I believed her. "Don't do anything I wouldn't do."

"Old you or new you?" she asked, flashing me a bright smile that felt like a hug.

"Let's try new me," I said. "If you're poking around in Dad's murder, I don't think old me is a good role model."

Avery shoved her phone in her pocket. "I like all of you, Sterling. Though I think new Sterling has a longer shelf life than the old version."

"Me too," I said, returning her smile. "Keep me posted if you find anything."

Avery shut the door behind her without answering.

Alone in my room, I looked around again, remembering Brax standing just outside my door. Shadow was fine, and everything in here looked untouched. But...

I strode across the room, pulled open my desk drawer, and dug under the notebooks to close my fingers around the peppermint tin. The sudden tension in my gut relaxed at finding it exactly where I'd left it. I opened it, closed it, and set it on the desk with a click.

Before I could think about it, I picked up my phone and tapped the screen until I got to Forrest's name. I hesitated only a second before hitting the icon of the phone.

Five minutes later, I was in my car, the peppermint tin in my bag, along with my toothbrush and a change of underwear.

I wasn't exactly sure if I was following my heart or my hormones. Was this what I needed? Or what I wanted? Either way, I wasn't going to figure it out sitting alone in my room.

Chapter Twenty-One

FORREST

She'd called, but when the knock fell on my door, I half believed I was hearing things. I opened the door, and there she was, standing on my doorstep, her blue eyes cautious but resolved. *Cautious but resolved* wasn't what I wanted from Sterling, but I'd take it for now. Her fingers clenched the long strap of her purse, and she looked up at me, lips parted as if she'd started to say something and lost her nerve.

That was okay. We didn't need to talk. We could get to that later.

I reached for her, taking her by the upper arms and pulling her through the doorway. Leaning to shut it behind her, I turned the lock. Sterling didn't step back or evade my grip. Instead, a second after the click of the lock, she leaned into me, her face raised to mine, her lids sliding closed and shielding her eyes. She didn't need to see. She just needed to feel.

We didn't get farther than my doorway before I

kissed her. Sterling was here in my house of her own free will, and I couldn't wait a moment longer. Her arms rose to circle my neck, and the urgency of her mouth on mine told me that despite whatever else was between us, at this moment, she wanted me.

I wasn't sure there was anything I wanted in life more than I wanted Sterling Sawyer.

I kissed her until we were both dizzy, holding her tight against me, her breasts pressed to my chest, and my hands splayed across her back, feeling every hitch of her breath, every beat of her racing heart.

My fingers found her zipper, and my head cleared enough for me to notice that we were still standing right in front of the closed front door. Not exactly the place for what I had in mind. Tightening my arm around Sterling's waist, I scooped her up and carried her through the house, up the stairs to my bedroom. Her lips were swollen, her cheeks flushed. She raised her free hand and went after the buttons on my shirt, her fingers nimble and quick. She had every one she could reach undone by the time I set her on her feet in front of my bed.

Her purse fell to the carpet with a thump as I finally pulled the tab of her zipper. Her dress unpeeled and fell to the floor. My mouth went dry at the sight of a strapless white lace bra against tanned skin, the peak of her dark pink nipples straining against the white lace. She was all curves and smooth skin.

Before I could touch her, her hands were at my belt. Getting naked was taking too long. I wasn't sure I wanted to take off her underwear—I loved the lace—but my pants had to go. Her warm fingers dove beneath the fabric at my waist, shucking my pants down my legs. The scratchy lace of her bra against my chest sent shivers over my skin.

I stopped and breathed in the smell of her hair. Everything that was Sterling enticed me. Stepping out of my pants, I scooped her up again and tossed her on the bed. She let out a laughing gasp, rolling forward to reach for me. I grabbed her wrists, transferring them into my right hand.

"Lie down," I said. She squirmed but followed my order, her teeth sinking into her swollen lower lip. I guided her hands up above her head, pressing them down against the mattress until her fingers curved to grasp the base of the headboard. "Don't let go."

"Or what?" Sterling asked, her eyes hot, bright and eager.

"Or I'll stop."

"Stop wh—" She cut off with a gasp as my mouth closed over her nipple, sucking through the lace. "Oh," she moaned, "okay."

She kept her hands where they were, gripping the headboard as I moved from one nipple to the other, sucking and nipping. Finally, growing tired of the bra and all that scratchy lace between me and Sterling's soft skin, I unsnapped it. The sight of her unbound breasts made my head spin.

I didn't know if she had the most beautiful breasts on the planet because they were hers or if they were really just that spectacular. It didn't matter. The truth was, no one would ever equal this woman. No one ever could.

She wasn't perfect, but everything about her was perfect to me.

I couldn't tell her that. Sterling was tired of hearing words from me. At this point, words just felt like excuses. I could only show her what I felt. Sex wasn't the best way to prove to her I was worth a second chance, but it didn't hurt. Not if we did it right.

She squirmed against me, arching her back to press those gorgeous breasts up into my hands. To my mouth. I obliged without argument. In bed, we'd always wanted the same thing. I lingered, touching, tasting until her moans sounded like pleas. And then I slid down the bed, hooking my fingers in her white lace thong, tugging it down her legs and pressing them wide, raising her knees and baring her body to me.

I dropped my head and licked.

She gasped my name. "Forrest, oh fuck, Forrest."

I pressed a finger inside her, then two, loving the way her hips rocked up, taking me deeper and rubbing her clit into my tongue over and over again, chasing the orgasm just out of reach. I closed my lips around her clit and sucked hard, my fingers stroking in and out until she came apart, sobbing out my name.

I shifted to the side, giving her space to recover from her orgasm while I grabbed a condom from my bedside drawer, thanking my earlier self for having the optimism to stash some just in case hell froze over and Sterling was ever in this bed. But I didn't know what was going on in hell. I was in heaven.

Condom taken care of, I moved back between her

legs, stroking a hand up the inside of her knee to trace a light stroke between her legs. She twitched, her fingers still curled around the headboard.

"Too sensitive?" I asked.

Her eyes foggy, she nodded.

I rose over her, nuzzling her elbow before kissing the inside of her wrist, taking in the tight grip of her hands on the headboard. "You're always such a good girl," I said, turning my head to capture her mouth.

Sterling growled low in her throat, kissing me back with the ferocity I'd missed so much. She loved it when I was bossy. No one told Sterling what to do. Except me. And though I knew a part of her hated my orders, they set her on fire every time. At least they had before, when she'd trusted me.

I had just enough brainpower left to wonder if her hands on that headboard meant she trusted me again, if only a little, before the head of my cock nudged her slick heat, and I stopped thinking about anything other than making her come.

"You think you can do that again?" I whispered, my lips at her ear. She nodded. "You can let go of the headboard now."

Her arms flew up as if on springs, coming down to wrap tightly around my back as I shifted my hips and filled her, inch by inch. Nothing would ever feel as good as Sterling. There was no pleasure, no prize on earth worth risking losing her.

I didn't last long. Neither did she. We moved in perfect unison until her nails dug into my shoulders, her head tipped back, and her body clenched tight around me. The pulse of her orgasm drew me with her, falling blindly into ecstasy.

When I thought I could move, I rolled to the side, bringing her with me. She shifted, pushing me to my back, splaying on top of me, her skin damp and her breath coming in gasps. I drifted for a few minutes as my heart slowed, and Sterling's breath evened out. Finally, she raised her head and moved to the side, hitching one leg over mine.

"That was nice," she said into my collarbone.

The laugh shook my chest. "Nice? That's all you can say? It was nice?"

"Mhm. Pretty great." She nodded sleepily.

"That was a hell of a lot better than nice," I said into her hair, stroking my fingers down her temple behind her ear to skim her neck, loving the way she melted into me. I got up to take care of the condom, sliding back into bed beside her and pulling her into my arms.

Then we dozed off, falling from nap into sleep, waking the next morning to the insistent buzz of the alarm on my phone.

Sterling jumped out of bed before I had my eyes open all the way, mumbling something I couldn't understand as she snatched her dress off the floor and leapt for the bathroom. I rolled to my feet, snagging my own clothes, and headed for the guest bath. If I waited to use my own, Sterling would sneak out the second I was behind the door. Instead, she emerged ten minutes later to find me in the kitchen, making breakfast.

The rich, bitter scent of coffee filling the kitchen told

me I was about to find out how badly Sterling wanted to escape my company now that the orgasms had faded. Sterling wasn't sure about me, but she loved her coffee in the morning. She stopped at the door of the kitchen, her purse clutched in her hands, eyes wary, the satisfied, relaxed woman who'd slept in my arms long gone.

Chapter Twenty-Two

FORREST

"Coffee?" I asked, holding out a steaming mug. As I'd hoped, she couldn't resist. "I'm making breakfast sandwiches. You want one?"

Sterling sat at the kitchen table and shrugged her shoulder. "Sure. Why not?" Then, giving in, she took a long sip of coffee. "You always made the best coffee," she said, going for a second, longer sip.

I slid a plate in front of her a few minutes later. She picked up half the sandwich, biting into it with a moan that reminded me of naked Sterling far more than the fully dressed woman sitting at my kitchen table. I already knew not only did she love her coffee, but she was also a sucker for breakfast sandwiches. Melting cheddar. Toasted sourdough. Fried eggs. I could gain a lot of ground if I could get her to stay long enough to feed her breakfast. So far, so good.

"How's it going with the cipher?" I asked, taking a bite of my own sandwich.

She swallowed, shaking her head, and sighed. "I can't figure out what I'm missing. But I know it has to be something because it doesn't make any sense," she said.

"Can I look at it?" I asked. It crossed my mind that I didn't have to ask. I could have demanded she give it to me. That might be a move I would have made a year ago. But now? In this new iteration of us? Sterling had been the one solving these clues, so that made it hers, too.

She reached for her purse and handed me the tin. I set the tin on the table and wiped my hands on a napkin before opening it. As before, it held only the card with my father's writing on it. The markings of the cipher didn't make any sense to me. This one wasn't alphanumeric, and I didn't recognize the pattern at all.

"Why is this one so much harder?" I asked.

Sterling chewed furiously on her last bite of breakfast sandwich and swallowed it, chased by a gulp of hot coffee. After another quick swallow, she blotted her mouth with a napkin and said, "It's the key. There has to be something, but it wasn't there. Or am I just supposed to know what the key is? Because so far, I don't."

So, we were missing a key. Okay. Carefully, I moved my empty plate and half a cup of coffee to the other side of the table and picked up the card with the cipher.

"What are you doing?" Sterling asked.

"I don't know," I said. "Just looking. Maybe there's something here."

"I looked already," she said, sounding a little sullen. It was unlikely I'd find something she hadn't, but so far, this had been Sterling's game. I'd only been along for the ride. Maybe new eyes would help.

I studied the inside of the lid, closed it, and examined the red and white of the logo and the old-fashioned script. Everything looked normal. I pulled out my phone and searched for the brand of peppermints to compare our lid to others. Image after image popped up on the screen, our tin matching a picture of a vintage peppermint tin of the same brand. I zoomed in on the picture but couldn't find any differences in the design. If the key was hidden there, I couldn't see it.

I flipped open the lid and examined the inside. The bottom was a thin layer of white wax paper cut with rounded corners to fit seamlessly beneath the first layer of mints. The mints were long gone, as was the top layer of paper.

"Did you look at this?" I asked, pointing at the paper.

Sterling rolled her big blue eyes. "Of course. I've looked at everything."

With a light touch, I nudged the edge of the paper, peeling it up and turning it over. The faint smear of graphite caught my eye. "Can you grab the magnifying glass? It's in the kitchen drawer." I raised my chin in the direction of the junk drawer where I'd tossed the magnifying glass after Sterling had used it the night she'd brought the Vitellius to my door.

She returned with it a moment later. "What do you see?" she demanded, leaning in to try to peer through the magnifying glass.

"I don't know," I said, afraid to guess. But there—small and faint, but very much there under the lens of the magnifying glass—the graphite smear resolved into a tiny series of letters and numbers running along the edge of the wax paper. "Here."

Sterling took the magnifying glass, holding it above the paper and squinting down. "I swear I looked at this. How did I miss it? Are the lights brighter in here?"

"Does it mean anything to you?" I asked, elated to have found something even though I had no clue what this new code meant. Was it a key or another cipher?

"I think this goes with the Jefferson cipher wheel, the one I have at home." Sterling replaced the wax paper and card with the cipher back in the tin. Surging to her feet, she tossed the magnifying glass in her purse along with the tin and grabbed my hand. "Come on, let's go."

I let her drag me out of the house, slowing only long enough to lock the door behind us. Sterling gave me a little shove toward the passenger door of her car. I got in without argument, not wanting to waste time. She slid behind the wheel and started the engine, a determined look in her eyes. That cipher had been making her crazy, I could tell. Now that she had a lead on the key, nothing was going to stop her.

I wanted to find the next clue, especially if it felt like another message from my father. But more, I wanted to see her face when she solved it and the one after that. I wanted to see her triumph, needed her to be a part of this journey of my father's.

Her tires ate up the miles between my house and Heartstone Manor. Sterling didn't say anything on the drive other than muttering under her breath once or twice that she swore she'd looked at the wax paper already. I was sure she had, too, but as she'd said earlier, the light in her bedroom wasn't great. In contrast, you could do surgery on my kitchen table. I liked a bright kitchen. Maybe she'd looked under her desk lamp and missed the tiny, pale gray scribbles. It was more than possible.

Sterling didn't say another word until we were in her room. She went straight to her desk, setting the peppermint tin in front of her. Pulling the Jefferson cipher wheel out of a drawer along with a pad of paper and a pen, she began the painstaking work of deciphering the code.

"This is it," she said when she was only a few letters in. "It's an address."

"Four, five, two, Laurel Lane," she read aloud, "Right, let me check this again." She'd written a row and stopped and gone back, checking the cipher wheel and the alphanumeric code again before slowly writing the last two letters: *RC*.

"I don't know what that last part means," she said, "but the first part is definitely an address."

I read from the screen of my phone. 452 Laurel Lane was an address deep in the mountains, less than an hour from Heartstone Manor. Based on the satellite view of the map, it looked like it was on at least a few acres of forested land. Nothing about the location rang a bell to me. I had no memories of visiting the place I saw on the screen, nor did I recognize any of the town or street names nearby.

"That must be where we find the key to the cipher on the index card," Sterling said. "Come on, let's go. It's not that far."

"Maybe we should do some research first," I said.

Sterling shook her head. "What's there to research? We have an address. We'll take my car. That's the one that the Learys aren't tracking. Hawk already checked it."

"You don't want to tell Griffen or Hawk where we're going?" I asked, following her down the hall to the main stairs.

Sterling slowed, appearing to think about my question before shaking her head and picking up her pace, "No, we're not going far. We'll be back by lunch."

"Sterling," I started, torn between caution and the same need that drove her. I wanted to follow the lead. I didn't want to wait and be careful and cautious. I didn't want to be sensible. What were the odds that this new place, 452 Laurel Lane, would be the end of our search? Unlikely. I had a feeling I'd know when we were at the end, and this wasn't it. This was just one more piece in the puzzle, and no one had any incentive to hurt either of us until we got to the end.

I closed my mouth, deciding to let it go. For the first time, it felt like Sterling and I were in this together. I felt the same driving beat in my bloodstream, the same need to solve the clue, to know what came next. What would I see when we got there? Would it come to life as a part of my past, the way the boathouse had brought back Sugar Mae and Bob? I wouldn't know until we got there.

WE DIDN'T TALK MUCH ON THE WAY, LETTING THE navigation app guide us through winding country roads, up the side of a mountain, and down a weed-infested gravel drive to a small, faded Craftsman bungalow surrounded by trees. There was a real estate lockbox on the door, probably holding the key, but it looked as if it hadn't been touched in months. The whole place had a faded, sad feel. The curtains were drawn, and old, dusty pollen was thick on the floorboards of the front porch. Whoever had lived here, they were gone. No one had been here for a long time. Sterling strode up the steps, leaving footprints in the dust. She raised her fist to bang against the door.

I followed her, eyeing the curtained windows and seeing no movement, crowding close in case there was someone inside and they didn't appreciate visitors. We waited, her knocks echoing through the house, but no one came to the door.

"It looks abandoned," she said quietly.

"It does," I agreed. "Let's try around the back."

We picked our way around the side of the house through the rocky yard. The grass was knee-high and half dead in the summer heat. I decided not to think about snakes or ticks or anything else that could be lurking out of sight. We tried the back door. No answer. Sterling eyed the windows. Locked.

Her gaze dropped to a rock in the yard, and I followed her train of thought. Before I had to talk her out of breaking a window, my gaze caught on the weathered wooden door half buried in the long grass. In a flash, letters after the address made sense.

"Root cellar," I said. "RC is root cellar."

Sterling turned from the rock to look at me, pointing down at the grass. Confusion faded from her eyes.

"Oh!" Going to her knees, she swept the long grass away from the wooden door, revealing a weather-worn handle. The door was secured by a simple slide bolt. "Bingo."

I pulled the bolt back and tugged on the handle. The door resisted, the thick, long grass growing over its hinges holding it down. Sterling curved her hands around the edge of the door as soon as I had it open an inch, and together, we yanked once, twice. On the third hard pull, the door flew open.

We stared into a black hole in the ground. "Please tell me you have a flashlight in the car," I said.

Sterling slowly shook her head, looking into the dark hole. "Only on my phone," she said, pulling the device out of her pocket. She tapped on the screen until a beam of light speared out from the back, illuminating the stone steps into the root cellar. Before she could start down, I got in her way.

"Let me go first." She started to argue, and I added, "I'll check for snakes."

"Good point," Sterling said. "You go first."

I didn't see any snakes, but that didn't mean they weren't there. The root cellar was pitch dark, not a single dusty window to let in any light. The air was chilled and musty even with the summer heat above. "Careful," I said, feeling Sterling move behind me. The steps were shallow and steep. Finally, there was dirt beneath my feet and the ceiling just above my head.

"How are we going to find anything down here?" Sterling asked, moving her phone's light across the walls like a searchlight, revealing nothing but damp stone and hard-packed dirt.

Long ago, there had been shelves lining these walls, probably covered in jars of canned vegetables and fruits, jams and jellies, root vegetables stored in burlap sacks. Now, it was mostly empty, with only broken wood and nails as a reminder of the shelves, not a jar or a sack to be seen.

"Maybe the key is in the walls, like hidden behind a stone?" Sterling asked. She looked around, her eyes wide, taking in the hundreds of stones that made up the walls.

"Maybe," I said. "We better start searching." After a careful sweep of the cellar for a bigger threat than dust and cobwebs, she headed for the closest wall and began to examine the stones.

We were so absorbed in our task we never heard the footsteps that must have echoed above, vibrations in the ground that couldn't penetrate our focus. I heard the creak of old wood, but it was too late.

I looked up just in time to see the door of the root cellar slam shut above our heads, the rough slide of the bolt locking us in.

Then, only silence.

Chapter Twenty-Three

STERLING

"Forrest?" I asked into the dark. I knew he was standing right next to me, but in the inky blackness, I felt completely alone. There was a thin blade of light from my phone, another from his, but I hadn't appreciated how much light the open door had let into the root cellar.

"Someone followed us. Or maybe they were already here? I don't know," he said, using the light from his phone to make his way back to the steep stone steps. He climbed a few feet up and shoved at the door. It rose half an inch before it stopped. He shoved again, the muscles of his shoulders bunching under his shirt as he threw his weight into his hands, pushing up.

"Don't hurt yourself," I said when he let out a growl and tried to shove at the door with his shoulder.

"I won't," he said. "But there aren't any windows down here. The door is the only way out."

That was very bad. I didn't need him to explain it to me. And it was my fault. I'd rushed Forrest out of the house, not wanting to stop for Griffen and Hawk, knowing they'd just slow us down. Hawk would want to send one of his people with us, which meant shuffling the schedule around. Griffen would want to research the property. While all of that was probably useful and smart, I hadn't wanted to wait.

Typical me, rushing headlong into disaster. And this time, I'd dragged Forrest with me. I was going to have to call for help. My pride hated it, but not as much as I hated the dark, dank cellar we were trapped in.

I stared down at my phone screen, stymied. No bars—not even a hint of a bar—just three dots where the bars should be. *Shit.*

"No signal," I said. "Do you have a signal?"

Glancing at his phone screen, I felt more than saw Forrest shake his head. "Nothing."

"Fuck." As our options fell away, a sickening thought occurred to me. "Can Hawk track my phone if there's no cellular connection?"

Forrest shook his head. "I don't know. Fuck. There's got to be a way to get through those doors."

I wanted to believe him, but root cellars were designed for storage and keeping animals out. There was no reason anyone would put a safeguard on the inside to prevent what had just happened to us. It wasn't what these were used for. I glanced at the door at the top of the steps. Even if it hadn't been bolted shut, it wasn't light—it had taken two of us to lift the door we'd opened. But maybe there was a way we hadn't thought of yet.

"Who would do this? The Learys?" I asked, thinking out loud.

Forrest let out a huff of breath. "Could be. Maybe they're trying to scare you."

I rolled that thought around in my head, but it didn't fit. Locking me in a root cellar didn't seem like Callum Leary's style. But then again, it wasn't like I knew the guy. Maybe Forrest was right. Maybe Callum Leary thought I'd be easier to deal with if I was scared.

I wasn't scared—not yet. Even so, I could admit this had not been one of my better decisions.

"We should have talked to Hawk and Griffen before we left," I said.

Forrest just nodded his head, a shadow in the dark.

I wanted to ask him why he hadn't stopped me, why he hadn't made me do the sensible thing instead of rushing off after the clue. But I kept my mouth shut. It wasn't Forrest's responsibility to stop me from being a dumbass. And more than that, I knew why Forrest hadn't stopped me—because he wanted me back. The last thing he'd want to do was piss me off. Yet again, this fuckup was all on me.

"I'm sorry," I said into the cold, dark room. "I'm so sorry. We should have told them what we were doing."

"You don't owe me an apology, Sterling," Forrest responded. "I could have said something, but I wanted to get here, too. I didn't want to wait. Now we just have to figure out how to open that door."

We worked on the door for what felt like hours, shoving and banging. I tried gouging at the hinges, but all the parts that mattered were on the outside. If anyone heard, they didn't come to our rescue. I thought about whoever had locked us in here. Were they waiting to see if we escaped? Would they meet us out there with a gun? Was this a prank or something far more insidious?

With a sigh, my palms bleeding and hands aching, I said, "I don't think we're going to get out of here."

A spike of fear went down my spine, the implications of my words became clear. No one knew where we were. We had no way to communicate with anyone. Our car was hidden in the trees, and we were locked in an empty, cold root cellar deep in the woods.

My impatience had gotten me into a lot of trouble over the years, but this might be my worst, and last, mistake. It didn't seem right that my story would end here. I had so much more I wanted to do.

I ran through how things would go at Heartstone when they realized I was gone. They'd try to track my phone, and they'd see the last known signal ping somewhere nearby. That gave me hope. Griffen and his team would find us. I was sure of it.

The question was how long that would be. A day? Two? And when they arrived, would this mystery person who'd locked us in here be waiting for them?

And further to that, who would want me and Forrest dead? The only person who knew where we were was the one who'd locked us in. If it was the Learys—and I wanted to hope that it was—they'd come back to let us out. I was no good to them dead.

The Learys needed us alive to finish solving the clues, so killing us simply didn't make sense. Plus, the clue very clearly led us here. Why would they lock us in instead of waiting for us to solve it and then come after us?

My thoughts whirling, I watched Forrest step resignedly away from the steep stone staircase leading to the door and sweep his flashlight around the room. The edge of the beam caught on something in the corner beneath the staircase.

"Wait," I said, "what's that by the stairs?"

The beam of light swung back, stopping to illuminate the edge of a box just barely sticking out from under the stairs. Moving closer, we saw a shallow storage area that had been dug into the dirt. The plain brown box inside was free of dust, the cardboard firm instead of soggy from the damp.

"This hasn't been here long," Forrest said, reaching for the box. He slid it out into the center of the room.

It didn't seem too heavy, but it wasn't light either. I went to open it. Forrest nudged me aside.

"Wait," he said. "We don't know what this is or who put it here."

"Oh, good point." Now, I was thinking of every nasty surprise that could be hidden in that box. A bomb? Snakes? Spiders? When Forrest reached for the flap, I grabbed his arm. "What are you doing?" I asked. "If it's not safe for me to open it, then why is it safe enough for you?"

I thought it was a reasonable question, but Forrest didn't answer. He shifted to move between me and the box, holding his phone at one end and poking at the flap with the other. It lifted and fell open, revealing a dark corner of the interior. I couldn't see anything inside, but at least nothing jumped out, and it didn't explode. Forrest did the same with the next flap of the box and the next until we could see inside. I wasn't expecting two plastic gallons of spring water and a family-size box of granola bars.

"Why—?" I started to ask when potential answers flooded my brain.

As if he was reading my mind, Forrest put my scrambled thoughts into words. "Whoever locked us in here doesn't want us to starve to death. Maybe that means they plan to come back and let us out. Now we know this wasn't a random prank." He pulled out one of the gallons of water, studying the cap at the top. "It's not sealed. They could have added something or refilled used bottles."

I eyed the granola bars. "All of it could be tainted."

Forrest nodded, frowning down at the box. After a long moment, he shoved it back into the corner beneath the stairs and stood. Letting out a short, sharp breath, he headed to the back corner of the room and began poking methodically at the stones that made up the wall.

"What are you doing?" I asked him.

"I'm looking," he replied. "I don't know if the clue is part of why we're locked in here, or it was just convenient for whoever wanted us out of the way. But at the moment, we're not getting out. We might as well search and make sure there isn't anything to find."

I joined him, starting in the opposite corner, going over every square inch of the wall, watching the battery on my phone drain lower and lower. Should I stop and conserve it? But what was the point when conserving the light would just drag out the inevitable? A dark voice whispered inside my head, *If you can't get out, you'll be stuck down here forever.*

As time stretched on and the chill settled in, my clothes saturated with damp and smelling of the musty cellar, the walls revealing nothing of their secrets, I began to doubt.

I didn't think it had been the Learys who locked us in. I couldn't figure out why they wanted to scare me, but if that was the goal, then by now, they would have let us out. It had been hours. It was cold, and I was hungry.

With every second that passed, the root cellar felt more and more like a dead end.

Chapter Twenty-Four

STERLING

"I don't think there's anything here," I said finally. "You don't remember this place, do you?"

Forrest's shoes scuffed on the dirt floor, moving closer. The heat of his arm was welcome as he wrapped it around me. "I don't," he said, "None of this is familiar or means anything to me."

"Then why would your father send us here?" I asked.

Forrest made a sound deep in his throat but didn't answer. "Someone's going to find us," he said finally.

The light on my phone went out, and I realized it had gone dead. "I hope so," I said.

Forrest's arm tightened around me, pulling me down into his lap as he sat on the damp earth and leaned against the stone wall.

"You'll get too cold," I protested.

"I'm fine." He held me close, and I let out a breath, absorbing his body heat.

"I'm sorry I've been such a jerk all these months," I whispered.

"You don't owe me an apology," he said. "I deserved all of it."

"Yeah," I agreed, "but I'm still sorry." And I was. Not for being angry and hurt but for letting it go on so long. We might not get out of this cellar, and I'd wasted so much time. This man cradling me in his arms wasn't a villain. He'd made a mistake, and he'd apologized. For so long, I'd said I wanted him to go away, to live a horrible, painful life without me. I'd wished for all sorts of vengeful things.

That was before.

And now?

Now, what I really wanted was Forrest. Not his misery or his abject apologies. Just Forrest. Preferably alive and not dead of exposure and starvation in an abandoned root cellar.

"We're going to get out of here. Griffen will find us," I said.

"Yeah, he will," Forrest said. "And I bet it will be soon."

I didn't think either of us believed it.

The light on Forrest's phone went out.

"Did it die?" I asked, hating the way my voice shook in the dark.

"No, but it's getting there. I don't want to lose the light completely."

He had a point. I hated the dark. And this wasn't regular, household dark, tinged with a faint glow from power buttons or night-lights. This dark was pitch fucking black, the walls closing in, cold and damp. I wished I'd given up the search earlier and saved my own phone battery. Today was my day for crappy decisions.

"You said you looked at it," Forrest said into the quiet dark. "The liner of the peppermint tin. Where we found the key," he clarified.

"I did," I said. "I swear I did. I know the light in my room isn't as good as your kitchen, but I looked with a magnifying glass. I should have seen it."

"But what if you did look," Forrest said, "and there wasn't anything there?

"How?" Realization unfurled inside me, and my stomach turned, "You mean—what if the code I found was a decoy? What if this wasn't sent by your father?"

"Could someone have added that code to the peppermint tin after you brought it back to Heartstone?" he asked.

My mind raced over the possibilities. "Who? I had it with me almost..." My voice died on the word *almost*.

Almost was a window of opportunity. My room didn't have a lock. I'd never really needed one. As a kid, I always jammed a chair under the handle when my father had his sketchy business friends stay at Heartstone. And later, we didn't have any visitors at all, and no one was interested in going into my room.

I'd thought of Heartstone as a safe place. Hawk and Griffen had worked hard to make it so.

"Who do you think it could have been?" I found myself asking, not wanting to give voice to the names floating in my head.

"I don't know. I don't know your family as well as you do. I can't see Tenn or Royal having anything to do with something like this. They love you, and they're so proud of you. I don't know your other siblings as well, but the only people I can think of are Ford and Brax," Forrest said, proving yet again that he was as smart as I thought he was.

Those were the names I'd been trying not to speak. And, of course, between the two of them, I wanted to assume it was Brax. My childhood tormentor, my nemesis. I wanted him to make the most sense because, though we weren't close, I didn't want to think Ford would ever do anything to hurt me.

But someone had. And it wasn't a childhood prank this time. I was getting colder by the second, as was Forrest. Could we really die of exposure in July? I shivered in the cold, damp air of the root cellar and understood that we could. It wasn't freezing down here, but it was cold enough that the temperature would probably get us before empty stomachs or dehydration, especially once night fell.

I knew how hypothermia worked. It killed faster than anyone thought.

Griffen and Hawk were in a race against time, and I'd made it very difficult to find us.

"Why?" I let myself breathe, trying to sort it out in my head. Trapping us down here wasn't going to get anybody any closer to Alan Buckley's fortune. And if the code written on the liner had been added later, at Heartstone, it definitely couldn't be the Learys who'd set us up to be locked in the root cellar.

"Who has to gain from getting you out of the picture?" Forrest asked. "Anyone aside from your siblings? What happens if one of you dies before the terms of the will are up? What happens to the money your father left you?"

"I think it goes back into the trusts that fund the Manor," I said. I hadn't really thought much about it, not planning to die in the next five years. Showed what I knew. "I think the result is the same as if Griffen kicks us out or we stay away from Heartstone for more than two weeks in a quarter. Anything left to us goes into the trusts for the house." I let out a long sigh. "But to be honest, I was pretty drunk the day Harvey played Dad's video will. I could have missed some of the details."

"How much time do you have left?" Forrest asked.

"The quarter just started," I said. "And I've only been away two nights. I have twelve days. If whoever locked us in is planning on waiting out the terms of the will, I'm pretty sure we'll be dead by the time they come back."

A dark thought, but it occurred to me that I might not be the target. What if this was about Forrest?

"Does anyone want to kill you?" I asked, struggling to imagine it.

"Not until I find my father's money," he said in a wry tone. "At the moment, I'm worth a lot more alive. But from that perspective, so are you. I don't think this is about my father's money. I think that was just a way to get to you." He paused. "Whoever did this was living at Heartstone or working there. Any chance one of the maids or Billy Bob is susceptible to a bribe?"

I rolled that idea around in my head. "They could be," I said, not liking the idea that April or Kitty might have set me up to die. Ditto for Billy Bob, cousins who could fix anything and worked for Savannah.

"Isn't there a nanny now?" Forrest added.

Paige. No, not Paige. She was quiet and lovely with Stella and the boys. But if it wasn't one of them, or one of Hawk's team—inconceivable—that left me with Ford and Brax.

I really didn't want to think it was Ford. I wanted to pin the blame all on Brax's smug, snotty face. He'd hated me since we were children, but this—this was beyond sibling rivalry. This was murder. Couldn't he just tear up my drawings or steal another doll? Did he need to lock me underground and starve me to death in the dark to make his point?

I sighed, not wanting to believe it. Yes, my family was unbelievably fucked up. But underneath that, they were my family. Would one of them really go so far as to try to kill two people for an inheritance?

I'd rather it be Brax than Ford, but the truth was I didn't know Ford. Not really. He'd betrayed all of us over and over, caused Griffen to lose everything and be exiled from his home, and sold Finn to kidnappers in a business deal. Who knew what else Ford had done that we hadn't learned about? Since he'd been home, he'd been so withdrawn. I wanted to think I could trust him. But the truth was...I didn't know. A wave of grief hit me. I was in the cold dark, trying to figure out which of my brothers would murder me and the man I loved. If I'd known how quickly our time would run out, I wouldn't have wasted so much of it.

"Forrest." I choked out his name. "I'm so sorry... I'm

so sorry... We're going to die down here, and it's my fault. I was impatient... I didn't want to wait, and—"

"Sterling, stop," he said, stroking his hand down my hair, his fingertips chilled where they grazed my skin. "I'll try again at the door in a little bit," he promised. "We aren't going to give up. We'll find a way out."

I let his words sink in, wash over me.

A few minutes later, Forrest nudged me off his lap and turned on the light on his phone, sweeping it over the floor. I could see by his expression he'd had a new idea.

"What are you looking for?" I asked.

"A rock with a sharp edge and some weight to it. Something I can use to chop away at the door. We're surrounded by stone down here. There should be enough to use as an ax and break through the door. I'll go at it where the lock is bolted in," he said, aiming his light at the dark circle of metal on the underside of the door.

The wood was thick, but I wasn't going to argue. We were out of options. At least Forrest had a plan. Searching in the thin beam of light, I found a sharp-edged, good-sized rock with some heft to it.

"Here," I said. "Take this one. I'll hold the phone."

Aiming the beam of light at the bolt Forrest thought secured the doors, I braced as he swung, the rock skidding off the dense wood, taking a shaving of splinters along with it. Not much, but he'd left a mark. He swung again, angling the rock to cut deeper, gouging the door around the bolt. A third swing, punctuated by a deep, reverberating thump and the rattle of metal on metal.

He had to be getting tired as he swung, over and over, his knuckles scraped and bleeding. "Getting there," he muttered, taking a moment to breathe and study the shallow groove in the door beside the bolt.

"Do you need another rock?" I asked, wishing I could do something, anything to help. I was half Forrest's size and had none of his muscle. If he got tired, I would take some swings, but putting me in at this point was a waste.

"No, this one has some life left in it. I'll get it, Sterling. Don't worry," he said and swung his arm again, putting his whole body weight behind the rock in his hand.

The door lifted at his strike and kept going, rising up and open. Forrest fell forward, catching himself in the open doorway, the rock tumbling to the ground by my feet.

Fresh, warm, humid air flooded into the root cellar, and from above, I heard a familiar voice as Callum Leary leaned in and said, "You two need a little help?"

Chapter Twenty-Five

STERLING

Callum Leary's smug grin faded as I stepped into the light, and he got a good look at me. Based on his expression, I must have looked exactly as awful as I felt.

"You know who locked you in there?" he called down.

"Not yet," I said.

"You planning to come out?" he asked.

"As soon as you give us some room," I shot back, not loving the way he loomed over the entrance. I was thrilled to see him—he was a human who was saving us. But I didn't trust him.

Forrest looked at me. "Go on. I'll be right here."

I stepped back and shook my head. "Hell no. I'm not going up there first."

"I'll be right behind you," Forrest reassured me. "I don't think—"

I cut him off. "It's not that. They need me. I'm not

sure they think they need you. I'm not leaving you behind. You go up first."

Forrest's eyes narrowed, and he crossed his arms over his chest. I didn't know if he didn't like the truth being thrown at him that way or if he was reacting to me pushing back. I didn't care.

"Okay," I said. "You don't like that reason? Try this one. Whoever's head pops up through that hole first is going to be the most vulnerable if they have bad intentions."

"That's your argument for why I should go first?" Forrest asked, raising an eyebrow.

"I figured it had a higher likelihood of convincing you." The truth was I hadn't liked the way Callum had treated him in our last meeting, as if Forrest was an obstacle. Disposable. I wouldn't put it past Callum Leary to separate us if he could.

Forrest sighed, his arms dropping to his sides. "You're right. Either way, this is fucked. I want you behind me. Like inches away."

"Trust me," I said. "I have no intention of getting trapped down here again."

As promised, I stuck to Forrest's back like glue, two steps behind him, as close as I could get without risking knocking us both over. The light above was dimmer than I expected. The sun set late in July, but we'd been down in the cellar for hours and hours. It was bright enough to see Callum and the man who had been with him at Willow Springs. As soon as we cleared the top of the staircase, I stepped to the side, putting space between me and Forrest. I wanted the focus on me. If they didn't think I cared about him, they wouldn't be able to use him as a lever. Hoping Forrest would understand, I turned to Callum.

"You're spending an awful lot of time down south. Don't you have business back home?"

Forrest sent me a warning glare but didn't close the distance between us. I hoped that meant he understood why I was five feet away instead of right next to him. I didn't have to wonder what the glare meant. He'd already made clear he didn't like me sassing the mobster with the gun. Fair enough. But sarcasm and attitude were my defense mechanisms, and Callum Leary scared the crap out of me.

Callum ignored my query. "You've had better days, Sterling. If we hadn't shown up, you two would have been screwed. I think that means you owe me."

"How did you find us?" Forrest asked, leaning forward a fraction as if he wanted to move. Toward me or Callum? I gave the tiniest shake of my head. *Please*, I tried to send telepathically. *Please just be quiet.*

Callum ignored Forrest, his focus on me. "Did you find what you were looking for down there?" Before I could answer, he added, "I'm prepared to make you a very good offer." His eyes flicked to Forrest, then back to me. "We don't need him. You said he offered you twenty-five percent. Why don't you let me make it fifty?"

"Why not seventy-five?" I countered. Sass. Anger. Meeting Callum where he thought I should be. That was how I was going to get us out of here safely.

"I like you," Callum said, crossing his arms over his

chest. "But seventy-five is a little too much, even for a pretty girl like you."

The way he called me a *pretty girl* grated on my nerves. The leer was masked in his eyes, but it was there. I could feel it as he looked at me. Gross, but I'd put up with it if I could use it. This was a battle, and I needed to use every weapon I had.

Callum's gaze slid over me in a slow scan, lingering on my tits. I fought off a shudder and rolled my shoulders back, lifting my chin. Not exactly flirting, but just enough to keep him distracted. *Ugh.* There was no contest between this man and Forrest Powell. There never had been and never would be. Forrest's promise of twenty-five percent was good even without the contract we'd written up. I trusted him.

Callum Leary, on the other hand, would lie to me in a heartbeat if he thought it would get him what he wanted. My life was only worth something as long as we hadn't found Alan Buckley's fortune. The second we did, I wouldn't have anything to negotiate with anymore. There wasn't the slightest chance in hell I was going anywhere with Callum Leary, ever.

Still, I stayed where I was, several feet away from Forrest, my arms crossed over my chest. It was bad enough that I was in their sights. I had to keep their attention off Forrest. I shifted, giving Forrest the back of one shoulder, almost fully facing Callum.

"Look, I know the South is great in the summer." I rolled my eyes. "And you just can't stay away. But you're wasting your time. I don't have a clue about the next cipher. It's a dead end all the way."

"Then what were you doing in the cellar?" Callum asked, lifting his chin in the direction of the heavy wooden door they'd opened.

"We don't know," Forrest said, "but we're pretty sure it had nothing to do with my father's scavenger hunt."

I cut in. "Someone sent us on a wild-goose chase."

"Someone? You don't know who?" Callum raised an eyebrow, his lips tightening at the shake of my head. "If we hadn't come for you, you two could have died. You know that, right?"

His eyes drifted back to the dark hole in the ground, and I shivered. Partly because I was still frozen by the cellar and partly because of the rapidly dropping temperature as the sun slowly set. We were still in the mountains. As much as I joked about southern summers, it didn't get that hot up here. The root cellar had been cold and was only getting colder. "Believe me, I know." I didn't want to look back at the open root cellar and remember the slide bolt scraping across the wood, sealing our fate.

"This was no wild-goose chase," Callum went on as if it wasn't obvious. "They wanted to do more than mess with you."

"Maybe," I said, shoving my hands in my pockets. I wasn't completely sure about that. I hadn't thought about the cold until we'd been locked in the cellar for a while. And whoever had locked us in left us food and water. They could have been pulling a prank and not realized how deadly the cold could be over time.

"I'd advise you to find safer company," Callum said. "Or join my team and let us keep you safe."

I almost answered with a grin and a wink out of habit. But suddenly, teasing and cute didn't seem like the way to go. This was no game, and Callum Leary was only putting up with my attitude because he still thought he could use me. Slowly, I shook my head, keeping my back to Forrest. "I'm not joining up with anyone. I'll keep myself safe."

Callum grunted and fixed his eyes on Forrest. I had no clue what he was thinking, but I knew I wouldn't like it.

"You're not going to tell me how you tracked us here?" I asked, drawing his attention back to me.

Callum gave me a swift grin and shook his head. "I think I'll let your security chief figure it out." He lifted his fingers in a salute. "We'll be around." Callum and his two goons turned and walked down the gravel drive into the deepening gloom.

I looked at Forrest, standing a few feet away, hands shoved in his pockets, glowering at me. "Ready to get out of here?"

He gave me a short nod.

"Fine," I said. I turned and began the short walk to where we'd hidden the car. The evening air was humid, carrying traces of the day's warmth, so much better than the cold, dank, musty root cellar.

I plugged my phone in and waited to say anything until we pulled out on the state road, Forrest driving, Callum Leary's sedan falling in behind us. "Is he guarding us or threatening us?" I asked, leaning to look in the side mirror.

"Both," Forrest said, his voice tight, the muscles in his jaw hard.

I reached across the center console and took his free hand in mine. "Hey, don't be pissed," I said.

"I'm not pissed," he countered in a voice that said anything but.

"I could tell you didn't like that whole scene back there," I said, pushing to get him to talk to me. I knew Forrest too well to think he'd liked staying in the background while I talked to Callum Leary. It would have gone against every instinct he had. I loved him for doing it anyway because he trusted me.

Forrest's jaw clenched, his eyes flicking off the road to meet mine for a second. "I'm not going to apologize for wanting to protect you," he said.

"Yeah, well, I'm not going to apologize either. I get that you want to take care of me. I even like it. But in this case, you need protecting more than I do." I squeezed his hand. "I'm not buying his bullshit. You know that, right?"

"Cut me a little slack, Sterling," Forrest said, letting out a huff of air. "Half an hour ago, we were locked in that root cellar, and if I couldn't get through that door, we were both going to die of exposure. Maybe not tonight or tomorrow. But..." He glanced at me, his eyes hot with emotion. "I'm not ready to lose you again."

I squeezed his hand and laced our fingers together. Shifting in my seat, I leaned to rest my head on his shoulder. It was a little awkward with the center console between us, but I needed the contact.

"You were going to get us out, Forrest," I reassured

him. "I watched you with that rock. You weren't giving up. We weren't going to die down there." I could still smell the dank must of the cellar. "I need a long, hot shower and clean clothes. And to never go underground again."

My phone rang, the familiar tone sharp in my ears. I looked down to see Hawk's name on the screen. "Signal must be back," I muttered as I picked it up, bracing for the lecture to come. Hawk was not going to be happy.

Chapter Twenty-Six

STERLING

"What the fuck, Sterling!" he barked before I could get a word out. "Are you okay?"

"We're both fine," I said, giving him a quick rundown of the hours since we'd left Heartstone Manor.

"You fucking left to follow a clue without letting anyone know where you were going?" Hawk roared into my ear.

When he put it like that, it sounded a lot worse than when I came up with the idea. And I couldn't deny that was exactly what had happened. "Yes, we did. And we're fine. We're headed back to Heartstone now. You and Griffen can both yell at me in person when we get there." Before he could say anything else, I hung up the phone and put it facedown on my lap.

"Hawk or Griffen?" Forrest asked with the hint of a laugh in his voice.

"Hawk," I said, shaking my head. Sometimes, it felt

like I had a million older brothers. I wasn't complaining. A text popped up on my screen.

Come straight back. Griffen's office in 30m.

I checked the map on my phone. We'd be pulling into the driveway in twenty-eight minutes. I replied with a thumbs-up emoji and put my phone down, sliding my fingers into Forrest's again.

"I'm sorry you didn't like how things went with Callum Leary," I said. "But I'm not sorry for protecting you. And I am one hundred percent sure that you were going to get us out of there if the Learys hadn't shown up. Everything's okay, so don't be mad."

He let out a half chuckle and raised our twined hands to his mouth, pressing a kiss to my fingers. "I'm not mad, Sterling."

"Okay," I said and let it go, falling into silence.

I spent the rest of the ride back to Heartstone, running through the possible suspects in my mind. Who had access to the peppermint tin? Who knew about the Jefferson cipher? Who could have done this to us?

The answer, depressingly, was almost anyone in Heartstone Manor. I'd talked about the cipher wheel with Ford in the billiards room, a room that had two open doorways in two separate hallways. Anyone could have been lurking, out of sight but close enough to eavesdrop. I already knew Brax had been nearby, but there was no reason to think he was the only one.

Except that out of everyone, he hated me the most.

And I'd left the tin in my room, the door unlocked. Not for days on end, but for good chunks of time. Nothing in my room had been damaged or disturbed, which was almost an argument against Brax. He'd never been able to resist screwing with me.

My gut was shouting it was him, but I didn't have any proof, and my gut wasn't exactly reliable where Brax was concerned.

"Hey," I said as a thought occurred to me, "when we get back..."

"We need to talk to Griffen and Hawk," Forrest said.

"Yeah, Hawk said he wants us in Griffen's office straight away. But I'm going to text him and tell him I need to change. They'll give me a few minutes for that. Before anyone knows we're home, we need to search Brax's room. If his car isn't in the garage, we should be clear."

"Why do we need to do that first?" Forrest asked. "Hawk didn't sound patient."

I winced at the memory of Hawk's bellow. *Not patient* didn't really cover it. But... "Griffen and Hawk are going to yell," I said with the practicality of a younger sister who'd been on the receiving end of more than a few lectures. "Everyone in the Manor will know we're in trouble. And whoever sent us to the root cellar will know they have to cover their tracks sooner than they expected."

"And you're sure it's Brax?" Forrest asked, shooting me a sideways glance. "Not Ford? Or someone outside the house who bribed someone on the inside?"

I let out a long sigh. It could be any of the above. "Yes. I think it's Brax." I waited for Forrest to argue, to tell me I wasn't rational about Brax or that we didn't have any proof.

Instead, he said, "Okay. We'll have to be fast."

Love bloomed in my chest, and I squeezed his fingers. This was why, even after things went so wrong, I'd always loved Forrest Powell. Even when I didn't want to, and even when I also hated him.

"We can do it," I said. "He only has a single room, like me. It's big, but it's not a suite."

We drove down the lane to Heartstone Manor exactly on time. I texted Hawk.

We're back. I need to change. I smell like a root cellar. Be in Griffen's office in ten.

Three rolling dots showed on the screen for far longer than they should have. I imagined Hawk grumbling at me, tapping at the screen, and then erasing his message. Finally, words appeared.

Be there in 5.

I'd have to make it work. Forrest guided my car around to the family garage beneath the guest wing, hitting the opener on my visor. We parked in my spot and got out, my eyes immediately going to the empty place where Brax's car would be.

"Come on, let's go," I said, grabbing Forrest's hand and pushing him through the mudroom door and up the back stairs.

The second floor appeared deserted, the sconces on the walls turned low. Most of the doors were shut, including Brax's. Hesitant, I turned the handle, wondering if I was going to have to ask Savannah for the key or borrow Scarlett's lock picks and come back later. But the handle turned, and a second later, we were in Brax's room. I flicked on the light.

"What are we looking for?" Forrest asked, scanning the room.

"I don't know. Evidence? Something that has the address of that house on it or... I don't know, maybe check his browser history."

"I don't see a computer here," Forrest said, looking through stacked papers and magazines on the sofa.

I didn't see a computer or tablet either. Brax's room was about the same size as mine, a large rectangle. The sleeping area was set up on one side, and a sitting area on the other. There was no desk or workspace, unlike in my room. Plus, Brax was sloppy. No moldy plates or cups were sitting around, but things were tossed everywhere, another strike against him in my book.

It was hypocritical coming from me, I knew. When Griffen came home a year ago, my room was the biggest trash pit in the house. Now that I wasn't drinking my way through life and had actually cleaned the place up, I loved the order of a neat room. Everything where it was supposed to go. Everything organized.

I glanced at the piles of clothes draped over the back of the sofa, the sliding stacks of unopened mail on the dresser. This level of sloppiness was just careless.

Or maybe I wanted to see Brax's every fault as a character flaw.

I went for the dresser, opening and closing the drawers. Forrest headed for the closet. I didn't find anything among the jumble of barely folded sweaters, socks, and underwear. A drawer stuffed with loose papers and mail, none of which looked remotely interesting, and the most recent of which was dated a few years before, a junk mail drawer he'd forgotten about.

I could hear Forrest off to my right, rummaging in the closet. I left the dresser and went to my knees to look under the bed. More nothing. Not even a dust bunny.

"Sterling." Forrest's voice was heavy.

I stood and crossed to the closet. "What did you find? Evidence? Something weird?"

"Both, maybe. I'm not sure." Forrest held a box, I guessed from the gap above, taken from the top shelf.

"What is that?" I asked.

"You tell me," he said, holding the box low enough for me to see inside and peel back a flap.

A Barbie separated from her head, another with her arms pulled off. A doll's dress written on with permanent marker and cut into pieces. Rage shot through me, impotent fury tinged with grief and hollow loneliness that brought me back to childhood.

I reached for the box, pulling it from Forrest's hands, stirring through the shreds of my past. So many little things that had disappeared. That little shit always played innocent, but here it was—everything I'd suspected Brax of stealing, broken to bits and shoved in a box in his closet. Memory came to life, and I heard echoes of Miss Martha, Darcy, and later Prentice. Calling me dramatic, asking me why I always had to blame everything on Brax, why it was always me causing trouble. Darcy, the only mother I had, her eyes chilly with disappointment because I was picking on her baby boy yet again. But here was the proof, and all these years later, it would do me no good.

"I knew it," I said, my voice catching as I sifted through the detached doll limbs and torn clothes.

"What are you doing in my room?" Brax demanded, his voice low and oddly flat. His eyes were a mix of fury and glee. He'd hidden these things, but I saw that a part of him was thrilled I'd found them. All these years later, his eyes flared with greed as he wrung out one more drop of my pain.

I wanted to throw the box in his face, but I couldn't abandon the wreckage of my toys now that I had them back. They were little more than trash, but they were mine.

"We're leaving," I said and tried to elbow my way past him.

Brax's hand shot out and closed over my upper arm, his fingers painfully tight. He shook me, almost knocking me off my feet. "I said," he spat in my face, "what the fuck are you doing in my room?"

Forrest stepped out from behind me, looming over Brax. Beside Forrest, my brother looked like a teenager, not a man.

"Don't ever touch her," Forrest said, his voice low.

Brax looked up at Forrest, his eyes wide, his cheeks gone pale. Abruptly, he let go of me. "She's in my room, going through my stuff," he said in protest.

"I don't care. You never touch her." Forrest shoved Brax to the side, guiding me out of the closet.

"What the fuck is going on in here?" Hawk growled from the door.

A quick glance told me Griffen was right behind Hawk, looking just as furious as our security chief.

"Sterling, you were supposed to be in my office ten minutes ago," Griffen said, his voice strung tight like a steel wire.

"We were on our way," I said. I swept out of Brax's room, the box clutched to my chest, Forrest at my side, Hawk, Griffen, and Brax trailing behind me. The short trip down the main stairs and through the front hall felt like it lasted an eternity.

"All right, Sterling," Griffen said once we were all in his office. "Why were you going through Brax's closet? I thought Hawk was clear that you should come directly to my office when you got back."

"I don't have anything to do with whatever trouble she's in," Brax said to Griffen.

"Somebody left a decoy clue in my room," I told Brax, "sending us to a root cellar out in Henderson County. They locked us in. We could have died." I watched Brax's face closely for some hint of guilt. Nothing showed but aggravation. He opened his mouth to say something.

"You wait," Griffen said to Brax, holding up a finger before turning back to me. With a level tone I could tell he was struggling to maintain, he said, "Please explain to me why you and Powell thought it was a good idea to chase this new clue without letting us know where you were going."

Forrest answered before I could. "In retrospect, it was dumb, but it hadn't occurred to us that someone was trying to kill us. At least not before we find the money."

"You're sure the intent was to kill you?" Griffen asked.

"Hard to say," I had to admit. "They left some water

and granola bars. Maybe they didn't realize how cold it would get underground. Maybe they were going to come back."

"Can I go?" Brax cut in. "I don't know what I have to do with any of this."

"What do you have there?" Griffen asked, nodding at the box in my arms and ignoring Brax.

I shoved it in his direction. "Look."

Griffen peeled back the flaps, shuffled through the contents, and looked at Brax.

"Why do you have Sterling's old toys in your closet?" he asked, his steely tone much more pleasant when it was directed at Brax instead of me.

Brax rolled his shoulders back and shook his head. "Because I was a shithead of a kid, okay? I took her stuff all the time. I'd break it. She'd accuse me. I'd lie. Everyone would tell her to stop being such a drama queen, and she'd start crying. It was fun," he said. He crossed his arms over his chest. "It was fun when I was twelve. I guess I never got rid of the stuff, but it doesn't mean anything now." He hooked his thumbs in his pockets and turned to me with the perpetual sneer I was so familiar with. "I'm not twelve anymore, not that you've noticed. Did you and your boyfriend find anything in my closet other than that?" he asked. His tone made it seem like I was the crazy one.

I shook my head, forced to admit that we had not.

Hawk looked up from his phone. "Logs show Brax was in Asheville all day, at his office in the morning and north of town in the afternoon. Showing property or playing golf is my guess, based on the coordinates."

I deflated as Brax looked away and admitted, "Golf." He looked up, flicking his golden bangs off his forehead and shooting a glare my way before adding, "With a client. So again, can I go?"

Griffen looked between us. "Sure," he said, sharing a loaded glance with Hawk, who watched Brax leave the room as he tapped something on his phone screen.

Before I could say anything, Griffen held up a hand, palm out. I bit my lip, forcing myself to keep my mouth shut. Maybe sensing how close I was to losing my shit, Forrest stepped beside me, sliding his arm around my shoulders. I leaned against him, suddenly tired, the adrenaline of the day draining out of me, leaving me limp and desperately in need of a hot shower.

"Walk me through this," Griffen began. "Someone snuck in your room and tampered with the clue?"

I explained to Hawk and Griffen about the wax paper liner, the cipher solved by the Jefferson wheel, the root cellar, and the slide bolt. I skipped over the hours of fear and cold and jumped ahead to Callum Leary, freeing us.

"I don't like that he's hanging around," Griffen said, "but I'm glad he was in the right place at the right time."

"I'll sweep everything for trackers," Hawk added. "And then I think you two should get out of here for a while."

Griffen looked up at him, eyebrows raised. "Leave Heartstone?"

"Sterling has twelve days left this quarter," Hawk said, referring to the number of days I was allowed to be away from the Manor before the provisions in my father's will kicked in and I'd be disinherited. "I think she should take that cipher she can't solve to Emmett and Lucas. If they don't recognize it, somebody at Sinclair should be able to point them in the right direction."

"You sure it couldn't be anyone on the staff?" Griffen asked Hawk. "Even the best people are susceptible to bribery."

Hawk shook his head. "Unlikely. I keep an eye on..." He paused, then said, "Finances. Nobody's taken a bribe that I can trace. Everything around here is normal except Ford being back and Brax being around more."

"See," I said. "I told you him being home so much was weird."

Griffen looked at the box on his desk. "I know he's always been a bully," Griffen said, "but toys from when you were a little girl aren't proof that he tried to lock you in that root cellar. That's a big accusation, Sterling. I can't just throw him out with no evidence." He glanced to Forrest. "What do you think?" he asked.

Forrest tightened his arm around my waist. "I think I'm good to go to Atlanta," he said.

So was I.

It looked like we were going on another road trip.

For over a year, Heartstone Manor had seemed like the safest place on earth. And now? Now, it seemed we were safer anywhere else.

Chapter Twenty-Seven

STERLING

Before we left the next morning, Hawk did a thorough sweep of my car, our devices, and even our shoes. With a snort of disgust, he discovered a tracker on my car and one inside my purse. That one was momentarily terrifying until I remembered sitting at the bar at Avery's place, drinking a seltzer, my purse hanging from the back of my chair. I'd lived in a small town my entire life. I hadn't thought twice about securing my purse. I wasn't exactly used to being stalked by criminals.

Hawk handed me my backpack and said, "I have it all set up with Lucas and Emmett. I texted you the address. Go straight there. Pull into the parking garage and say who you are through the intercom. They'll let you in." He paused, then added, "Don't be shy." He tilted his head at my backpack, my laptop safely inside. "I don't know why you haven't told anybody what you've been up to with those classes, but these guys can help if you're interested in moving in that direction. Don't be afraid to be yourself."

Hawk wasn't the touchy type, except with my sister, but his words made me feel such a confusing combination of gratitude and embarrassment and love that I threw my arms around him in a tight hug.

Hawk's arms came up slowly, and he gave me a tight, short squeeze in return.

"Thanks," I said and got in the car beside Forrest.

"You know where we're going?" Forrest put the car in gear, his eyes lingering on Hawk, then shifting to me for a second before pulling onto the long drive to the gates.

"Yep." I dropped the address from my text messages to Forrest's phone, and he set up the navigation app.

"What was that about?" Forrest asked as he tapped the screen.

"What?" I asked, playing dumb.

"You giving Hawk a hug."

I couldn't tell whether he was jealous or just curious. And I didn't know how to answer. I didn't want to tell him what it was about, considering that I hadn't told anyone what I'd been up to. But Hawk's words had struck me. *Don't be afraid to be yourself.* I didn't entirely know who *myself* was. But the Sterling Sawyer the world knew was not a newbie hacker and computer geek.

I'd heard a lot of names applied to me, both by people who knew me and people who didn't. And it was jarring to realize that few of those names applied. *Nobody* knew me. I wasn't the spoiled party girl I'd been. I wasn't the kickass, financially independent coder I wanted to be. I didn't know who I was. So, no one did.

Except that wasn't true. Hawk knew me. Quinn knew me. Griffen knew me. Forrest knew me. But not all of me. Because Hawk was right—I was hiding the truth because I was scared.

I looked at the backpack at my feet, then back to Forrest, who patiently waited for an answer. I thought I loved him. I thought I'd forgiven him. But if that was all true, why didn't I just tell him?

I ran through it in my head. *I've been studying coding, and it turns out I'm pretty good at it. And Hawk wants me to talk to Lucas and Emmett because I'm interested in cybersecurity, and they can give me advice.*

The words sounded fake, like anyone who heard me say them would bust out laughing. *Sterling Sawyer? The girl with the big boobs and the blonde hair who threw great parties and could drink the guys under the table? That girl is into coding? Not likely.*

I pressed my lips together and felt a stab of remorse. After everything I'd put Forrest through for lying to me, I couldn't bring myself to tell him the truth. It was still too new, too raw. And I couldn't risk him laughing, even if I thought it unlikely he would.

I opened my mouth, and instead of telling Forrest why I'd hugged Hawk, I lied. "Just wedding planning stuff," I said casually. "Hawk is really sweet, building the arbor for Quinn. It's going to be small, but I want to make it perfect for them."

Not entirely a lie. All of that was true, just not what we'd been talking about. Did the tiniest bit of relief cross Forrest's face? I couldn't tell. I didn't feel relieved. I felt a little sick.

All my demands for honesty and I folded as soon as my pride was at risk. But I didn't want to be laughed at. I wasn't missing the irony. I had made so many poor choices and refused to be embarrassed by them. Now I'd made a smart choice—to finally apply my brain to something I was good at—and the idea of telling anyone paralyzed me.

It was a lot more painful to be laughed at for trying, for reaching for something I cared about, than to be laughed at for not doing anything. I couldn't fail if I didn't try, right? But now—now I was fucking trying. And it was terrifying.

I snuck a sideways glance at Forrest. "What?" I asked, seeing something in his eyes that said he wasn't done.

"Do you ever think about coming back to work at the inn? Doing what you were doing before? Working in event planning?"

I shook my head, feeling even worse about my lie. "No," I replied. "It was fun. I learned a lot, and I think I'm good at it, but it's not what I want to do. Too many people, always having to be on. And I like being in charge of my own schedule." All of that was true, but it wasn't the whole truth.

I should tell him, give him the honesty I demanded of him. I half opened my mouth, then snapped it shut, pulled up my phone, and went to the board of pictures I'd been collecting for the wedding. It didn't make me feel like less of a wuss, but at least it made what I'd said about Hawk a little more true.

Hawk was making progress on the arbor, which

meant I had to get my butt in gear. Just because they didn't want fancy didn't mean I couldn't pull together something special.

The miles flew by, Forrest playing DJ. We'd always shared taste in music, so I had no objection. I scrolled through idea boards, occasionally showing things to Forrest and asking his opinion. He wasn't into fashion or decorating, but he had a good sense of style.

That was one of the first things I'd noticed about him when he'd started working at the inn—he didn't look like he spent an hour getting dressed every morning, but he always looked good. The kind of good that told me he might worry about coordinating his socks with his ties, but he put thought into the things he chose to have around him and on his body, and he cared enough to get it right.

He agreed with almost all of my choices for the wedding. I teased him with a pic of hot pink tulle swags, but he just looked at me and shook his head with a curl to the side of his mouth. "I don't think Hawk would go for that," he said dryly, and I giggled, knowing he was right.

So many people said a wedding was the bride's day, but I knew this one was as much for Hawk as it was for Quinn, if not more. I had a feeling my sister would have happily trotted down to town hall and stood in front of a judge. She wanted to be Hawk's wife, and that was it. She didn't particularly care about the wedding, but Hawk did. He wanted it to be perfect for her, and she wanted it to be perfect for him. Sometimes, I thought they'd kill me with adorableness.

I looked over at Forrest, calmly navigating the twelve-lane freeway into Atlanta. I liked to think of myself as sophisticated, but every time I was here, the sheer width of the roads blew my mind.

Forrest didn't seem troubled. He didn't fold. It was another one of the things I loved about him. He wasn't showy, and he wasn't loud, but he had a spine like steel, and he didn't give up when things got hard. Most men would have left after we broke up. They would have given up. Cut their losses.

Not Forrest.

How long would it have taken me to talk to him if I hadn't solved the clue on the Vitellius? I didn't know, and now that we'd come this far, I knew I wouldn't have been able to stay away forever. I would have cracked sooner or later. Sooner, probably.

We got off the freeway in Buckhead, turning up one road and down another until ahead on the right, I spotted the building Hawk had described in his text. Four stories of mirrored glass with accents of gray and black. Forrest turned down a side street and pulled into the entrance to the underground garage. An impenetrable metal gate blocked the way from floor to ceiling. Lowering his window, he leaned out and hit the red button by the intercom.

"Can I help you?" a crisp female voice asked.

"Forrest Powell and Sterling Sawyer to see Lucas Jackson," Forrest said.

"Oh!" Now, the voice was welcoming. "You made good time. Pull up ahead and to the right and park in one of the guest spots. The button for the offices is marked in the elevator. I'll be there to let you in." The intercom clicked off, and the metal door slowly rose, revealing the dark interior of the garage. Forrest eased the car forward, the bright light of the summer morning fading as we entered the inner sanctum of Sinclair Security.

Chapter Twenty-Eight

STERLING

"This place is pretty slick," Forrest said as we parked.

I tried to picture Griffen or Hawk here and found I could, easily. Their dark SUVs were a match for the rest of the vehicles in the garage. I could see them getting on this same elevator to go up to the office. For a good chunk of the years, Griffen had been away, this was where he was living a life I knew nothing about, a life where he did things I'd never ask him to tell me. Given everything that had happened since someone had murdered our father, it was lucky he had. As much as I agreed with Avery and didn't want to be locked down, I was glad we had Griffen and Hawk's skills. I wanted freedom, but more than that, I liked being alive.

The elevator carried us smoothly up to the floor with Sinclair Security's offices. The doors slid open to reveal a small, dark-haired woman with a short bob and blunt-cut bangs. She was tiny, not just short like me, but built on a small scale with delicate bones and curious, sky-blue eyes. She wore a white dress with navy blue nautical detailing and a full skirt. The red crinoline beneath matched her lips. She was fresh and glamorous and the last thing I'd expected to see at the front desk of this elegant office.

"Hi," she said, holding out her hand. "It's so nice to meet Griffen's sister, Sterling. I've heard so much about you."

I rolled my eyes, liking her immediately. "That's a scary thought."

"No, not like that." Her eyes flashed with humor. "Griffen adores you. I'm Alice. Alice Sinclair. I run this place, though my husband Cooper would disagree."

"Not a chance," said the tall, dark-haired man who came up behind her. His eyes were ice-blue but warm as they looked down at Alice. He slid an arm around her shoulders and held out a hand. "Cooper Sinclair. It's good to meet you both." He shook my hand and then Forrest's. "We miss your brother and Hawk around here."

"I know they miss all of you," I said. "Though I'm glad we have them at Heartstone."

"I'm glad you do, too," Cooper said. "It seems like you need them more than we do, at least for now. I knew I wasn't getting Griffen back, but I had hopes for Hawk."

I grinned up at Cooper. "I'm pretty sure my sister Quinn isn't giving him back."

Cooper let out a sharp laugh. "She's a smart woman. It was good to see Hawk so happy. For that, I can live with losing him to the wilds of North Carolina."

Alice looked up at her husband. "You have a call in five minutes."

"I know," he said, "but I didn't want to miss meeting Sterling and Forrest. I'll walk them back to Lucas's department."

Alice nodded, then looked to me. "We have one of the safe house apartments free if you need to stay overnight." I drew in a breath, ready to say we could get a hotel, and Alice shook her head. "Hawk specifically ordered me to tell you that if you're staying in town overnight, you're staying here. He also added that if you have an issue with that, I should direct you to call him."

I let out a huff of breath. I definitely had an overdose of big brothers in my life. On the other hand, being offered a Sinclair Security safe house was a pretty good deal.

"Thank you," I said. "We'll take it."

"We don't really know what our plans are," Forrest added. "But we'll let you know."

Alice's eyes popped from my face to Forrest's, and she gave me a sunny grin. "You look like Griffen," she said. "It's in the eyes. Not the color, but the way you look at me reminds me of your brother."

I held that close to my heart, beating back all my insecurities as we followed Cooper down one long, gray-carpeted hallway and then another. My brother had belonged here. Maybe I could, too. Or somewhere like it. We came around a corner into a sea of small offices and open desks, computers everywhere. I saw people with headsets, multiple screens around them, laptops open here and there, wires, circuit boards, soldering guns.

Excitement fizzed through my veins. I didn't know what most of this stuff was for, but I wanted to. I wanted to know everything about what they were doing.

A thousand questions tumbled in my brain. Every single one evaporated as a man stepped into view—a man or a mountain? He had to be six and a half feet tall, and wide, his biceps stretching the sleeves of his olive-green T-shirt. Shaggy dark hair over sharp cheekbones almost hidden by a black beard. Surprisingly bright apple green eyes framed by thick lashes that reminded me of Forrest's —long and dark and thick. Lashes to die for. Why did men always get the best lashes? He was handsome in a terrifying way.

Marshaling all my courage, I stuck out a hand. "Sterling Sawyer," I said.

"Lucas Jackson," he answered, giving me a firm shake and confirming his identity.

I'd seen Lucas from a distance when he'd come to Heartstone, but that was nothing like seeing him up close. He turned to Forrest and held out a hand.

Forrest took it and shook firmly. "Forrest Powell. Good to meet you."

"Yeah, you too. I'm curious about this cipher you've got."

Cooper squeezed my shoulder. "I have a meeting. It was great to meet you both." To Lucas, he said, "Let me know if there's anything I need to know."

"Got it, boss," Lucas said.

Another man joined the group, and I backed up a step in surprise. "The last time I saw you," I said to the newcomer, "you had blue eyes, kind of like Cooper's, and your name was Jay. And then you kidnapped my sister."

"Emmett Blake." The man I'd known as Jay held out his hand. He had the grace to look a little sheepish, an expression that didn't sit comfortably on his serious face. Emmett Blake's real eyes were a warm brown, his dark hair brutally short. He was tall, as tall as Forrest, though not as tall as Lucas, and lean.

I remembered his wiry build, the feeling of barely contained energy. I wasn't exactly clear on why Emmett Blake wasn't in prison for kidnapping. In fact, he'd bypassed all authority in Sawyers Bend, and Hawk had ushered him straight here to Sinclair Security. Where, from what I could see, he'd fit right in.

I'd asked Quinn what had happened to him a few days after the kidnapping. She'd been oddly tight-lipped about her mysterious kidnapper, only saying that not everything was what it seemed, and things worked out the way they were supposed to. Bullshit answers. When my sister didn't want to talk, she was a vault. And if she was fine, I was fine, so I hadn't pressed.

"I'm sorry for all of that," Emmett said. "I had some things to work out." He looked to Forrest, studying him for a long moment before his eyes drifted back to me. "Hawk filled me in on what you two have been up to. I shared it with Lucas. I think we might be able to help you." His eyes flicked back to Forrest. "In a few different ways. Tell me about the ciphers."

Lucas led us to a conference room at the side of the big open room filled with desks. We sat around the table.

"Do you have any pictures?" Lucas asked as I started to explain about the statue of Vitellius.

I looked to Forrest. He gave a nod, and I pulled out my laptop and opened the file where I'd kept my notes. I walked Lucas and Emmett through our progress, sharing the few pictures and notes we had, finally, sliding the peppermint tin onto the table between them.

"And then we found this one," I finished. "But unlike the others, it doesn't have a key. We thought we found a key." I filled them in on the debacle of the root cellar and Callum Leary's rescuing us.

"And you don't know who at Heartstone Manor created the decoy clue?" Emmett asked.

"I have my suspicions," I said, "but I can't prove it."

Lucas and Emmett shared a long look but didn't say anything.

Lucas looked to me. "Show me what you've got for us." His eyes narrowed and landed on me, and I felt my cheeks flush. I thought I knew what he meant, but—

"Show you...?" I asked, stalling.

"Show me what you've done to try to solve this one," he pressed, his gentle tone encouraging as my stomach flipped with nerves.

"Well, I, um, I..." The heat on my cheeks grew, and I looked at Forrest, the fear from a few hours ago roaring back. I was embarrassed and terrified I was going to be laughed at. These people were some of the most elite hackers on the planet. Lucas Jackson ran the whole IT division for Sinclair Security. I didn't know about Emmett, but Hawk had said this was what he specialized in. I couldn't show them my amateurish fumbling, the code that hadn't worked.

Lucas's eyes narrowed. "Are you going to sit here and tell me you didn't write something to try to crack it?"

I shook my head, swallowed, and heard Hawk's voice: *Don't be afraid to be yourself.* I closed my eyes, lines of code flashing in my mind, and knew there'd never be a better time or place to take the leap and show them what I'd been working on.

Chapter Twenty-Nine

STERLING

"No, I, uh, I wrote a program—" My eyes skipped to Forrest's face and back to the screen, registering his look of surprise. But I quickly turned away, not wanting to see it change into anything else.

Clearing my throat, I started again, this time with more confidence.

"I wrote a program to try to crack the cipher. I tested it on a few ciphers I found online, and it worked. But it can't do anything with this one. I've looked everywhere for a key, and I don't know what I'm doing wrong," I said, my shoulders slumping as I finished. The same frustration I always felt enveloped me, a feeling that swamped me every time I hit run on the program and nothing happened.

"Show me how it works," Lucas said, leaning over my laptop.

I walked him through my rough code. "I tried it with

this cipher." I clicked and pulled up one of my test ciphers. "See, it works."

I knew it was slow as programs went, but I was proud of it. Pushing aside my fear, I plugged in another cipher I'd used to test the program, a simple alphanumeric cipher that used a shifting alphabet code. Within forty-five seconds, my program spit out the answer.

"It worked on this one too." I entered a different code, one that used a simple key, and again, this time in a minute and a half, my program spit out the correct answer. "But this—" For the millionth time, I pasted in the code on the index card in the peppermint tin. And for the millionth time, my program hung.

Emmett nudged my hand away from the keyboard and scrolled through the code. "You wrote this?" he asked, looking to Lucas and back to me.

I shrugged in agreement, my cheeks still hot.

"It's not bad for a beginner," Emmett said.

Lucas agreed. "It's pretty damn good for a beginner. How did you figure this out?" He pointed to a section of code I had labored over.

"I, um, found some open-source code I thought would work and tweaked it," I admitted.

"Clever," Lucas said, scrolling through the rest of what I'd written. When he was done, he sat back and crossed his arms over his chest. "The problem isn't with your program. Your program is actually pretty fucking good. The problem is that you're not dealing with an alphanumeric cipher. This is a polygraphic substitution cipher."

I'd seen the term but didn't know what it meant.

"What are you thinking?" Lucas said to Emmett.

"Either a Pollux cipher or fractionated Morse," Emmett said.

I'd never heard of either of those. "What's the difference?" I asked.

"Both ciphers," Emmett said, "have more than one key. Or rather, there's a key to decipher the key. The Pollux cipher uses fill-in-the-blanks, in a sense, and the fractionated Morse cipher uses Morse code. You couldn't solve it with your program because you were only looking for one key."

"I don't know what that means," I said, feeling my brain stretching to try to make sense of what Emmett meant.

"Here, let me show you. Hold on a second." Emmett left the conference room, grabbed something off a desk in a nearby office, and returned. "We work with ciphers more than you'd think. In the old days, I came across them a lot. Check this out." He opened an app on his laptop that was a hell of a lot slicker than what I'd cobbled together. "Give me that." He looked at the cipher on the index card, typed it into a box, and clicked a few menu items. "There's a key to the key, basically. We have to figure out what it is."

So, I'd been on the right track. A spike of warm gratification shot through me.

"I've looked everywhere," I said. "With every other cipher Forrest's father left, there was a hint or a clue of some kind. With this one, it's just the card with the cipher."

Lucas leveled his gaze on Forrest. "Then the key is probably something that you would have known. Right?"

"That makes sense," Forrest said. "So far, it's felt like my dad expected us to do this together. Except for the clue that ended up being a decoy, I've either known or recognized everything, even though I thought I'd forgotten a lot of it. It seems like he planned for us to do this a long time ago."

Lucas and Emmett exchanged another extended, silent look. I wondered what they were communicating.

"All right," Lucas said after a moment. "This is the fun part. Let's start going through things you would have known back then. Do you remember your street address growing up?"

"I do," Forrest said and told them.

Emmett typed it into the search box. First, just the numbers, then only the street name, finally, everything together. Nothing.

"Middle name," he demanded.

Forrest answered. Nothing.

"Childhood dog."

Still nothing.

"Cat."

Dead end.

They went at it for a while: Forrest's school, his favorite book, Alan's favorite band.

"What about your mother?"

"Emily," Forrest said. "Back then, she still used my father's last name."

Emmett typed in "emilybuckley" with no capitals or spaces. For the first time, something happened when he hit enter. The cipher rearranged itself into a different alphanumeric code, then to Morse code, and then into something entirely new. *Treasureislandp178*

"*Treasure Island* page 178," Lucas said. "What the fuck are you supposed to do with that?"

Forrest sat back in his chair, letting out a long, weighty sigh. "We read it together," he said. "The year before he died. He had an old edition. It was illustrated. It was really cool, actually."

"Do you still have that copy?" I asked, my stomach clenching at the thought that we might lose the trail simply because so much time had passed. The book could have been donated, thrown away, or lost.

Forrest closed his eyes for a long second. When he opened them, he said, "If I do, it's at my mom's house." He pulled his phone out of his pocket, looked at the three of us. "Do you mind if I step out and make a phone call?" Without waiting for an answer, he rose and left the room.

I watched him through the glass—the light in his eyes dimming as I assumed his mother answered the phone, the way his brows pulled together while he waited.

"So, what are your plans?" Lucas said, interrupting my study of Forrest.

I dragged my eyes to Lucas's and raised my brow, not wanting to assume I understood what he meant.

"Hawk says you've been taking coding classes," he clarified. "And that you've studied a little cybersecurity, and you liked it."

"Yeah, I, um..." Hawk's words echoed in my mind again, and I sat up straight. Lucas had said I was clever.

He hadn't laughed. This was a shot for me, a chance to be this new Sterling. I wouldn't know what could happen unless I opened my mouth and talked to him. "As you can tell from my program," I said, "I'm still a beginner. But I love it. I've been checking out how the security system works at Heartstone, and I want to know more. I was hoping, um, Hawk said that you two might be able to tell me what I need to learn."

"That depends on what you want to do," Emmett said.

"I don't know," I countered. "I don't know what all my options are, but whatever it is you guys are doing in here looks pretty cool. And Hawk said you wrote all the code for the system we have. Is that true?" I asked Lucas.

"Yeah, I did. Emmett has done similar work, but that's not all we do here."

"I want to know all of it," I said in a rush, my brain driving my mouth, leaving no room for insecurity or fear. "I want to learn everything."

Lucas sat back, crossing his arms over his chest. "I like your program," he said. "And there aren't many people's judgment I trust more than Hawk and your brother. So, here's what we're going to do. If you want."

I nodded, ready to agree to anything.

"You're going to keep taking those coding classes," Lucas went on. "You need to lay a good foundation, and the program you're in is a solid start. Emmett and I will add on a few classes you'll find through different sources. And when you're done with all of that, we're going to train you. If you make it through all the training, we'll put you to work."

"Really?" I said, afraid I'd misunderstood. "You'll train me? Teach me the stuff I don't know? And then you'll give me a job?" I felt queasy at asking so bluntly, but this was too important, and I didn't want to misunderstand.

"Yeah, if you can learn what you need to know," Lucas said. "And given the way you've run through these ciphers, I'm sure you'll soak up everything we can teach you. Then hell yeah, we'll put you to work. I know you've got the thing with the will, but we can do a lot of this remotely. We'll figure it out."

"Thank you." My heart pounded furiously in my chest. This was so much more than I'd hoped for. "I won't let you down," I promised.

"I don't think you will," Lucas said.

Forrest came back into the room, his phone in his hand. "Good news and bad news. The good news is that my mom says she has everything from my room before we moved boxed up in the garage at her house in Oregon. The bad news is that she doesn't want anything to do with this." He looked to me. "If we want to find that book, we're going to have to go to Oregon and hunt through her garage ourselves. She didn't exactly hang up on me, but it was close."

My heart, still thrumming from the sudden change in my future and the possibilities, took a second for his words to sink in. He sat beside me, and I reached for his hand. I knew Forrest had been close to his mom and that the only thing they never discussed was his father. "I'm sorry you had to ask her," I said quietly.

Forrest just shook his head.

"I think you two need to get out of town," Lucas said. "Until you know who sent you into that root cellar, I don't think you should go back to Heartstone Manor." His eyes flicked to me. "Not unless you have to. And with the Learys involved, Oregon seems like a great place for a vacation. You can go through those boxes on your own. As long as you've got a phone with a camera, you can touch base with Emmett or me if you need to." Lucas stopped and looked at Emmett, his chin lifting and dropping in the tiniest increment.

Emmett let out a breath. "There's more. When Sterling cracked the code on the Vitellius, Hawk asked me to do another dive into you." Emmett looked at me. "He thinks of you like a little sister. He trusts your judgment. But he wanted to make sure this one wasn't hiding any more secrets."

"I'm not—" Forrest started.

"Yeah, I know." Emmett gave a semi-apologetic shrug of one shoulder. "This isn't about you. It's about your father."

"He's been dead a long time," Forrest said.

"That's one of the things I was looking into." Emmett sat back. "The official story is that your father committed suicide."

Forrest gave a curt nod, and I tightened my fingers on his hand.

"I don't have any definitive proof," Emmett went on, "but I don't think your father killed himself. I don't know if there was corruption or just laziness, but there are too many things that don't add up."

"Like what?" Forrest asked, his voice gruff.

"Like the fact that your father paid in full for a luxury European tour a week before he died. Your father was on the frugal side for a man of his means. I've seen his spending records. I can't see him plopping down that kind of cash, knowing he wouldn't be around to enjoy it, especially since it was going to be a surprise. I based that on the fact that you and your mother didn't go on the trip or even attempt to cancel it and get a refund."

Forrest shook his head. "We didn't know about that. We'd talked about going, but it was... There wasn't a firm plan."

"There were other transactions that indicated he planned to be alive well after the day he died. There's this scavenger hunt with the ciphers that it looks like he intended to do with you. And then there was the crime scene. The police report said he was killed by a self-inflicted gunshot wound. But when I dug into it, the gun they found at the scene hadn't been fired, and he didn't have any residue on his hands. I don't know why no one followed up on that. I'm still poking around. I'll let you know if I find anything else, but I think..." He looked to me, then back to Forrest. "I think it's likely that whoever took the Vitellius ended up killing your father."

My heart sank as I realized what Emmett was saying. "You think my father killed Forrest's father or had him killed?" I asked.

"Theoretically, it could have been anybody. But it's established knowledge that your father took the Vitellius from Alan Buckley."

I glanced at Forrest. This time, it was he who squeezed my fingers.

"My guess is he thought it would be easy," Emmett said. "He thought the number on the bottom was the account number, and having the statue was as good as having the money. Then, when it turned out not to be that simple, I think he went after your dad. And either your dad wasn't willing to give him what he wanted, or more likely, Prentice or whoever he sent lost patience. I can't prove any of this in court. I can dig for more, but..." He paused, maybe waiting for a response from Forrest.

Forrest just looked poleaxed.

Lucas stood, looming over us. "You should talk to your mother," he said. "If what she remembers lines up with what Emmett's found, we can always push this. I'll talk to Cooper."

Forrest nodded. "I guess we're going to Oregon," he said, his hazel eyes shifting to me.

"I guess we're going to Oregon," I agreed.

Chapter Thirty

FORREST

"I've got you set up," Alice said, handing me a stack of printed paper. I glanced down to see the name of an airline and flight numbers. "Two tickets to Eugene and a rental car waiting on the other end. You have just enough time to get to the airport."

"Alice," Sterling said with a laugh, "you're amazing."

"I know," she agreed. "You have bigger fish to fry right now and can't hang around, but you have to promise to come back once all this is settled. Quinn told Lucas's wife, Charlie, all about you, and she's been dying to meet you. Now that Lucas met you first," Alice's eyebrow raised, and the side of her mouth quirked, "Charlie won't be patient. Anyway, I have a feeling we'll be seeing a lot more of you."

I didn't know what Alice Sinclair meant by that, but it looked like Sterling did. "Thank you, Alice," I said, reaching out to shake her hand. "I'm assuming you'll send me the bill."

She winked. "It'll be in the mail."

"Thanks, really."

"Any time. You guys are as good as family, and I can't wait to see how this turns out." Alice waved us off as we got in the elevator to begin the next step of our journey.

Another time, I would have been drawn in by her engaging smile, ready to laugh along with her. But at that moment, I was dazed, too much coming at me at once. I didn't even know where to start. I'd already been unsettled to learn that Sterling knew how to write a computer program—not just one program, but multiple programs good enough to crack a basic cipher.

I knew from the way Griffen and Hawk talked about him that Lucas Jackson was the next thing to a computer genius, and he'd thought Sterling's program was good. That meant she knew what she was doing. Why hadn't she told me? I thought I'd earned back her trust, at least a little, but now that seemed like a distant possibility. Sterling had a whole life she was keeping from me. Maybe I was just a means to an end. I didn't know anymore.

I'd barely absorbed that new information when I'd had to talk to my mother, had to confess that I was still chasing my father's legacy. I'd hated hearing the pain and disappointment in her voice.

She'd sighed. "Of course, I have your things. Just don't ask me to help you with this."

My heart was a lead weight in my chest. I was a terrible son to shove this in her face again. Losing my father had shattered her. She'd poured all her love into me, unwilling to risk her heart on another partner. When her second husband, Jerry, had snuck under her guard with his shy humor and gentle teases, she'd let go of some of her grief. She loved Jerry. I loved him for giving my mom back a part of herself she'd lost when my father died.

The mention of Alan Buckley, even though he was seventeen years gone, always dragged her into the past. The depth of her pain, even across the phone, reminded me that this was no game. If the Learys and our stint in the root cellar weren't enough to tell me that, hearing my mother's voice go flat was a sobering reminder.

And then to find out that my father might not have killed himself, that he could have been murdered?

I couldn't keep my head straight.

Sterling tucked the flight information in her purse and linked her arm through mine as we left the elevator and made our way back to the car. Moving on instinct, I opened her door, waited for her to get settled, closed it, got in the car, and programmed the map to bring us to the airport.

We were standing in the security line before I pulled out my phone and texted my mother. I started to type a few times before I settled on what to say.

I'm coming out to look for the book. Sterling is coming with me. Can we stay with you?

I hoped bringing Sterling would soften her up. My mother had been so angry when she'd found out what I was up to in Sawyers Bend and also furious that I'd lost the woman I'd told her so much about. She'd been thrilled I'd finally found a woman who caught my interest, as she put it, so excited to meet Sterling. I'd been frantically trying to figure out how to untangle the lies I'd told, and then it had all been over.

My phone remained silent as I loaded our bags onto the X-ray belt and took off my shoes, going through the ritual of setting my things out in the bin and waiting to be waved through the metal detector. On the other side, I checked my phone as I collected it from the bin. No text from my mom, and we were getting close to our boarding time.

"What gate?" I asked Sterling.

She pulled out our boarding passes, squinted down at the page, and said, "B24. Hey, Alice booked us in first class."

I winced a little at the thought but didn't mind.

"I'm sorry for the bill Alice is going to send you," Sterling said. "But considering the length of the flight, I'm not complaining."

"Me either," I said, happy I'd be able to stretch my legs out in front of me.

The flight was already boarding by the time we reached the gate. My phone beeped just as I shoved our bags into the overhead bin. Sitting, I checked the screen. My mother.

Of course, you're staying with me. Send me your flight information. I'll kill the fatted calf for dinner.

Sterling looked over my shoulder as I responded to her text. "She's still mad at you?"

"Yeah," I admitted.

"How can you tell?" she asked, rereading the text for a clue. In explanation, I scrolled back to older texts. After a few pauses for them to load, I got to those we'd exchanged the weeks before my lies were exposed. My mother's rampant use of emojis screamed off the screen.

Sterling smiled down at the phone. She reached to scroll forward in time, reading the stilted texts we'd exchanged in the past twelve months. "Why haven't you been home to see your mother in a year?"

I remembered mentioning that at Sugar Mae and Bob's and the surprise on Sterling's face. "The only person more pissed at me than you about all the lies I told last year was my mother," I said. "She was furious that I had anything to do with the Sawyers, that I had lied about who I was, that I was chasing after the statue my father had died over. And most of all, she was mad that I lost you."

"Me?" Sterling asked, looking up, her eyebrows pulling together. "Why am I on the list?"

"I told her about you," I said, smiling a little at the memory of how excited she'd been. It wasn't like Sterling was the first woman I dated, but the issues with my dad aside, my mom and I were close. She'd known Sterling was different even before I did. I sighed at the memory. "I lied to her about where I was working, who I was working with, put her off on visiting. But I told her about you. She was excited, wanted me to bring you out to meet her. Then the truth came out and—"

"She was pissed, huh?"

"When she found out I lied...oh yeah," I replied, shaking my head at the memory of my mother's rage. Her disappointment. "She was excited that I'd met someone, and the idea that I screwed that up over memories of my father... She wants everything with my father to have stopped the day he died. She doesn't want him in the present. I think it hurts her too much. I think she needed to leave him behind for herself. But I can't do that."

"Of course you can't," Sterling said. She curled her hand around mine, her thumb rubbing the backs of my fingers. "He was your dad, and you loved him. He loved you. This scavenger hunt he sent you on..." She shook her head. "He really loved you. I'm sorry...my father..." She bit her lip and closed her eyes.

I wondered if she was trying to shut out the idea that her father had killed mine. If that had happened. Probably not with his own hand, but I was betting that if there was any proof out there, in the end, it would point straight at Prentice Sawyer. And none of that had anything to do with Sterling. I turned my hand to squeeze her fingers. "Sterling, no. Your father was a miserable human being, and that has nothing to do with you."

"I'm not sure about that," she said. She opened her eyes, the blue shimmering behind a veil of tears. "I don't envy you your grief, Forrest. I grieved Darcy, and I still miss her every day. It sucks, but I envy you your dad, because you're right—my dad was a miserable human being. And I'm sure if I knew everything he'd done, I wouldn't be able to sleep at night. But I'd probably be able to forgive some of it if he'd loved me even a fraction of how much your dad loved you. I know you didn't have him long enough, but what you had was pretty amazing."

My throat locked shut, and I shook my head, not denying her words, just too overwhelmed to say anything. I lifted our joined hands and kissed her fingers. If she walked away from me when this was all over, I wasn't sure I'd survive it.

The flight attendant stopped at our row, offering our choice of drinks. I could have used a drink, but noticing Sterling's choice of soda versus alcohol, I went for the same. Drinks in hand, I ignored the passengers boarding the flight and asked the question that had been bugging me for the past few hours.

Turning to Sterling, I rubbed the back of her hand on my cheek and asked, "Why didn't you tell me about the programming? When did you start doing that? You weren't doing it when we were together."

"No, I...I would have told you," she said, but her words were hesitant. "Or maybe— I don't know."

"So why didn't you say anything? Still don't trust me?" I hated the thought of that, but I needed to know.

Sterling gave an embarrassed laugh. "Not you specifically. I didn't tell anyone. Hawk only knew because he had to go through all the web traffic when Emmett— It's a long story, but Hawk found out. That's how he knew and how Lucas and Emmett knew. But I was afraid. I was afraid you'd think it was stupid," she said in a rush. "It's so not me."

Sometimes, this woman made my heart ache. She was so smart, so full of love, so much of everything that was good. It astounded me that she'd grown to the age of twenty-six and couldn't see that in herself.

"You weren't afraid to show me that you could break the ciphers," I pointed out.

"I was," she admitted. "But there was no way I could hide that if I was going to talk you into letting me see the

Vitellius. The coding stuff was easier to keep quiet." She drew in a steadying breath and let it out slowly. "I've been studying coding for about eight months. I didn't tell anyone because, at first, I didn't know if I'd be able to do it, and I didn't want to fail at another thing. And then when I figured out I could do it, that I liked it, it just seemed so out of character. And I was afraid... I was afraid of being laughed at, I guess. I wasn't sure what I wanted from it. It started with curiosity, and then...then I guess it's turned into hopes. But I don't...I don't know what I'll be able to do with any of this. Not really. Working in event planning at the inn was the first real job I've ever had. I don't know what I'm doing trying to create a career out of some classes I've been taking."

"There's so many different things you can do with it," I said. "But you wanted to talk to Lucas and Emmett. You want to get into cybersecurity?" Her eyes lit up, and I knew I was right.

"I do, and Lucas and Emmett liked my code," she said, almost to herself, as if she needed to convince herself of the truth.

"You can learn anything they can teach you," I said, utterly confident I was right. She was Sterling. She could do anything.

"You don't know that," she said, taking a quick sip of her soda and shaking her head with a smile as the attendant offered her headphones.

"I do because I know you. I know how smart you are, and I know how you are when you're determined. You didn't know anything about event planning when you came on at the inn."

"I knew how to throw a party," she said.

"Not the same," I argued. "But you figured it out, and then you kicked its ass. You've only been coding for eight months, and already you're writing programs that Lucas Jackson thinks are good." I paused, letting that sink in. I was incredibly impressed with her but not particularly surprised. "You can do anything you set your mind to, Sterling."

"Thanks," she said quietly and settled back into her seat. "I guess we'll see." She slipped into thought, sipping her soda as we took off. A while later, she asked, "I hope your mom doesn't mind me just showing up with you. I don't want to make things worse between you."

"You won't," I said.

"Will she like me?" Sterling asked in a soft voice that made me want to unsnap her seat belt and pull her onto my lap.

I raised our joined hands again and kissed her fingers. "You, she's going to love you. It's me she's not that thrilled about."

"What's she like?" Sterling asked.

As much as I'd told my mom about Sterling, I'd never shared that much about my mom. I'd avoided any but the most general mentions of my past in my efforts to hide who I was. Now, I tried to think of how to describe my mother and gave up. "She's great," I said. "But you'll see soon enough."

The rest of the flight went by slowly. We napped, ate dinner, and watched a movie. It felt like days had passed by the time we landed, the wheels bouncing on the tarmac, Sterling's hand tightening around mine as we rolled to a stop at the gate.

I texted my mother when I was in line to get the rental car, letting her know we were almost on the road.

I made lentil soup and fresh bread instead of fatted calf. See you when you get here.

That was it. It seemed she'd thawed a little, but not all the way. She was still pissed. It was there in every missing smiley face and heart emoji. When this was all over, I'd have to figure out how to make it up to her. I glanced over at Sterling, chewing on her lower lip, I thought, nervous about meeting my mother. I was hoping my mother would love Sterling as much as I did. I was looking forward to a future where my biggest problem was the two of them ganging up on me. I could only hope.

Chapter Thirty-One

FORREST

It was a ninety-minute drive to the coast, where my mom and Jerry had their place. We pulled in a little after I'd guessed we'd be there, coming to a stop in the gravel drive in front of their house, the deep navy of the Pacific Ocean far in the distance, below the cliffs beyond the house. Once, this property had been part of hundreds of acres overlooking the coastline, with sweeping views surrounded by wild nature. Years before, the land had been subdivided, and Jerry had managed to snag ten acres with a sliver of the cliffs to call his own. A handful of outbuildings had come with the land, and he'd used one of them as his pottery studio, but he hadn't built anything until he'd convinced my mother to marry him. Then they'd designed a modern house, all angles and wide cedar plank siding, with tall plate glass windows that looked over the land and the ocean beyond the cliffs.

Around the house, they had a kind of farm. I say "kind of" because it was nothing the two of them couldn't manage easily. There were chickens and a goat. The area she'd set aside for vegetables was at least fifty percent bigger than the last time I'd been out. Speckled around the property were the outbuildings, all of them with dark green siding built in a style that far predated the contemporary main dwelling.

When my mom had met Jerry, she'd thought he was a potter, teaching a ceramics class she'd signed up for as a way to fill her time and keep her creative juices flowing. She'd assumed Jerry was a poor artist and been chagrined to find out that he'd actually started and sold a successful company selling kombucha. His distinctively branded bottles were found all over the Pacific Northwest. He wasn't Sawyer-level wealthy, but he'd had a healthy bank account and the desire to spoil my mother with as much compost and as many farm animals as she could handle. These days, she was mostly retired, puttering around her land, growing things, playing with experiments in the kitchen, and generally causing trouble.

At the sound of our doors closing, my mom strode out of the house onto the deck. The familiar sight of her sent a stab through my heart and brought unexpected tears to my eyes. It was the first time in my life I'd gone so long without seeing her, and fuck, I'd missed her.

She stood on the front deck in a pair of old jeans—probably Jerry's—that hung from her hips and were patched at the knee, held up by a braided leather men's belt. Over that, she wore a flowing grass green tank top, her mostly gray hair long and wild in waves and curls almost to the middle of her back. She'd added streaks of hot pink since I'd last seen her. Except for the gray, she looked years younger than her age. Her eyes were sharp as they landed on us.

"Finally." She strode down the steps from the deck and down the walkway to come to a stop in front of Sterling. She gave Sterling a slow once-over with hazel eyes so like mine, taking in every detail of the woman beside me. When she got to Sterling's face, she smiled. "Sterling Sawyer," she stated with a hint of Georgia in her voice, "I heard you don't take after your daddy."

Sterling smiled back and said, "God, I hope not." She held out her hand.

My mother ignored it and pulled her into a tight hug. "I'm Emily. It's good to finally meet you," she said. "I'm glad he brought you home."

Sterling's hands rose to tentatively pat my mother's back. I didn't think she'd been expecting the warm welcome. To be honest, neither had I. I wasn't sure what to expect. It had been a long time since I'd brought a girl home to my mother. Not since high school. And never anyone like Sterling. Never the woman I loved.

My mother's welcome for me was significantly less warm. She leaned in and wrapped her arms around me, giving me a tight, quick squeeze. "It's good to have you home." Letting me go, she stepped back. "Come in. We'll have dinner soon," she said, turning and leading us into the house. "Jerry's out helping a neighbor with his fence. He'll be back soon. Can I get you something to drink? Tea? Wine?"

"I'd love some tea," Sterling said. "With the time

change, I keep forgetting it's almost my bedtime. I feel like we've been traveling for weeks. It's hard to believe we were in Sawyers Bend this morning."

My mother pulled out a teapot and a matching set of teacups that I recognized immediately as Jerry's work.

"These are beautiful," Sterling said, admiring the deep red glaze that faded to orange and then to a bright yellow at the lip of the mugs.

My mother smiled. "My husband Jerry made them. He's an amazing potter."

"Oh, that's so cool. We have some wonderful potters at home. The area I live in attracts artists." Sterling lifted the mug and studied the rich color of the glaze. "This is really gorgeous. I'd love to see more of his work."

"Oh, we've got it all over the house," my mother said, pride evident in her voice. "There's some in a gallery in town, too. He still teaches classes now and then. It's how we met."

Sterling and my mother talked as my mother put together tea and filled a plate with my favorite ginger snaps. She might be angry with me, but she was still my mom. I sat at the table, silent, absorbing the awesome weirdness of my two favorite women getting along, happily chatting. I'd always thought they'd like each other. Had, in my most optimistic moments, dreamed about Sterling being welcomed in my mother's kitchen, the two of them enjoying each other. But now, after the last year of solitude frozen out by both of them, it just felt surreal.

My mother poured tea and set our mugs in front of us, and then I recognized the look on her face. It was time to talk business. Mom Business. She raised one dark eyebrow, her sharp gaze moving from Sterling to me.

"Explain," she said.

"Explain?" I asked, raising an eyebrow back.

"Don't get smart with me, young man," she said. "Explain why you're still wasting your time chasing daydreams."

"They aren't daydreams, Mom," I said. "Dad left behind a code—"

My mother smacked her palm on the table so hard that the plate with the cookies jumped. Ripples ran across the top of my tea, and my mom's eyes went from sharp to stark with pain. My stomach twisted. I hated this part of it, hated that she'd never been able to hear a single word about my dad.

"Forrest," she said, her voice tight, "I've barely talked to you for a year. I recognize that is mostly my fault. I was angry, maybe angrier than I have a right to be, considering that you're an adult living your life. But I cannot understand why you would risk your career and the woman you told me you'd fallen in love with, chasing some fantasy of your father's. There are no accounts filled with money. I don't know what happened to all of it, but it's gone. He didn't leave us anything. He just left us."

Her voice cut off with a choke, and she swallowed hard, blinking away the gathering moisture in her eyes.

"I'm not wasting my time," I said evenly, trying to control my frustration. "And I don't care if there isn't any money. This isn't about the money." I looked to Sterling, for whom this was very much about the money. "If there isn't any money, I'll—"

Before I could finish, Sterling cut me off. "Shut it, Forrest. I don't care about the money either."

I saw in her eyes that she was telling the truth.

"Emily," Sterling started gently, "I don't know if there's any money. We'll find out, I hope, eventually. But I decoded the clue on the statue of Vitellius, and Forrest and I have been following all of the clues his father left. It isn't daydreams. It's important." She looked at me, emotion heavy in her eyes. "He left this for Forrest. He wanted Forrest to do this. It's not a waste of time, but I'm sorry that it makes you sad."

My mother didn't say anything, but I could tell she was listening.

"Mom," I said, "Sterling's right. I have to do this. I have to follow this trail Dad left for me. It's been full of memories. We went to the lake house. I saw Sugar Mae and Bob. I'd forgotten about them."

My mother lifted a hand to shield her eyes as if it was too bright in the kitchen. Her shoulders hitched, and I hated myself anew for forcing her to deal with all of this, to feel these things she hated to feel. But she had to know.

"They miss you," I said quietly.

"I miss them too," she whispered. "They were good friends. I just...I couldn't stay, I couldn't... Forrest...I'm sorry... I'm sorry I haven't been able to let you have your father. I just..." She dropped her hand and lifted her eyes, shattered with pain.

My heart flinched. I didn't want to think, didn't want to imagine what it would be like—to lose Sterling. And not the Sterling of today, but a Sterling I'd married and had a child with, had a life with. And then to have her be gone, to have her leave me in such a final way by her own choice.

No, I couldn't fathom what that would do to me. And my mother didn't know what Emmett Blake had discovered.

"Mom," I said, afraid that I was only going to cause her more pain. "Have you ever considered that Dad may not have killed himself?"

My mother shook her head, tendrils of hot pink and gray brushing her cheeks. She tucked her hair roughly behind her ears. "Forrest, we can't rewrite the past."

"I'm not," I said. I looked to Sterling and back to my mother. "Sterling's been doing most of the work solving these codes and ciphers Dad left behind. But we came across one we couldn't crack."

I wasn't telling her the story about the root cellar or any of the reasons we left Sawyers Bend. That would only get me in more trouble.

"We brought the latest cipher to some security people Sterling's brother used to work with. And they, um... They looked into me since Sterling and I are..." God, this was awkward and complicated to explain. "Anyway... when they investigated me, they looked into what happened to Dad."

I explained what Emmett Blake had found. My mom was shaking her head before I could finish telling her about the gun that hadn't been fired.

"No," she said. "Forrest, no. I don't want to hear fairy tales. I don't want revisionist history bullshit. The past is the past. Your father left us, and I will never forgive him for that. I will never be at peace with it. And I won't let you sell me some story. I won't let you give me hope. I'd rather have the truth, and the truth is that he's gone." Her eyes burned with anger and pain, tears pooling on her lashes.

"Mom...can't you just listen?" I pushed, hating that I was hurting her all over again.

"I am listening," she said, "but you don't have any proof. The police looked into his death all those years ago, and no one ever said it was anything other than suicide. I won't have it." She smacked the table again, the teapot and mugs rattling at the impact. "Do you hear me? Unless you have real proof, I won't discuss it. Do you have anything more than shadows and ghosts?"

I let out a long sigh and shook my head.

"Then get out. Just give me a few minutes. Please. And then I don't want to discuss this again." She stood, wobbling a little. "You two go poke around in the garage, see if you can find your boxes while I finish up dinner. We'll eat the cookies later."

I stood. "Mom...I'm sorry. I wasn't sure if I should tell you—"

She cut me off with a shake of her head. "I was so mad at you for lying last year and causing yourself so much trouble. I can't be mad at you now for telling the truth. Even if it's only your truth. But I need a minute. Please."

I nodded, sick to my stomach at her distress, my heart aching. I'd hurt her by lying, I'd hurt her by staying away, and now the thing that I'd thought might make her feel better had only hurt her more.

I hated it. I hated myself more than a little for doing what I'd done.

"Give a shout when dinner's ready," I said and led Sterling back out the front door, across the yard, past the chicken coop to the old garage.

Chapter Thirty-Two

FORREST

"You did the right thing," Sterling said as we walked.

"I'm not so sure about that," I said. "I hate that I made her sad all over again."

"Yeah. Me too," she agreed. "But I understand. I don't think you ever get over that kind of sad."

"Maybe." I opened the side door of the garage. The space had been split in two. One half was Jerry's studio, the walls there lined with shelves holding everything from glazes to projects in various stages of finishing. A pegboard on the wall held all sorts of tools, and the potter's wheel sat in the middle of the room, covered by a sheet. The other half of the garage was taken up by more shelves stacked with boxes and plastic storage bins.

"I haven't been in here in ages," I said, trying to remember the last time I'd come in the garage. It had been years, and everything had been rearranged since.

Sterling pulled out her phone and started texting. "I'm asking Emmett if there's any chance of getting something to back up his suspicions. Maybe something solid enough that your mom will believe it." Sterling hit send on her text and then looked up at me. "She's afraid to hope. She's been so angry at him for leaving her. The idea that he was taken, that's a whole new hurt, you know."

I did, considering I was grappling with it myself. To me, the idea that he hadn't left me willingly made all the difference. But maybe not so for my mother. Or maybe, as Sterling said, it was just that simple—the hope that she'd been wrong all this time was too much. And maybe forgiving my father would be a whole new kind of pain, a new kind of grief. There'd been enough of both in my mother's life.

Sterling's phone beeped. "Emmett says he's working on it." She looked up to see me standing in front of a shelf, reading the labels on the bins.

"She must have reorganized all of this stuff at some point," I said. "These bins don't date from our move from Georgia to Oregon, but they're not new either."

I lifted one that said *Forrest Toys* and pulled it off the shelf, setting it on the floor. Sterling pulled over an empty bucket, turned it upside down, and sat on it.

"Let's see what's in here," she said.

I pulled off the lid to find stacks of board games, an ancient pack of Uno, and a tin covered with faded pictures of dominoes. I opened it to find it filled with stone arrowheads and shark's teeth.

"This is all my stuff," I said, brushing a finger over the sharp edge of a tooth.

"I don't understand," Sterling said, rummaging through the bin. "These are your things from when you lived in Georgia?" I nodded. "Why didn't your mom unpack it and put it in your room here?"

I wasn't sure I knew. Thinking back, I said, "When we came out here, we lived with my grandparents. My mom was..." I shook my head slowly at the memory. "She wasn't in great shape those first couple years after my dad died. We lived with Pop-Pop and Grandma. They didn't have a lot of room. My mom and I shared a bedroom for a while." I trailed off, remembering hearing her cry herself to sleep.

So many nights, I'd joined her, silently weeping in my own bed. As much as I'd loved my grandparents and my mom, I'd hated everything about being in Oregon. I'd hated leaving home, hated being without my father, hated losing my friends and going to a new school. Everything had been in pieces.

I drew in a slow breath and let it out. "Pop-Pop ended up building onto their house, and I got my own room. We were going to move out, but then Grandma got sick, and we stayed. I guess we just never unpacked a lot of this stuff."

I dug through the bin, lifting out old, thin cardboard boxes of puzzles, looking for that copy of *Treasure Island* from my father's code. Instead, I found a layer of stuffed animals. I reached in and pulled one out, finding an owl with amber plastic eyes, bushy eyebrows, and pointed ears.

"My father bought me this," I said, my words rough, my throat tight.

Wet heat prickled in the backs of my eyes, and I blinked, feeling Sterling's hand land on my shoulder.

"He—" I opened my mouth to tell her my father had won me this at a town fair. The owl had reminded me of the one on a poster at the library that I loved when I was a kid. I'd seen it at the fair and wanted it, and my father had paid over and over for handfuls of darts until he'd popped enough balloons to get it for me.

I wanted to tell her, but my voice strangled in my throat. That wet heat gathered in my eyes rolled down my cheeks. My shoulders hitched as I tried to breathe.

Sterling's arm slid around me, her cheek against my shoulder. "I'm so sorry, Forrest," she said. And I felt the heat of her own tears leaking through my shirt.

I wrapped my arms around her and held on until the storm of emotion drained away. When my chest loosened and my eyes dried, I brushed the heels of my palms against my cheeks, embarrassed to have lost it like that in front of her.

"Sorry," I started to say.

She pressed her lips to my temple, then to my cheek. "Don't be sorry, Forrest. You loved him. I'm so sorry you lost him." Her lashes were spiky with tears, her eyes as bright as sapphires.

I wanted to tell her how much I loved her, but now wasn't the time.

"I didn't think this would be so hard," I said, looking at the storage bin between my feet, filled with the remnants of my childhood. "I feel like a jerk for putting my mom through this."

"You're not," Sterling said, "though I get why you feel that way. This is the legacy your father left for you. Of course, you want to follow it. It's yours. And I understand why it hurts her that you have to. That doesn't make you wrong."

"No," I agreed, "it doesn't make me wrong." A knock sounded on the door, and I looked up to see my stepfather, Jerry, his graying hair pulled into a loose ponytail at the nape of his neck. He wore a pair of leather thong sandals on his feet and an untucked, faded chambray shirt over a pair of jeans, so like my mother's, I was sure I'd been right in guessing where hers had come from.

"Good to see you, Forrest. Sterling," he said with a welcoming nod. "Looking forward to getting to know you. I'm Jerry. Emily says soups on. She made a strawberry rhubarb pie for dessert to go with those ginger snaps."

He didn't comment on my red eyes or Sterling's spiky lashes, and none of us said a thing about my mom's puffy, bloodshot eyes when we got to the kitchen. There were times when my family's ability to ignore reality grated at me. This was not one of them. We all needed a break.

Dinner was easier than I thought it would be. We didn't talk about why we were there, or my father, or the fact that all of us had been crying. Instead, my mom and Jerry gave Sterling a friendly third degree, and she played along, charming them both. She told them about working for her sister Quinn in the guide shop, the thriving artists' communities in western North Carolina, and her new career goals, managing to fill them in while avoiding any mention of ciphers or clues or why we'd been in Atlanta.

Then we got to everything I'd been doing in the last year, which sadly wasn't much other than work. But I loved my job at the inn and went into detail on a few of the projects my mom knew about.

Before I realized how much time had passed, I looked over to see Sterling, her jaw wide in a yawn.

"Sorry," she said. "I know it's only eight here, but it's late for me. It's been a very long day."

"You two need a good night's sleep," my mother said, her eyes narrowing slightly. "You can get to business tomorrow. How long can you stay?"

I looked to Sterling, who answered, "I have to be back at Heartstone Manor in eleven days."

"Well," Jerry said, "you're welcome here for as long as you have."

"Thanks," I said, and meant it.

"Jerry put your things in the guest room," my mother said. "I'll see you both at breakfast bright and early."

"The chickens will have us all up at dawn," I explained to Sterling as we climbed the stairs. My mom and Jerry's bedroom was on the first floor, and I was grateful for the distance.

Sterling disappeared into the attached bathroom as soon as she'd opened her small suitcase. She emerged from the shower with her hair dry, piled on top of her head in a messy bun, strands of gold falling around her damp shoulders.

"Flying always makes me feel gross," she said.

I couldn't resist reaching out to touch all that damp, smooth skin, but I didn't linger, heading for my own quick shower before joining her between crisp white sheets.

"This day has been about a million years long," she said, turning into my arms.

"At least," I agreed, rolling, gently pushing her onto her back.

Her eyes widened in surprise. "We're in your mother's house," she said.

"I know, but she and Jerry are all the way downstairs, and I'm pretty sure you know how to keep quiet." I pulled her out of the straps of the camisole she had chosen to sleep in, dragging it down from her shoulders to hook under her full breasts. "Can you?" I asked, looking up into her eyes shadowed in the near dark.

I saw her face shift as she smiled down at me. "I don't know," she said. "Can I? I guess we'll find out."

Braced on my elbows, I pressed her breasts together, squeezing the tips of her nipples until her head dipped back. I surged up to bite her throat, tasting the vibration of her moan before I kissed her.

"Shh," I reminded her and fell into the kiss, her mouth mobile and eager, as needy as I was.

I kissed her until I couldn't breathe, then moved down her body, tracing the line of her neck, the curve of her shoulder, the side of her breast, sucking the hard peak of her nipple until she squirmed beneath me, letting out a squeak when my teeth grazed her sensitive skin.

I lifted my head to whisper, "Shh."

Sterling growled, the lust and rebellion in the sound sending a spike of desire straight to my cock. And I slid down, dipping my tongue into her belly button, from one hip bone to the other, and then down to taste the salty, slick heat of her.

A groan rumbled in her chest, and I lifted my mouth, kissing her inner thigh. "Uh-uh," I said, and she raised her arm, covering her mouth and rolling her hips up. I got the message. She'd keep herself quiet if I got back to work.

More than happy with that arrangement, I dipped my head, slid a finger in her tight heat, and sucked the pearl of her clit into my mouth. Her body shook with the effort to stay quiet.

She tightened around me, a high, desperate sound escaping as I drove another finger inside and lifted my mouth to press my palm against her clit, fucking her with my fingers, almost losing it as she tightened around me in fast, hard pulses of orgasm. Her body relaxed as my fingers slid free, the only sounds were her harsh breaths and the thud of her heartbeat. Finally, she whispered, "I think you killed me."

"Complaining?" I asked.

She shook her head. "Never." I wasn't expecting it when she sat up, closing her hands over my shoulders and pushing me down on my back. "My turn," she said. "I proved I can keep my mouth shut. Can you?"

Then she was between my legs, her mouth closing over the tip of my cock, her quick tongue licking, her fingers wrapping around the base to squeeze hard. My vision whited out, and I let out a low moan. A second later, the bed shifted, and Sterling sat up.

"Uh-uh." She wagged a finger at me. "Remember? Quiet," she reminded me, a hint of glee in her tone.

This was payback, and I was in for it. "I'll be good," I promised.

Unlike Sterling, I didn't cover my mouth. I clenched my teeth together and reached down to thread my fingers through her soft hair, feeling the hum of her throat as she sucked and licked and brought me closer and closer to the edge until she pulled me over, taking everything I had.

When I could breathe again, she crawled up my body and slid into my arms, her thigh splayed over mine.

"That was hot," she said against the side of my throat.

"Fuck yeah, it was," I agreed.

"Wake me up later, and we'll do that again," she murmured as she slid into sleep against my shoulder.

Hours later, deep in the night, after making sure I put on one of the condoms I'd brought, I drew her to the surface with kisses. Touching, tasting, I filled her slowly, her legs wrapping my waist and her arms around my shoulders. It was slow and sweet and silent.

I DIDN'T REMEMBER FALLING ASLEEP AGAIN, JUST Sterling in my arms and then the bright light of morning. The light stabbed my eyes, softened only by the scents of coffee and bacon.

I rolled over to see Sterling, her cheeks flushed, her lashes barely parted, lips still swollen from our kisses in the night. "I'm starving," she whispered.

"Me too. And my mom makes a killer breakfast."

My mother seemed like herself again, her eyes clear, her hair in a loose braid. She wore a tie-dyed sundress, her feet bare as she flipped bacon and buttered homemade sourdough toast. Sterling poured coffee, and the four of us stuffed ourselves full.

Food consumed, I sat back, sipping my coffee, about

to suggest to Sterling that we head out to the garage when Jerry laid a hand on my shoulder.

"I know you have plans for the day," he said, looking to Sterling, "but can I borrow you for a minute before you get started? I got a shipment of supplies yesterday. I could use some of that young muscle bringing it to the studio."

"Of course. I'll be back," I said to Sterling, wondering if she would mind me leaving her alone with my mom.

"We're good," Sterling said before I could ask.

I looked at my mother, sending her a silent plea to keep her embarrassing stories to herself. Hoping her answering wink meant that she would, I followed Jerry out the door.

Chapter Thirty-Three

STERLING

I was only a little nervous about being left alone with Forrest's mom. So far, she seemed to like me. What could go wrong? *Famous last words.*

I stood, picking up my plate. "Let me help you with the dishes. This was an amazing breakfast," I said.

"No, no," Emily said, taking the plate from my hands and setting it on the counter. "Sit. Let me pour you another cup of coffee." Emily refilled the carafe and brought it to the table. "I owe you an apology."

I sat back down and held up my mug, watching the thick, dark liquid as she poured. I had to love a woman who made coffee so strong the spoon would stand straight up in it. I added a heavy dash of cream and sipped, smiling. "You don't owe me any apologies."

"No, I do," she insisted. "That conversation yesterday wasn't appropriate for your first visit here. None of us are rational on the subject of Alan's death. Me, least of all. We lost him. It was devastating. And I suppose as much as I love Jerry, all these years later, I'm still not over it. I'm sorry you got caught in the middle of that."

"You don't need to apologize. This has been hard for Forrest, too. He wants to follow the clues his father left, and still..." I thought of the look on Forrest's face when he'd recognized Bob and Sugar Mae—the sadness and the longing. "I think he's had to grieve all over again," I said.

"I'm sorry for my part in making it harder," Emily said, her eyes, so like Forrest's, heavy with regret. "I've always loved him so much, but when it comes to his father, I haven't been the best parent. I wish I could go back." She shook her head slowly. "But we can't, can we?" Leaning forward, she braced her forearms on the table, her hands wrapped around her coffee cup, her eyes level on mine. "I need to know, are you going to kick him to the curb again?"

Taken by surprise, I sat back in my chair, lifting my coffee mug for a slow sip, stalling. I knew the answer. I'd known the answer for a while, but it didn't feel right to tell Emily when I hadn't talked to Forrest yet.

"I know my boy shouldn't have lied," Emily went on. "He knows he shouldn't have lied. He got in over his head, and he made a stupid decision. He's always been a good boy. Worked hard and didn't get into too much trouble. Looked out for me. His grandparents. If anybody ever deserved a second chance, it's Forrest." She added cream to her coffee and stirred, giving me a chance to respond.

I didn't know what to say. All I could do was wonder what it would be like to have a mother-in-law like Emily. I wasn't used to this kind of parental relationship—the open love she had for Forrest, the way she'd hugged me. I wanted to be a part of this family. I could be. But that was for Forrest, first.

I couldn't tell Emily what I was going to do about him—not until I talked to him—but I could give her the part of the truth that was mine alone. "He loves you so much," I said. "My mom died before I was old enough to remember her. My stepmom was great." I sighed, thinking of Darcy and her warm hugs. "But she wasn't mine. And then I lost her when I was nine. My dad was..."

I shrugged. My father didn't need any further explanation.

"I envy you two," I went on. "I know things have been hard. I know you've been through a terrible loss, but I still envy what you have."

I sat back, setting my coffee mug on the table, crossing my arms over my chest.

"I'm not great at trust," I admitted. "And Forrest lying about who he was, why he got to know me, it hit me where I don't have a lot of defenses. I was angry. I was really, really angry. But," I let out a breath, "I spent the last year trying to get over your son. And so far, that hasn't worked out very well. I'm not perfect—understatement of the century. I was pretty much a mess until not long before I met him. I've been working hard to get my life together, but...I'm not sure I'm the best person to judge him for one mistake."

"So, you're going to give him another chance?" Emily pressed.

I shrugged and picked up a piece of toast that I hadn't

finished, taking a bite and chewing slowly. After swallowing, I said, "I think it's safe to say we're figuring things out."

Emily nodded, apparently satisfied, and started clearing the plates in front of her. "You won't do better than my Forrest," she said.

I took another sip of coffee and then stood up myself, grabbing the other two plates on the table. "I'm pretty sure you're right."

Forrest opened the back door, his eyes going straight to me, his lips curving in a smile as he saw that I wasn't traumatized by being left alone with his mother.

"Jerry's all set," he said.

Emily nudged me in Forrest's direction. "I've got the dishes. You two go do what you came here for."

Forrest reached for my hand, and I slid my fingers into his, letting him pull me out the door.

We had a book to find and a code to crack.

Chapter Thirty-Four

FORREST

Sterling and I grabbed cold cans of soda on our way back to the garage. It wasn't hot, not yet, but the day was warming up. I stood in the doorway, surveying the shelves of boxes. How had one kid accumulated so much crap? I didn't know, but I was going to find out.

I pulled the first of the plastic storage bins off the top shelf and set them on the floor. Sterling dragged over the bucket she'd used the night before and sat. I did the same with a nearby step stool.

One by one, we opened the neatly labeled bins and went through what was left of my childhood. Baby blankets. My christening gown. Picture books. A bin of artwork, pages and pages I imagined had been sent home from school, dutifully admired by my mother, and then packed away. Only a parent would see anything worth saving in my childish scribbles. I hadn't been meant for a future as a painter.

I found another box with my mother's wedding

album. A white candle, the wick barely burned, beside a bouquet of dried flowers. I probably should have closed it, but I pulled out the album and opened the front cover. Sterling slid her bucket to sit beside me, her cheek warm against my shoulder as we flipped through the pages. They'd been so young, both of them. My mother's beaming smile shone through the decades, my father beside her, not just happy but enormously pleased with himself. Love and pride were clear in his eyes when he looked at his bride.

It was hard to imagine they'd ever been apart. I was only halfway through the album when I closed it, feeling like I was violating my mother's privacy. I knew without asking that she wouldn't want us going through this box. Not yet. Maybe never.

Sterling seemed to understand. She took the album from my hands gently and nested it in the box as it had been, careful not to disturb the flowers.

"Maybe someday she'll be ready to look at this again," Sterling said.

"Maybe," I agreed.

I lifted the bin back onto the shelves and opened another to find uniforms and patches from Cub Scouts and my short tenure in Boy Scouts, a stack of soccer gear buried in the bottom. We uncovered a bin of Halloween costumes, revealing my youthful obsession with cowboys and knights in shining armor. With a twinge, I thought of my lies and losing Sterling for so long. Some knight I'd turned out to be.

Sterling smiled down at the plastic helmet and sword

in her hands. "I bet you looked cute with this." She flashed me a grin.

"My mom probably has pictures somewhere," I said. "I'm sure she'd love to embarrass me."

"I want to see them." Sterling opened another box and let out a whoop.

"Did you find it?" I asked, leaning over her shoulder.

"*Treasure Island*? No, but look, books. We must be closer."

Closer, maybe, but there was more than one bin of books, and while they weren't big, they were packed full. Painstakingly, we went through them, double-checking all of the covers beneath the dust jackets. And then there it was, halfway through the third box, my much loved and very dog-eared copy of *Treasure Island*.

My father had read it to me when I was no more than nine or ten, a chapter at a time before bed every night. Later, not long before he died, I'd reread it by myself. Now, here it was, maybe a key to finding what he'd had left behind, what he'd died for.

I handed her the book, and she turned to page one hundred seventy-eight. I wasn't sure what I was expecting to see. A note in my father's handwriting. Something.

There was nothing. It was just a page like any other. Except it wasn't. Page one hundred seventy-eight held the scene where they found the treasure. That couldn't be a coincidence. The next code had to be here.

I let out my breath in a gust of frustration. "What am I missing?" I asked out loud, both to myself and to Sterling, squinting down at the familiar lines of the story.

Sterling didn't answer, her eyes glued to the page. Her finger was running down it line by line, moving back and forth. Something caught my eye.

"Sterling," I prompted.

She grunted, her eyes still flicking back and forth over the page.

"Look," I said, pointing to a capital A at the beginning of a sentence. ***A**nd thereupon we all entered the cave.*

Then, to a lowercase d. *I behel**d** great heaps of coin...* And to a lowercase m and r. *How **m**any had it cost in the amassing, what blood and sor**r**ow...*

"Do you see?" I asked, flipping to the prior page and back again.

"Oh," Sterling breathed, reaching to trace the letters with a fingertip, catching the curves and lines on those letters—deeper, wider, darker than the rest of the type in the book, showing the grooves of indentation from his pen. The one and seven in the page number had received the same treatment.

"Do you have a notebook?" Sterling asked. "I need my laptop. Hang on."

She jumped up and sprinted from the garage, returning in a few minutes with her bag slung over her shoulder, a little out of breath. Sitting back on the overturned bucket, she pulled out both her laptop and a notebook.

"How many of them are there?" Sterling asked.

We made our way through line by line, finding four of the slightly distorted letters just in the first paragraph. And between them, an entire word with each letter ever so slightly shaded. Not enough that it jumped off the page, at least not until I knew what I was looking for.

"I think it's a Caesar cipher," Sterling said. "I have one here, but it's a pain to read, so I made a program instead." Digging in the front pocket of her backpack, she pulled out a thick coin and shoved it at me.

Once in my hand, I realized it wasn't a coin. It was two discs, one set inside the other, both with the alphabet engraved on the edges. A hole in the center coin revealed a number beneath. Sterling leaned over and spun the center coin.

"You line it up to the number that's the key, and the alphabets align," she said. "One set of letters is the code, and the matching letter is the solution. But it's hard to read the numbers through that hole or hold it still while I turn it to read the letters."

Flipping her laptop open, she navigated to a file and double-clicked. It opened to a black screen with two text boxes outlined in white. One asked for the code, and the other the key.

Turning from the Caesar cipher coin in my hand, she typed A, D, M, R into the code box. Into the box labeled *KEY*, she typed seventeen and hit enter.

RUMI appeared below the boxes.

"Rumi?" Sterling asked, raising an eyebrow. "Like the poet?"

Something teased at the back of my brain. "I think..." I struggled to make the picture in my memory snap into focus, but it refused. I closed my eyes, remembering our old house in Willow Springs. A book with a golden-yellow cover floated to the surface of my mind. My heart sank when I remembered where I'd seen it last.

"I think my mother has a collection of Rumi's love poems," I said. "I remember it from when I was a kid. My father must have given it to her."

"Shit," Sterling said, and I silently echoed her sentiment.

"Do you think she kept it?" I asked more to myself than to her.

Sterling looked around, then popped to her feet and scanned the labels on the boxes we hadn't gotten to. "That's pretty sentimental. I would have if I were her. Any chance your mother has books packed away here?"

I hoped Sterling was right. The amount of stuff my mom had saved—particularly from her wedding—told me she hadn't erased my dad's memory from her life as much as I thought she had. A book of love poems, though. I could see that being incredibly painful. And if she'd gotten rid of it, then what would we do?

There was only one path forward. We'd look ourselves, and if we couldn't find it, we'd have to go to my mom.

"She could have some in here," I said.

I didn't see any, but we went through the rest of the labels and opened a few more bins. We found ancient cookware, a tea set that I thought had been my grandmother's, and a stack of quilts. But none of my mother's books or more personal items.

"I hate to say this," Sterling said, "but I think we have to ask your mother. I wonder... At first, it seemed like your dad meant to do this with you—which makes a lot more sense if he was murdered—"

I nodded in agreement. It felt like that to me, too.

"But now I wonder if it wasn't meant for the two of you," she continued. "Once it was obvious that you were part of the key to solving it, it seemed weird it was only for you. You were a kid. What were you going to do with all that money?"

"Good point," I said. "Unless there isn't any money, and it was just about the fun of the treasure hunt. But either way, I could see him wanting my mom to be a part of it. And we don't know how long he planned to wait for us to try solving the clues."

"True," Sterling agreed. "So, what do we do now?"

I hated causing my mom pain, hated the look in her eyes when we talked about my father. She was still so raw and so angry. I couldn't picture asking her for help, but the thought of not doing that, of walking away and leaving this unfinished, was equally untenable.

"Forrest," Sterling asked, shaking me out of my paralysis. "What do you want to do?"

"We're going to have to talk to her," I said, knowing we didn't have another choice.

Chapter Thirty-Five

FORREST

I found my mother in the kitchen, doing something with a cutting board piled with fragrant herbs. The spicy green scents of thyme and oregano filled the kitchen. She turned, her hair floating out around her slender frame in a cloud of gray and pink.

Her chin came up, but her eyes were cautious as they met mine. "What did you find?" she asked.

"We found what we were looking for," Sterling said gently. "There was another clue in Forrest's copy of *Treasure Island*."

My mother was silent, but her eyebrow raised in question.

"The clue," I said, "was Rumi. We think it means—"

"—the poet," my mother finished for me. She let out a long sigh, seeming to deflate, her shoulders rounding forward, her chin dropping. Setting the knife on the cutting board, she turned, heading for the hallway that led to the bedroom she shared with Jerry. The space was bright and open, the ceiling a tall slant, no more than my height on one end, soaring to twenty feet on the other side of the room. Tall, plate glass windows made up the wall that faced the ocean, the deep navy spreading across the distant horizon.

Sunlight flooded the room, but as my mother entered, she brought darkness, her sadness clinging to her like a fog. I expected her to head to her closet or the bookshelf, but she went to the neatly made bed, sat on the side, and pulled open a bedside drawer. She rifled through it and, from the bottom, pulled a slim volume. The cover was the deep yellow-gold linen I remembered. Down the spine in gold-pressed letters, I could see *Love Poems of Rumi*.

"He gave this to me," she said. "On our fifth anniversary. He always loved Rumi." She rubbed her thumb over the words on the spine. "I always thought it was odd. He could be so unsentimental, so logical and orderly. Not the kind of man you'd think would be into love poems." She let out a huff of breath and wiped at the bottom of her eye, her fingers coming away wet. "But he was a romantic at heart." She flipped through the book. "I don't see anything." Shaking her head, she looked to me. "I haven't read this in years. Not since, well." She shrugged, cut off in a choke, and she swallowed. "But I don't—"

Sterling laid a soft hand on my mother's arm. "May I?" She reached for the book, and my mother slid it toward her, her eyes squeezing shut.

Sitting beside my mom, Sterling opened the book in her lap, carefully leafing through. With a glance at me, she shook her head. But as she opened the cover and closed the book again, something jumped out at me.

"Sterling—" I held out my hand, and silently, she

passed me the thin volume. I opened the front cover all the way and looked at the endpapers, the sheets of paper that were glued to the inside of the hardcover of the book and served as the very first and last pages. They didn't match the rest of the book, and they didn't match the cover. Instead of a plain paper or some fanciful design that would go with a volume of poetry, these endpapers looked like pencil sketches of vintage maps. Were they printed maps or actual pencil sketches? I used my phone as a flashlight and studied the endpapers, but I couldn't tell. I ran my fingers along the edge of the front cover.

Sterling's breath drew in sharply, her eyes bright as they met mine over the book. Taking the volume from my hands, she caught her finger beneath the last page and turned the book, so instead of the front, we were looking at the last page and the inside of the back cover. Immediately, I saw what we'd missed. The endpapers in the back were the same vintage maps as the front, but here, the edge was raised, almost lumpy.

"Mom," I said. She drew her attention from her memories and focused on the book in my hands. "Look at this." I flipped the pages from the flat, clean endpapers of the front cover to the raised, uneven endpapers in the back.

"I don't remember there being maps in the book," my mother said slowly. "It was..." She closed her eyes as if trying to think. "It was a weird, swirly paisley."

Taking the book from my hands, she turned it in her lap and wedged her fingernail under the edge where the glue had begun to give way. Slowly, she worked the endpapers free of the glue, up around the corner and down one side. When she'd freed almost half, she lifted the endpaper and tilted the book. A small, folded packet of paper slid out, landing in her lap. She let out a gasp, her eyes wide with wonder.

Shoving the book into my hands, she picked up the packet of papers, unfolding them slowly. There were two, the first a sheet of notepaper that read *ALAN BUCKLEY* at the top. My chest squeezed as I recognized it from his desk at our old house. The second page was almost translucent, a printed receipt with the logo of a travel agency at the top. The lines of the receipt were filled with notes and dates—an itinerary from almost two decades ago.

The trip to Europe Emmett Blake had discovered. Before I could think too much, my mother shoved my father's note at me, her eyes full of tears.

"Read it," my mother whispered.

Sterling moved to look over my shoulder, and together, we read my father's final words.

To Forrest and Emily, my dearest, truest loves,

Congratulations on solving the final clue. I always hoped my obsessions would pay off. I promised you riches, success, and adventure, and I can finally say I've delivered on all three.

This trip is just the beginning for the three of us. It's time to start a new chapter in our lives.

I love you both so much. Thank you for your faith in me. I hope you'll feel it's been rewarded.

Love,

Alan

Sterling looked up at me, tears streaming down her

face. "He never meant to leave you," she said. "He was going to start a new adventure—" Her words cut off, and her shoulders hitched. "I'm sorry. It's just, I'm so sorry."

I knew without her having to explain that she was thinking of her father and his role in what I now knew was certainly my father's murder.

Because the man who wrote this letter, the man who'd planned this trip, day by day, with the travel agent —that man had not taken his own life.

My mother reached out, her fingers closing around mine. "He didn't leave us," she said, her voice filled with grief and wonder.

"No," I agreed, feeling the wet heat on my own face to mirror hers. I moved to sit beside her on the bed, Sterling on my other side.

"I misunderstood everything. I got it all wrong, and I kept him from you. Kept his memory locked away out of anger, and he—" She choked on a sob, and I hugged her, pulling her damp cheek to my shoulder.

"You didn't know," I said, wishing I had the right words to comfort her. It was easy to look back and say she should have known, and so impossible when things had seemed so clear. He'd lost his company to Prentice Sawyer. The police were certain he'd taken his own life. Everything seemed to add up, and she'd been in so much pain.

"You only knew what you knew," Sterling said, reaching out to take my mom's hand in hers. "I'm so sorry, my father—" Sterling choked on the word, her eyes squeezing shut.

"Oh, Sterling, no," my mother said as I wrapped my

arm around Sterling, holding her close. "You have nothing to be sorry for."

"Your father was a monster," I said, brushing my lips across the top of her head. "And you grew up to be you despite him."

"I have part of him inside me," she whispered, turning her head into my shoulder and letting out a ragged breath.

"Barely anything," I said. "Griffen isn't a monster. Neither are Tenn and Royal, or Quinn, Parker, Finn, Avery..."

Sterling gave a watery laugh. "I noticed you didn't mention Ford or Brax."

"I haven't decided about Ford," I said, honestly. "But Brax definitely takes after your father."

Sterling straightened, wiping her eyes. "I'd understand if you blamed me," she said.

My mother simply said, "We don't. And I don't want you worrying over it, understand? His sins are his own."

Sterling nodded and gave her a weak smile, her eyes drifting down to the papers in my mother's hand.

We sat there, the three of us, rereading my father's letter, studying the itinerary for the European tour that had never happened. My mother traced her finger across the letterhead on the thin paper. "They probably called after he died. I would have assumed it was a sales call." She let out a ragged breath. "I'm so sorry, Forrest." She looked to me, her eyes filled with remorse.

"Don't be sorry, Mom. You did the best you could," I said, wishing I had better comfort than that.

"I should have known. Because your father never

gave up." She reread the letter. "We fought about how much he was working," she murmured, "and he kept promising. 'Soon,' he said. So many times. 'Soon.' But there was always one more hurdle, one more goal. And soon never came." She let out another long sigh. "I'll be right back."

My mother pushed to her feet, her legs a little wobbly as she walked into her bathroom. Through the open door, I saw her turn on the water and splash her face.

"You okay?" Sterling asked.

"Yeah," I said, looking down at the letter in my father's strong, distinctive hand. "I think I am. I've been so angry at him for leaving us. For so long, I wondered why, what I did to make him leave. Wondered if I could have changed his mind, done something to make him want to stay."

Sterling's hand closed around mine. "Forrest, no."

I let out a laugh I didn't feel. "I know it wasn't about me. Kids always blame themselves. I get all the psychology of it, and still...still, I've never been able to stop myself from wondering if I'd been just a little better. But there wasn't anything I could have done because he didn't choose what happened to him. He didn't leave us."

I looked up to see my mother standing in front of me.

"It's going to take a while for that to get through my head," she said, her face and eyes red from her tears.

Sitting back down on the side of the bed, she picked up the book and leafed through it, studying the endpapers at the back where the note and the itinerary had been hidden.

"What are you looking for?" I asked, watching as she

peeled back the endpaper all the way and ran her fingertips over the exposed cover.

"I'm looking for some clue about what happened to all the money," she said, one eyebrow raised as if surprised I'd ask.

Sterling and I looked at each other in shock. After all this time chasing the big payday, it seemed both of us had forgotten that was what we'd expected to find at the end. To me, learning my father hadn't killed himself was priceless. I didn't care about the money, but Sterling...

She smiled across at me, shaking her head. "I don't care about the money," she said in a whisper.

"But it's odd, isn't it?" my mother said. "We all assumed that ugly little statue had the key to Alan's missing fortune. And while this is a lovely..." She drew in a ragged breath and pushed it out, straightening her shoulders as if she could throw off these ugly, raw emotions and get back to practicalities. "He sold his company, the one he started before the VoIP business Prentice stole from him. He was paid for it. I know that much. If the code on the statue of Vitellius wasn't hiding the money, where is it?"

Sterling took the letter from my mother's hand and reread it, turned it over, looked again at the itinerary. "I don't see anything we missed," she said. "It's just a letter. Maybe this really wasn't ever about the money at all. The money could be a completely different thing. And..." Sterling handed the papers back to my mother. "Maybe my father screwed Alan out of what he owed him, and there was never any money to find." She gave my mother an apologetic glance. "Knowing my father, that seems like the most likely answer. If he had something to do with Alan's death, I wouldn't be surprised if he'd somehow arranged to steal the money."

"All this work," I said, "and there's no payday."

A small, secret smile curved across Sterling's mouth, and she shook her head. "Oh, I think we got our payday. This is better than the money."

My mother smoothed her fingertip over the indentations of my father's writing. "Well done, you two. I'm proud of you," she said, gaze on Sterling.

My heart squeezed as a flush hit Sterling's cheeks, her eyes shining at my mother's praise.

My mom shifted her gaze to me. "I may not have approved of all the decisions you made on this journey of yours, but I'm so proud of you for taking on the challenge your father set in front of you. And proud of you for seeing it to the end. If you hadn't, we never would have known the truth." She stood, brushing her hair back from her tear-damp face. "Why don't you two go for a walk? Forrest, you haven't shown Sterling the cliffs. I need to share this with Jerry. He'll want to see it."

"Of course," Sterling said, popping to her feet. She looked at me and then at my mother. "I need to wash my face." She disappeared down the hall, leaving us alone.

My mother caught my hand as I stood. "Forrest, I'm sorry about this past year. I'm sorry for being so hard on you. You did the right thing."

"I didn't... I messed everything up," I said, not sure how she could call anything about the past year *the right thing*.

"Oh, honey," she said, shaking her head, "I forgive

you. I know I've been blinded by hurt and anger at your father. I couldn't see clearly, but now I understand. And it's okay. Maybe now you can forgive yourself."

She raised an eyebrow, and I shook my head. "I don't know how to make it up to her," I said. "How to make it up to both of you."

"You don't need to." She held out the letter. "Alan had plans and hope. We would have had so much fun." A tear ran down her cheek. "Life is short, sweetheart. We know better than anyone. Don't waste any more of it blaming yourself. You've done right, and you've done wrong. You've done a whole lot more right than wrong, so forgive yourself."

Her words spread through me, a healing balm. "I wish I could have done things differently," I said.

Her arms slid around my shoulders. "Well, you can't. You can only go forward from here. I love you so much, Forrest. I've missed your father every day he's been gone. But I'll always have a piece of him in you, and that's the greatest gift he ever gave me."

I soaked in her love, her forgiveness.

"I have something for you," she said. "Stay there."

She disappeared into her closet, and what she held in her hand when she returned caught the light in a blaze of color. "You don't have to use it, but that's the ring your father gave me. And when you get around to proposing to Sterling, if you want..." She set it in my palm—a circle of gold topped by an emerald-cut diamond faceted so that it burned like fire.

I picked up the ring and held it to the light, hope

surging in my heart. I looked at my mom over the ring. "We're not there yet. I'm not sure she's forgiven me."

My mother smiled. "You worry too much. She's a smart girl, and I've seen the way she looks at you. She's not going to let a good thing get away. And you, my sweet boy, are the best. You don't have to use it if you had something else in mind."

All at once, I knew she was right. This was right. "Sterling will love it. Thanks." I wrapped my arms around my mom in a tight hug, feeling so lucky. We'd lost my dad, cruelly and before his time, but all these years we'd had each other. And maybe, if I could pull it off, I'd have a future with the woman I loved.

I let my mom go and tucked the ring in my pocket.

"Go on," she said. "Take your girl for a romantic walk. Who knows, maybe you'll put that thing to use."

Chapter Thirty-Six

STERLING

Forrest came out of his mother's room with a smile on his face. He was lighter, as if he'd shed a weight I hadn't known he was carrying.

"She needs a minute," he said.

"I'm sure." I couldn't get my head around how she must feel. What a mindfuck this had to be. "It's a lot to take in," I said.

"Yeah. At least Emmett threw the idea at me yesterday, so I've had a chance to absorb the possibility. My mom didn't think there was a chance when we brought it up. She's reeling. But she texted Jerry. He's on his way in."

"Will that be weird?" I asked. "Him comforting her over her first husband?"

Forrest smiled. "Not really. Jerry's never been jealous of my dad. He told me once that he's sorry we lost him and grateful he got the chance to love my mom. He said life isn't fair, but it's the only one we've got, so we might as well make the best of it."

"Wise man," I commented. "Maybe I should start drinking kombucha and throwing pots."

"You're wise enough as you are," Forrest said. He shoved his hand in his pocket and looked down at me for a long moment. "Do you want to go for a walk?"

"Are there really cliffs?" I asked. I had seen the ocean in the distance but hadn't seen any cliffs through the trees.

"There really are," he said. "They're pretty cool, though we can't get too close. Come on, I'll show you."

I followed Forrest out the kitchen door. He led me to a path I hadn't noticed, winding between Emily's garden and a chicken coop.

"I'm sorry there wasn't any money," he said as we followed the trail.

"I don't care about the money," I said. I'd said it before, and I meant it, but not like this. I looked up into his beautiful golden hazel eyes. "The money isn't important. I can make my own money."

His eyes warmed, and I knew this time he believed me. Raising on my toes so I could reach, I clasped my hands to the sides of his face, pulling him down for a kiss. His lips, warm and soft, pressed to mine, his arms winding around to draw me close. I leaned back, and I told him the truest thing I knew.

"There was a prize at the end of your dad's codes," I said. "At least there was for me because I got you, and you're everything I want. I love you, Forrest. I loved you a year ago. I wouldn't have been so angry if I hadn't loved you."

"Sterling, I'm sorry—"

"Shhh," I said, putting a finger over his lips. "You're interrupting my moment. I know you're sorry. I know you won't lie to me again." I thought of my secret coding classes and added, "I won't lie to you either because I love you and I trust you, and I don't want to screw this up again."

"I love you too," he said, and this time I didn't break our kiss. Not until we were both breathless.

"Show me your cliffs," I said, feeling settled for the first time in forever. "And then we'll go back and really celebrate with your mom and Jerry." I took a step, but Forrest didn't follow.

He slid his hand into his pocket. "Sterling," he said. Then he shook his head. "I'll show you the cliffs."

"Okay," I agreed, wondering what he'd been about to say.

He pulled his hand from his pocket and twined his fingers with mine. "It's not far," he said.

We walked side by side down the neatly trimmed path. The woods ended abruptly, opening into a narrow field of waving grasses. Beyond the grass, the land just disappeared, a jagged edge at the end of the world, nothing but deep, navy ocean beyond.

"Oh my God," I said. "I've never seen anything like this before." The drama of it took my breath away. On my side of the continent, the ocean met the land with grace, one sliding into the other. I looked to my left and saw the ocean bashing itself against the stone of the cliffs, exploding in spray. It was feral, powerful, and absolutely gorgeous.

I took a step closer, then pulled back. We were fifty

feet away and plenty close enough. The land at the edge of the cliffs looked unstable, with overhangs of grass and dirt. From what I could tell, the base of the cliffs was lined with sharp rocks. It would take one misstep, and you'd never be seen again.

Forrest turned to me, his hand in his pocket again, the other raised to cup my chin, his eyes serious. "Sterling—"

"I hate to interrupt your romantic moment," came a voice from behind us. "But no— I really don't."

I looked over to see my brother Brax standing at the edge of the woods twenty feet away, a gun in his hand.

"What the fuck? Brax?" I said stupidly, my brain knocked out of gear.

"What are you doing in Oregon?" I heard Forrest say.

"I'm here for the money, you moron." Brax shook his head, scorn dripping from his words. "Here's the deal," he said and looked straight at me. "I know you found it. I saw you go rushing to the house with that book in your hand and then come out here looking all dopey and happy. I'll make you a deal. Give me the account number, and I'll go away. I know you won't miss me, and we both know Dad didn't leave us a goddamn thing. If those trust funds aren't empty now, Griffen will have cleaned them out by the time the will terms are up."

"No, he won't," I said without thinking. "Why would you say that?"

"Oh please, you're so trusting," Brax smirked at me. "I was going to say you're an idiot, but you're not, are you? You were smart enough to solve the codes. You just weren't smart enough to realize I was watching you the whole time."

"It was you who sent us to that root cellar," I said. Despite the circumstances, triumph swirled through me, giving me the guts to face him down over the barrel of that gun. "I knew it was you."

"Duh," Brax said with an exaggerated roll of his eyes. "Everyone else is so lovey-dovey these days. Family above everything. Fuck that." He tossed his golden hair off his forehead. "That's not how we were raised. Everyone's out for themselves. You, me, Griffen, Ford. All of us. Just like Dad was."

Was that really what he thought? I'd hated Brax for as long as I could remember. And still, that was just sad.

"No," I said, "we're not all out for ourselves. We're a family. You were there when I accused you of sending us to the root cellar, when we found my toys in your closet. Griffen stuck up for you because he loves you. Because you're his brother."

"Bullshit," Brax said. "How are you going to tell me everyone's not out for themselves? You're only with Powell here so you could get a cut of whatever his dad left because he couldn't find the money without you."

I shook my head but didn't bother to argue. I knew how wrong Brax was, and so did Forrest. That was what mattered.

Forrest stuck his hand in mine and squeezed. I kept my focus on Brax.

"Dad was always out for himself," he continued. "Ford screwed over his own brother to take his place. I figured Ford would help me get rid of you. But he went soft in prison." He rolled his eyes in disgust. "He told me you deserved better. Right. Whatever."

"Why couldn't you just leave me alone?" I asked. I never truly understood the reason for Brax's hatred. It wasn't like I was the only sibling. There were ten of us for him to despise. "Why do you hate me so much? We could have died in that root cellar."

I eyed the gun in his hand. I couldn't imagine he planned to pull the trigger. Waiting for us to die from hypothermia was a distant death, one he could tell himself was an accident, a tragic prank. Shooting us was murder. I didn't think Brax had that in him. Was the gun even real? He couldn't have flown out here with a real gun. Could he?

He laughed. "Yeah, I know. Crazy, right? I wasn't planning to kill you. Not then, at least. I just wanted to get you disinherited." He grinned with glee. "Banned from all Sawyer property, sent away. Banished." He paused again. "That would have been fucking fantastic."

"You were barely home anyway," I said. "Why did you care if I was around?"

"Because you—" He jabbed the gun in my direction.

I tried not to flinch, wanting to hear what came next, needing to know why.

"You took everything, and you weren't even a real Sawyer. You were the fucking bastard child of that slut, Trina. Bad enough that Dad flaunted her all over town. People were still talking about it even after she died. And then we got you," he said, venom dripping from his voice. "Such a perfect baby girl with your curls and your pink dresses. Mom loved you like you were her own. Always talking about what a little princess you were."

His voice was bitter now, filled with resentment and anger.

"So beautiful and so sweet," he continued in the same tone of voice. "Like you were better than me when you were trash, and no one but me could see it. And then you got older, and you were such a little shit. All the tantrums and drama, and still everyone loved you."

I shook my head. He could have been describing himself. He'd been Darcy's precious baby, her little prince. I was the only one who knew what an asshole he was. Everyone else had adored him when we were young. Apparently, not enough to stop him from hating me.

The gun shaking in his hand, he imitated a woman's voice, his face twisted in a sneer. "Brax, why can't you be nicer to Sterling? Brax, stop picking on Sterling." Back to his regular voice, he said, "Like you deserved more than me. Her attention. Her love. And she could never see what a stupid waste of—"

"That's enough," Forrest cut in, moving between me and Brax's gun.

Brax pivoted and leveled the gun on Forrest. I lunged forward, my only thought to get in between a bullet and Forrest, but Forrest's arm shot out like an iron bar, stopping me in place.

"Don't fucking move," he said through the side of his mouth.

I curled my fingers into the back of his shirt and tugged, stepping backward, pulling Forrest with me, an inch at a time. If we could get to the trees...

Chapter Thirty-Seven

STERLING

"Don't move," Brax warned us again, "or I'll pull this trigger and kill you both. Give me the account number."

Easing out from behind Forrest's protective stance, I asked again, "That's all you want?"

"I want a lot of things," Brax said. His eyes were cold now, devoid of any emotion. "Top of the list is to never see your face again." He paused, "So, I figure, give me the money, and I'll go. I'll take off, forfeit the rest of whatever my inheritance is, and none of you will ever see me again."

"If only it were that simple," I said. "There isn't any money, Brax."

"What the fuck do you mean? How—"

"We were all wrong," Forrest said. "It was a game. A puzzle he wanted me and my mother to solve. It was never about the money."

"I don't believe you," Brax said.

He looked at the gun he had pointed at us, his

eyebrows raising slightly as if he was surprised to see it in his hand. With a half shrug, he dropped his arm to his side.

"You know what's funny," he said in a conversational tone that seemed out of place, considering he'd just threatened to shoot us. "When I locked you in that root cellar, I wasn't trying to kill you. I just figured I could stick you down there long enough for you to violate the will, lose your inheritance, and get banished." He shrugged. "That seemed like enough of a prize to me. You know, just a step up from decapitating your Barbies."

The light in his eyes when he said that last part let me know he'd enjoyed every minute of tormenting me when I was a child.

"But then," he went on, "Griffen said you would have died of exposure. I thought it would bother me, the idea of killing you. I mean, you are my sister, technically. But it didn't. Not really. If anything, I was disappointed you didn't die. The money would be nice, but I do pretty well working for Sawyer Enterprises. If I can't have Alan Buckley's fortune," he smirked and raised the gun again, "then I might as well just get rid of you. A quick trip off the edge of the cliff and—boom—problem solved."

"You can't just shoot her," Forrest said, his voice filled with disbelief.

"Oh no," Brax said with a roll of his eyes, "I'm going to shoot both of you. Obviously." He raised his other hand and braced the pistol.

Forrest shifted as if planning to shove me behind him or out of the way. A crack sounded through the air. I lurched, my knees going out from under me. I didn't feel any pain, but would I? The movies always made it look like people got shot and didn't notice for a few seconds.

Forrest and I both hit the ground. I rolled to my knees, scanning myself and searching Forrest for a sign of injury.

There was nothing. Had Brax missed?

Frantic, I glanced over to see Brax wavering on his feet, his mouth open with an O of surprise, his eyes fixed on the edge of the woods. A bright red circle blooming on his chest, he fell to his knees with a thud and pitched forward, the gun spinning out of his hand to rest in the grass.

"Stay down," Forrest whispered.

Callum Leary strode from the woods, a gun in his hand very much like the one Brax had pointed at us a moment before.

"I was tired of listening to him talk," Callum said, coming to a stop in front of us. "Annoying little shit."

"Is he dead?" I asked, looking at Brax lying prone in the grass.

"If he's not, he will be soon enough," Callum said, sounding mostly disinterested in Brax.

I should have been scared of his bored tone. He'd shot my brother. But at that moment, I was just grateful he'd stopped Brax from killing us.

"Now that he's out of the way," Callum said, "I'll take the account numbers and any passwords your father left you. And given that I had to come all the way out here and save your life, I won't be cutting you in."

"There isn't any money," I said for what felt like the millionth time. "I wish there was, but—

"I heard the story you told the shithead." Callum's dark eyes studied Forrest, then me, as he processed what we'd said. Finally, he shook his head. "I'm not buying it. All this work, and it was a game? No way. I'm a businessman, so let's do business. You give me the money, and I let you keep your lives. I think that's fair."

"It would be," Forrest said, "if we had anything to give you."

"Try again," Callum said, closing the distance between us, lifting the pistol, and aiming at Forrest. "I'm going to count to three—"

"Don't bother," a new voice cut in.

My adrenaline was pumping so hard that I had a hard time processing what was going on. I strained my eyes. The voice was familiar, but I couldn't see behind me from my position on the ground.

"Who the fuck are you?" Callum demanded, shifting the gun to point at the newcomer.

I turned to see Emmett Blake standing behind us, a very big gun in his hand.

"Emmett?" I asked. "What are you... How..." I couldn't find the right words.

"He was tracking you, but he didn't know we were tracking him." Emmett raised one eyebrow a fraction at Callum. "You're good at leaving trackers. You might want to get better at looking for them."

"Fair." Callum Leary stepped back, dropping the gun to his side. "My men?" he asked Emmett.

"Neutralized," Emmett said simply.

"Meaning?" Callum pressed.

"Meaning they're alive, but they won't be able to help you."

Callum gave a short nod. "Then we'll talk later," he said to Forrest and me.

"No, you won't," Emmett cut in, his gun still trained on Callum. "They weren't lying. There isn't any money." Without taking his eyes off Callum, he continued. "We dug deep, and there's no record of any accounts created around the time Alan Buckley acquired the Vitellius. It looks like he may have reinvested the income from his first startup in one that failed a year later. There isn't anything to find. If you're smart, you'll go home and spread the word that the pot of gold at the end of the rainbow had chocolate coins. There's nothing for you here."

Callum shoved his hands in his pockets, his gaze resting on my face and then Forrest's for a moment before he shook his head and took a step back. "Well, this was a fucking waste of time."

"That's what you get when you go chasing legends," Emmett said evenly, his gun still aimed at Callum. "Sometimes you win, and sometimes you lose."

"Yeah, well," Callum nodded at Emmett, then turned to Forrest and me, "it's been fun."

"Not really," I said under my breath, watching his back as he headed to the woods.

Emmett, his eyes still trained on Callum, gave a signal to someone in the trees I couldn't see. He must have gotten a signal back because he lowered his gun and turned to us.

"You were following us from Atlanta?" I asked.

"Not at first," Emmett said. "But when we found out they were following you, we thought it was best. Turned out we were right."

"Thanks for saving our asses," Forrest said, helping me to my feet.

"Not a problem," was Emmett's response. He looked to me. "I owed you one."

"True enough," I agreed, remembering the day he kidnapped my sister. "Now we're even."

"That we are," he agreed. "For now."

I thought about the training he and Lucas had promised me. I couldn't think of a better reason to owe Emmett Blake. I started to smile until I caught sight of Brax, facedown in the grass. "Is he—?"

Emmett crouched beside him, pressing his fingers to Brax's neck. After a minute, he shook his head. "Ambulance is on the way, along with the police, but I don't feel a pulse."

I waited to feel something. Sorrow. Regret. Grief. All I felt was glad to be alive.

"The police?" Forrest asked. "Are my mom and Jerry okay? Did anyone—"

"Your mother and stepfather are fine. No one came near the house. My guys in the woods called the police and ambulance when Leary shot Brax. We got it on video. Callum Leary won't be back to bother you again."

I looked behind me, the waving grasses almost obscuring the view of Brax's body. All those years of mutilated Barbies, taunts and cruelties, and despite everything... "It didn't have to be this way," I said, "except he wouldn't let it be any other way."

Forrest's arm slid around my shoulders, his lips pressing to the top of my head. "He brought it on himself," he said quietly. "You couldn't have saved him."

"No," I said. "We'd better go explain to your mom why her place is going to be crawling with the police. Maybe she'll feel sorry for us and let us have some of that rhubarb pie."

"Sounds good to me," Forrest said with a nod at Emmett.

As we followed the path back through the woods, Emily and Jerry's house coming into view through the trees, I realized that all of us—all of us except Brax—could leave the past behind.

Forrest's father had dreamed of a future filled with love and adventure. He couldn't share that future with us, but we were still here, and we had each other. That future filled with love and adventure was waiting for us. Right after we explained everything to the police.

Epilogue

STERLING

"I love Saturdays," I said, rolling over in our bed in Heartstone Manor, my cheek pressed to Forrest's chest.

For the first time in my memory, everything was right in my world, and I was exactly where I wanted to be.

"Let's stay here all day," I said, letting out a contented sigh.

Forrest's hand came up to stroke down my hair, and he kissed the top of my head. "That works for me. It's been a busy few weeks."

He wasn't kidding. I was ready to take a break from being busy for a while. We'd stayed in Oregon with Emily and Jerry for almost a week, using as much of my time away as we could, considering the possibility of delayed flights. Oregon was a long way from North Carolina. It wasn't like we could jump in the rental car and drive back in a flash if our flight was canceled.

Emmett and the team he brought with him pretty much took care of the aftermath of Brax and Callum's attempts to claim Alan Buckley's fortune. Forrest and I talked to the police about Brax and what had happened, but they didn't really need us. They had Callum Leary in custody and some very high-definition video. We were only needed to substantiate the evidence they already had. The quest for the secrets of the Vitellius had been Callum's pet project. With him out of the picture, the rest of the Learys weren't interested in us.

I was trying to be sorry that Brax had died. Maybe it was callous to say all was right in my world when my brother had died right in front of me, but he'd been a real shithead of a brother and a crappy human being, cemented by his plan to shoot me and throw my body over the cliffs. It was hard to feel sorry he was gone.

Maybe someday, when the memory of the dark barrel of that gun pointed at my forehead had faded some, maybe then I'd feel bad. I wasn't there yet.

I could have stayed in Oregon for a lot longer than a week. Learning the truth about Forrest's father had bridged the distance between Forrest and Emily as nothing else could have. Seeing their relationship up close—the open affection, the way she was excited to hear every detail of his work at the inn, and most of all, the smile on her face when her son walked in the room—all of it was a revelation. I hadn't grown up with love like that. There'd been some love in our house thanks to Darcy and Miss Martha, but not enough. Not like that. Emily delighted in Forrest, and he had an easiness with Jerry that was sweet to see.

And on top of all of that, Emily seemed thrilled that her son and I were together. I'd never really thought about the parents of anyone I'd dated, maybe because I'd never taken my dates all that seriously. But where Emily was concerned, what she thought mattered.

I was in love with Forrest and didn't plan on being parted from him ever again if I could help it. If I got my way, someday, Emily would be my mother-in-law. I wanted that. I would have claimed Forrest even if his mother had been an evil witch, but I couldn't deny that I was thrilled she wasn't. I leaned into every hug, soaking in her maternal affection.

It wasn't hard to adore Emily. She was fun and loving and wise and weird in the coolest ways. She had full conversations with her goat, which seemed to be two-sided based on his head nods and vocal responses. She made vats of homemade yogurt and always had fresh sourdough bread. After Emmett saved us from Callum, we'd returned to the house, shaken by the scene on the cliffs. When she heard what happened to Brax, Emily pulled me close and rocked me from side to side, rubbing my back, saying, "Oh, you poor, sweet baby. Oh, you poor girl."

I wasn't ashamed to say I wept. A lot. I didn't think I'd ever had an embrace like that. Not since I was a toddler. While a part of me was a little homesick—Parker had been sending me pics of Shadow, who she swore missed me—a part of me wanted to stay, to sink into the rhythm of the little farm, eat sourdough toast and yogurt with fresh berries. To learn to throw pots and collect eggs from the chickens and get Emily's hugs three times a day. But home wasn't Oregon, and I had a wedding to plan back in Sawyers Bend. Forrest could handle a lot of his job remotely, but I could tell he was eager to get back to the inn. Emily and Jerry promised to visit Sawyers Bend in the fall for leaf season and the annual craft fair. Jerry was already making phone calls to potters in the area to tour their workshops.

We'd arrived back at Heartstone Manor to find a beautiful arbor in Quinn's clearing, with flowers and low bushes already planted around it. It was wider than I'd expected, with four sturdy posts and an arching roof of woven peeled branches. And because it was for Quinn, Hawk had added hammock hooks. I wouldn't be surprised to find Quinn's double hammock hung there now and then, the two of them cocooned away from the world.

The arbor was done, and Quinn had her ring. As far as Hawk was concerned, it was go time. Thanks to Tenn and Savannah's wedding, Griffen was ordained and could perform the ceremony. We briefly discussed waiting, given Brax's unexpected death. His body came home while Forrest and I were still in Oregon, and the rest of the family had a small service without us as soon as I'd assured them I didn't want to be there. All agreed that we could grieve Brax and still celebrate Quinn and Hawk's marriage. Everyone was just waiting on me.

Considering it was her wedding at stake, Quinn gave me the week off from work. I spent it grabbing anyone I could—mostly the kids since they had summer off, and Scarlett and Parker because they made their own schedules. Together, we decorated the clearing in a midsummer night's dream theme, fairy lights in the trees and flowers everywhere. I filled tin buckets with tulips and lined them up to create an aisle, hung lanterns from low branches, and draped swaths of tulle on the arbor.

Avery brought her nice event chairs over from the brewery, and Royal and Tenn connected me with the musicians they used at the inn to play violin for the ceremony and bluegrass for the party afterward. At Quinn and Hawk's request, Finn planned the barbeque to end all barbeques after the wedding, right in the clearing where we held the ceremony.

Fortunately, most of the guest list was already cleared by the security team. Quinn had a few local friends, plus Cooper and Alice Sinclair, Evers and Knox Sinclair, and their wives, Summer and Lily. Lucas came with his wife Charlie, who—exactly as he predicted—I hit it off with immediately. Emmett Blake came along with them.

Two days before the wedding, Parker had shown up when Quinn and I were going through some details on the flowers.

"I know you said you have a dress," she'd started, and Quinn rolled her eyes in friendly exasperation.

"I don't really care about the dress," Quinn said for the millionth time.

"I know," Parker said with her own eye roll. "And I love you and your endless supply of cargo pants, but you are not getting married in a sundress."

"It's a beautiful dress," Quinn protested, defending the cute white eyelet sundress I knew she loved.

"It is a very pretty dress," Parker agreed, "but you've worn it twenty times, and this is special."

Quinn leveled a look at Parker. "It's not the dress that makes it special."

Parker didn't credit that with a response. "I can return it if you don't like it," she said.

"What are you talking about?" Quinn asked.

Parker held up a translucent plastic bag that appeared to be filled with white tulle. "Help me out, Sterling," she said.

She lifted the hanger at the top of the bag, and I pulled up the plastic, revealing the dress that was so perfectly Quinn, my eyes teared with joy for her. Light layers of tulle floated from the bodice to the floor. This wasn't a princess's gown. It was fit for the fairy queen Quinn was at heart.

The straps were the width of my thumb and held up a structured bodice made from layers of white tulle, covered with a confection of appliqué vines and flowers that concentrated on the bodice and flowed down the skirts. It was light and fresh and would move around her like a cloud.

I glanced over to see Quinn staring at the dress, her eyes shining.

"Okay," she breathed. "You were right."

"I know," Parker said with a smile. "Let's go try it on and make sure it fits. You don't have much time for alterations."

It fit almost perfectly. Parker put in a pin or two where it was needed and took the dress back, promising to have it ready for Quinn's wedding.

And that was that. We were pretty much done.

I'd seen a lot of weddings in the last year. In some ways, Quinn's was the most low-key. But of all the weddings, this one was the most magical. For one thing, it was the only one that took place in the woods. Early evening on their wedding day, with the sun just beginning to set, Griffen walked Quinn down the aisle to Hawk, standing in the arbor, Quinn's dog Ginger at his side. Leo had been left in the gatehouse for the wedding, as he was most decidedly an indoor cat.

The ceremony itself was short. I didn't remember most of the words, fully absorbed by the incandescent joy on Quinn's face, the matching expression on Hawk's as they said, "I do," the clearing just beginning to light up with the warm glow of fireflies. They walked back down the aisle under a cloud of rose petals and let me drag them off for a few wedding pics before the musicians switched from classical to bluegrass, and the party really got started. As the sun sank below the mountains and the fairy lights blinked on, we feasted on barbeque, and I danced with Forrest under the moon until Quinn and Hawk snuck off into the woods for their wedding night.

They'd decided to postpone their honeymoon for the winter when Quinn's business would be at its slowest, and they could spend two weeks in the cabin where they'd fallen in love. For now, they were taking a long weekend in the mountains, just the two of them and their huge backpacks. Not my idea of a honeymoon, but Quinn and Hawk's idea of heaven.

It had only been a few days since the wedding, and I'd been doing a lot of thinking. There was nothing like a death followed by a wedding to start me down the path of reevaluating my choices. Endings and beginnings. Full circle. My life story thus far was a long list of bad decisions and wrong turns. I could blame my father's crappy parenting and my own lack of direction, but it didn't matter who was to blame. That part of my life was over. I knew who I was now. I loved and was loved. I knew what I wanted and where I wanted to go. And so much of that revolved around the man lying beside me.

My head had been so busy lately, not just with the wedding but with my own plans. There were so many ways to ask for what I wanted. I rolled to my side in bed on that lazy Saturday and looked up into Forrest's warm hazel eyes, rich with gold in the morning light.

He smiled down at me, lifting his palm to press to my cheek, his fingers sliding into my hair. "I love you," he said.

I smiled, and just then, I knew exactly what my next step needed to be. Sometimes, simple was best.

"Marry me," I said.

Adorably, his eyes flew wide open, and he stuttered, "W-what?"

"Marry me," I said again and grinned. "Or rather," I rephrased, "would you please marry me, Forrest Powell?"

He grinned back, his eyes bright. But instead of answering me immediately, he rolled away from me to face his side of the bed, opened and shut a drawer, then rolled back, light flashing from what was in his hand.

It was perfect. We were perfect.

"I was going to give this to you that day on the cliffs," he said. "But after everything that happened, it didn't seem like the right moment. And then we got back, and Quinn and Hawk were getting married, and it felt better to let them have their time. Now that they're married, I planned to try again, but you beat me to it." He lifted my hand and slid the ring on my finger. "Yes, Sterling Sawyer, I would love nothing more than to marry you."

A tear welled in my eye and skated down my cheek. I leaned up to press a kiss to Forrest's mouth, lingering, my heart so full I couldn't catch my breath. Pulling back, I looked down at the ring on my finger. A generous emerald-cut diamond on a gold band, it could have been plain, but for the size—a touch bigger than it needed to be—and the fire inside the stone. The diamond was the highest quality I'd ever seen, cut so every facet caught the light.

"It's so beautiful." I tilted my hand and watched it turn the morning light into spears of rainbow. "Where did you find it?"

"It was my mother's," Forrest said. "It's the ring my father gave her. She gave it to me for you. If you want something else, that's okay."

My heart swelled, so much I thought it would burst. "No, I love it. It's gorgeous." I splayed my hand on his bare chest, admiring the picture it made. "Emmett said your father was frugal, but clearly not when it came to this diamond."

It was exactly what I would have chosen myself. Big, but not obnoxiously so, and elegant through and through.

"Your mom really gave you her ring?" I asked. "For me?" That was huge, at least to me—to know that Emily wanted me as a daughter-in-law enough to give me a ring she must have treasured.

"Yeah," he said, his voice gruff. "She knew I was going to ask."

I loved that he'd been thinking about it for a while, too.

"She's a smart lady, your mom," I said.

"Yeah, she is. Now we have something to celebrate." He closed his hands around my upper arms and tugged me to lie over his chest, bringing my mouth even with his own. He kissed me, his lips lingering until I sighed.

"I love you so much, Forrest," I said as he rolled me to my back, and we celebrated our engagement. Thoroughly.

After, Forrest swore he didn't tell Savannah a thing, and I knew I hadn't, but somehow she and Finn had figured it out. By the time I made it to the kitchens to show off my gorgeous ring, Finn was already baking my favorite layered coconut cake in celebration.

Dinner that night was an impromptu engagement party. My heart squeezed just a fraction as I remembered Hawk and Quinn's engagement dinner only a few weeks before. This time, no one looked annoyed at me or otherwise. Ford sat at the end of the table opposite Brax's empty seat, a faint smile on his lips, his eyes avoiding the space where Brax should be. I grieved the brother Brax could have been, but it was hard to miss the man he'd chosen to be. I wasn't planning to waste a lot of time grieving my would-be murderer.

Forrest and I wanted to take our time setting a wedding date. For one, I couldn't decide what I wanted. When it came to the event itself, Forrest claimed not to have an opinion, saying he simply wanted me to be his wife and getting there was up to me. I wasn't sure that was entirely true, but I'd find out once I got to planning. First, I had to figure out what kind of wedding I had in mind.

If I wanted to marry him anytime soon, it would have to be something small. I already knew Hawk would kill me himself if I tried to throw a big bash. The security for something like that would be a nightmare.

So, I could wait and hope we managed to catch my father's killer and eliminate the threat against our family, or I could get married soon and have a small family wedding like everyone else had.

I was impatient to take the next step, to say the hell with it, find myself a beautiful dress, and throw my own wedding at Heartstone Manor. It was certainly a grand location, and I knew I could make it beautiful. It didn't hurt that all my favorite people were already allowed on the estate. But I thought I wanted more than that, and we weren't in a rush.

We went back to normal life, a new normal, one we'd never had before. I worked for Quinn, handling the office and helping her organize clients for hiking or fishing trips. Then, as soon as they were on their way and it was quiet again, I'd pull out my laptop and get back to my coding classes. I emailed Emmett when I had questions, especially once I started the cybersecurity unit, and found I had a million of them, every answer leading to more questions. It was fascinating.

One night, I asked Forrest what we would do if I actually got a job at Sinclair Security. He just kissed me and said we'd figure it out. "There are hotels in Atlanta. It's all an adventure as long as I'm with you."

Everything would have been perfect except for my dreams. They started not long after Forrest slid his mother's ring on my finger. Near nightly, I had dreams of sitting in Emily's bedroom watching her peel back the endpapers on the book of Rumi's love poems. Dreams of the letter Forrest's father had written him. I didn't understand what I was so focused on.

The letter was a beautiful, heartfelt message of hope and love to his family, but why was it haunting me? Was I captured by the idea of a father loving his wife and child that much? Maybe. It had made an impression on me, but one worthy of repeated dreams? The last time I dreamed of something like this, it had been the Vitellius invading my sleep night after night until I remembered the secret panel.

I woke one morning, a little over a month after we got engaged, unable to shake my dream from the night before. It had been particularly vivid. Maybe because we'd spent a good part of the day packing up things of Forrest's, dividing them into belongings he was bringing to Heartstone and things he'd put into storage. We didn't want to be apart, and I couldn't leave the Manor, so he was going to keep his house and rent it out. He loved it, and so did I, so once the terms of the will were up, we could move in together there. But for now, it wasn't hard to find good tenants in our area. Plenty of people wanted to move to our idyllic town and were looking for rentals before they bought something.

We'd gone through a box packed with things of his father's. Random items like binoculars and an old fountain pen; the kind of things a young boy would have held on to, to remember his father. In my dream, I'd been sitting on the bed next to Emily, the binoculars pressed to my forehead. Allen Buckley's handwriting had been undulating in my vision, words popping off the page to disappear and reappear.

It bugged me all through breakfast until, finally, I turned to Forrest and said, "Do you have the letter? The letter your dad left?"

"I do," he said. "My mom gave it to me. She thought I should have it."

"Can I see it?" I asked. "I keep dreaming about it." I shook my head and made a twirly motion with my pointer finger at my brain.

Forrest went still, his eyes narrowing. "What are you dreaming?" Before I could answer, he said, "Let's go look at it."

We left the breakfast table to head straight up to my room.

Forrest took it from his briefcase and handed it to me, separating out the itinerary of the trip that had been folded with it.

I sat at my desk, aiming the lamp at the page. "Do we have your magnifying glass?" I asked.

"Yeah. Hold on. I think I know what box it's in." Forrest found it after a minute and handed it to me.

I held it over the letter, moving it in and out, making the words change in size from small to huge as they had in my dream. I didn't even know what I was looking for. This was probably a waste of my time, but the picture in my head wouldn't go away, like a puzzle that needed to be solved.

I spent another minute or so and sighed to myself. There was no puzzle here. There was only Allen Buckley's handwriting. His words were a combination of print and cursive, all of it angular, the strokes of his pen bold and strong.

Then, something caught my eye. I leaned in until my nose was almost touching the page, squinting at the letters.

Some of the print letters were randomly capitalized.

It was done so smoothly that they blended with the rest. It was possible it was simply his natural pattern. I didn't have another handwriting sample for comparison. But in some spots, the capitals didn't quite match the rest of his handwriting.

I could feel the excitement build and warned myself not to jump to conclusions. Until I had firm proof, I had to proceed methodically. I pulled a notepad from my desk and began to list the printed capital letters, one after the other. It didn't take long before I said, "Forrest."

I didn't need to get his attention. He was already leaning over my shoulder, watching my progress. "Those aren't random letters," he said.

anD

Always

Would

Success

ON

triP

OuR

Thank

mE

Rewarded

"Dawson Porter," Forrest read, already typing it into

his phone. He stared at the screen, turning it to me after a long pause.

The top search listing read *Dawson & Porter, specializing in wills, estates, and trusts.* An Atlanta address was listed below.

Forrest looked at me, his eyes wide with wonder and a shade of panic.

Holy shit.

"Your mom never found the money," I said. "Call them."

He clicked the number on the screen of his phone and turned on the speaker.

A moment later, an efficient female voice said, "Dawson & Porter, how may I direct your call?"

Forrest said, "My name is Forrest Powell. My father was Alan Buckley. He passed away a long time ago, but I have reason to believe he may have had business with your firm that his family was unaware of."

"One moment," the receptionist said.

Classical music played as we were put on hold. We waited, eyes locked on each other, not speaking, not breathing, not moving. It felt like a million years passed before a new voice interrupted the music, this one older, male, with the strong cadence of Georgia.

"Forrest Powell, formerly Buck Buckley. The last time I saw you, you didn't come up farther than my knee. I've been waiting a long time for this call. I'm William Dawson. In addition to being a client, your father was a friend."

Forrest shook his head, though William couldn't see

him. "I'm sorry," Forrest said. "I don't remember you. All of this is a surprise. Do you know why I'm calling?"

"I think I do, but you're going to have to tell me," William said.

I glanced at Forrest. The riddles continued. What was Forrest supposed to say?

"I—we, my fiancée and I—have been working on the clues my dad left behind. My mother was with us when we found a letter he left. We thought that was it, but then my fiancée saw the code in the letter and the name of your firm—" Forrest fell silent.

William was quiet just long enough for me to wonder if that would be enough, or if there was some other clue we needed to find.

Finally, he said, "Well done. I'm sorry I couldn't contact you after your father died. The terms of the trust are very specific. I'm only able to release information to you once you contacted me. Now that you have, I'll need you and your mother to come to the office in person so we can verify your identity. Then we can go over the details."

"Details?" Forrest asked, his voice hesitant, as if he couldn't quite digest what was happening.

"Yes, the trust your father left is a bit complex. We'll need you to bring more than one form of ID and..." He listed acceptable forms of ID and dove into some of the legalities and limitations.

I didn't register any of it. I wasn't sure Forrest did either.

As if sensing our distraction, William said, "We'll go

over the specifics when you can come to the office." He cleared his throat. "You should know, the amount your father put in trust seventeen years ago was substantial. In the intervening years, thanks to our good stewardship and healthy financial markets, it's grown to an amount that is..." He paused, clearly unwilling to give us a number over the phone. "Quite a bit more than just substantial." He cleared his throat again. "But as I said, we'll go over the details when you're here. I look forward to seeing you then."

"Sounds good," Forrest said. "I'll speak with my mother and make arrangements from there. Thank you, William."

"You're very welcome. As I said, I've been waiting a lot of years for this call. I look forward to meeting you again. Goodbye, Forrest."

The call ended, and Forrest and I stared at each other in disbelief.

"You did it," he said.

I shook my head. "We did it. We did it!"

"I wonder what twenty-five percent of 'more than substantial' comes to," he said with a raised eyebrow.

I held up my left hand, admiring my ring. "I think I have my share right here," I teased. "You and your mom can have the rest."

"My future wife is too generous." Forrest stood, pulling me to my feet and drawing me into a quick waltz around our room.

I laughed, tipping my head back, dipping low as he swung me down then up into a twirl. "I don't need the money," I said, reaching up to frame his face in my hands.

"I already have everything I need right here." Forrest's mouth met mine in a long, slow kiss.

It was a while before we managed to call Emily and let her in on the big news, but I thought she'd understand.

When I'd woken that morning, all those weeks ago, knowing I could solve Alan Buckley's code, the money was all I cared about. Now, it was nothing next to the true prize at the end of Alan's scavenger hunt. I'd found so much more than Alan's lost fortune.

I'd found a prize without price.

Love.

TURN THE PAGE FOR A SNEAK PEEK OF RECKLESS HEART,
BOOK EIGHT OF THE HEARTS OF SAWYERS BEND

Reckless Heart

SNEEK PEAK

CHAPTER ONE

AVERY

My small, cluttered office didn't feel like the place to have a serious meeting, but I couldn't think of another option. I sure as hell wasn't going to do it in front of my employees. Definitely not in the taproom where anyone could walk in. This time of the morning, we were unlikely to have a crowd, but in a tourist town, you never know. There were a lot of reasons people visited Sawyers Bend, and the active foodie and brewery culture in the area was at the top of the list. I'd had more than one group stop in for a breakfast beer.

I was stressing about the location of the meeting because I didn't want to think about the reason we were having it in the first place. I mentally reviewed my arguments, hating that my mouth was bone dry and my heart thudded in my chest. Why should I be nervous? I'd fired more than a few employees since I'd started my brewery. Why was this one any different?

Because it was. Hiring Matthew was arguably the worst mistake I'd ever made, both as a woman and as a business owner. He had to go. It had taken me far too long to reach that conclusion, and my gut told me he wasn't going to go quietly, hence the dry mouth and pounding heartbeat.

The pen I fiddled with shot out from between my fingers, rolling across the desk to fall on the floor, and I added sweaty palms to the mix along with my dry mouth and thudding heart.

"Fuck, Avery, get your shit together," I told myself. "Everybody messes up. Time to clean up and move on."

Firing Matthew was the right thing to do. My gut knew it. My head knew it. So why was I dreading saying the words? I couldn't answer that question, and as knuckles rapped on the doorframe, I knew I was out of time.

I looked up to see Matthew's familiar, charming smile spread from ear to ear, a shock of his golden blond hair falling in his eyes.

"What's up, boss?" he said, folding his lanky frame into the chair beside my desk. "I was just about to head out to the orchard to go over plans for the Halloween party. The new fall brew is going to make a splash. It's fantastic. We make magic together."

He winked, and my stomach squeezed, reminding me exactly why I was firing Matthew. We hadn't developed the recipe together unless you counted his standing behind me, second-guessing every choice I made as collaboration, which Matthew did. As far as I could see, his presence had only served to get in my way until he could take credit once the job was done. And I was pretty damn sure that if the new recipe wasn't as amazing as we thought it would be, he would quietly slide into the shadows, leaving me to take the blame. Because that was how Matthew worked.

I'd finally reached the point where I could recognize the formula. Step one: Compliment me enough to get me excited so I'd work my ass off. Step two: Swoop in and take the credit. But this was my brewery. My work. And I was done letting him manipulate me.

"Matthew," I said, threading my fingers together and resting my hands in my lap. "I appreciate everything you've done here at Sawyers Bend Brewing, but I think it's time we part ways."

I expected shock and anger. I expected rage, even. I was prepared for it. I didn't expect Matthew to fold his arms over his chest and lean back in the chair, giving me a gentle, condescending smile.

"Ave, baby, I think you were right to break things off between us. At least for now. I haven't given up completely." He winked. How had I ever found this man charming? "But you can't deny that I'm a hell of a brewmaster, and I've made all the difference around here."

A spurt of rage burned through my chest, firing hotter as I had to concede and recognize he wasn't wrong. Not entirely. He was a great brewmaster. I'd learned from him, and Sawyers Bend Brewing was better for his tenure here. But that wasn't the whole story. Being good at his job wasn't enough.

I tried for a professional smile. I could guess from his expression that what I managed was more of a stretch of my lips over gritted teeth. "Matthew, you're an excellent brewmaster. But at the end of the day, I don't think our visions match. I think you'd be happier somewhere bigger."

Matthew shook his head and tried again. "Ave, sweetheart—"

His use of my nickname grated. "My name is Avery, and I'm not your sweetheart. Do I need to point out that this is part of the problem?"

He gave a confused shake of his head, and I didn't know if he was being obstinate or he just didn't get it. I had a feeling it was door number two, which didn't say a lot about my taste in men. I was pretty sure he had no idea what a dick he was. How could he when he had so much to offer? Brewing expertise and orgasms—what more could a woman want? How about mutual respect or letting me run my own goddamn business rather than coming in once I'd gotten some traction and trying to take over the whole place?

I'd had such high hopes when I hired Matthew. He had the kind of experience I needed to take the next step in the world of craft brewing. Sawyers Bend Brewing had been barely more than a hobby back then. I'd been able to cover expenses only because my brother Ford had strong-armed our father into cutting me a break on the rent. I'd hired my first employee a few months before I took the leap and brought in Matthew as brewmaster.

I could see now that I'd hired him because I'd been terrified I'd fail. And failure wasn't an option. Not in our family. And so, when the self-proclaimed god of brewing had chosen me, I'd said yes. Even then, there were red flags. Ones I should have paid attention to.

If I were being honest, deep down, I knew it was taking every ounce of earned confidence in myself to take this step today. I could do this on my own. I didn't need him.

Even now, we still worked in small batches and served a local market. I created the recipes, worked with artists on the labels, and ran the bottling machine. I had a hand in every aspect of the business. I didn't care how much expertise Matthew had. He wasn't taking any of it from me.

He'd been great at first. A team player eager to help me expand my reach. The change had started slowly. A lingering hand on my shoulder or one of those flirty winks. Late nights talking beer and strategy. My hormones had gotten the better of my business sense. I'd been going through an endless dry spell.

Running my own place on a shoestring budget didn't leave me much time for socializing, and I had a strict policy about hooking up inside the industry. The brewers in the area had created a strong community, including places smaller than mine all the way up to national corporations. In this world, being a Sawyer wasn't an asset, not when I was also a woman in a traditionally male-dominated field. The last thing I needed was a messy romantic relationship to get in my way. But the first time Matthew kissed me, standing right here in this office, I'd given in to the flash of lust. For a while, things had been great. We'd run the brewery together. It had felt like a partnership. Things had been good in bed and great at work.

And then, little by little, Matthew started taking over. I hadn't noticed at first. He'd encouraged me to focus on recipe development and let him handle little details and small tasks until, eventually, it was Matthew representing the brewery while I was quietly in the background, working my ass off and getting none of the credit. Slowly, the suspicion had grown that Matthew didn't want me, he wanted my brewery.

On top of that humiliating realization, it had occurred to me that while we worked well together, I didn't really like being with him that much. To be fair, the sex was pretty good—a hell of a lot better than no sex at all—but it wasn't life-changing. And neither was Matthew. He was an asset to the brewery, but as a person, he was boring. All he could talk about was himself. What Matthew wanted, what Matthew thought. He wasn't interested in being a partner. What he really wanted was an audience.

A month ago, I'd ended our personal relationship. He'd taken that so well it had confirmed that his real interest lay in Sawyers Bend Brewing. Once orgasms were off the table, my vision cleared, and I realized that Matthew's skills as a brewmaster weren't enough to put up with the rest.

"You know we make a great team," Matthew said, bringing me back to the conversation. "I can't leave you on your own, Avery. This place will fall apart."

The soothing tone in his voice had my hand itching to fly up and smack the smug expression from his face.

"I was hanging in there before you showed up, Matt. I'll make it work without you," I said, managing to keep the fury out of my voice.

"You won't be able to hire another brewmaster with my experience," he said, shaking his head. "Not with what you're willing to pay."

"Probably not," I agreed with a hint of a smile. "One of the things I've realized over the last year is that I miss being the brewmaster."

Matthew scoffed. "Avery, you were barely making it before I showed up." He leaned forward, bracing his elbows on his knees, his expression so sincere I knew he believed what he was saying, which only made it that much more infuriating. "You could be so much more than a small-time brewer. You have so much talent. You have an instinct for the process, for flavor and timing that's unique and can't be taught, but you just need guidance. With my help, you can be so much more."

"I don't want to be more." My chest burned a little as I spoke the lie. I did want to be more. I just didn't want the more Matthew envisioned.

I'd known this was over the day he let it slip that his long-term plan was to build up Sawyers Bend Brewing to sell to a multi-national. Hell no. Not happening. Did I want to reach more beer lovers with my craft brews? Abso-fucking-lutely. Could I create great beers? I had no doubt. But this was my place. I hadn't built it up from nothing so I could sell out and let a conglomerate slap my logo on their beer in exchange for a fat check.

"Like I said, Matt, I think we have different visions for Sawyers Bend Brewing. I'm sure you won't have any trouble finding a spot somewhere else." Matthew had a good reputation in the industry, and he wasn't short on employment options in this area of the country. Between Western North Carolina, Georgia, and Tennessee, there were plenty of breweries who would love to get their hands on him. They were welcome to him. I was done.

He studied my face, his features gradually hardening as he finally read my resolve, and he understood he wasn't going to be able to get his way. The friendly expression in his eyes flicked off as his gaze chilled.

"You're going to regret this," he said, his voice low and hard.

I raised an eyebrow as my shoulders relaxed. "Really? That's what you're going with? I'm going to regret this?" I let out a sigh. "Maybe I will. But I won't know until I do it." I stood, ready for Matthew to exit my brewery and my life.

He rose from the chair, stepping closer, looming over me. "Don't expect me to come back and save your ass when this place goes under," he said.

I gestured to the door. "Thanks for your concern," I said dryly. "I'll be okay. I appreciate everything I learned from you, but it's time for you to move on. If I regret it, that'll be mine to live with."

"I've invested too much in this place to walk away," he protested, refusing to back up when I stepped forward, trying to urge him to the door. A frisson of alarm skittered down my spine. Was he going to attack me? Would he dare? I had two part-time employees in today, and neither were close enough to hear if I called out.

"You've invested your time for which you were

compensated," I said, keeping my eyes locked on his. "I'm not going to change my mind."

Cold fury flashed across his face before a vaguely genial expression took its place. The ease at which he hid his true feelings was spooky and made me even more sure this was the right move. He shoved his hands in his pockets and shook his head.

"I made you what you are, Avery. Without me, you're nothing. One way or another, you're going to pay for this." He turned and strode through the door.

As much as I wanted to let him make a dramatic exit and then never see him again, practicality had me trailing him as he left, crossing from my office to the other side of the warehouse-style building that housed the brewery, stopping only to grab his wallet, keys, and jacket as he went. The heavy metal door slammed behind him.

Letting out a long, slow breath, I tried to shake off my unease. The hard part was over. Matthew was gone, and I was free to start a new chapter as a brewer. I was ready for this. I didn't need Matthew.

I looked around the brewery, drawing in the smell of hops and malt. This was my home. The invader had been tossed out. All was right in my world. Wasn't it?

Sure, it was, I told myself. It had to be.

Shaking off my unsettled mood, I ran down a list of things I had planned for the day. I needed to check in with the orchard we were co-hosting the annual Halloween party with. Verify the delivery estimates for the new labels. Sweet talk Hank from the hardware store into installing new locks now that Matt was gone. Call my local hops supplier and see if he could increase my usual order. And when that was all done, I'd man the taps until Cammie showed up to cover the taps until close.

I expected phone calls or texts as word got around about me firing Matt, but my phone stayed silent. Customers came in, drank beer, left with a six-pack or some merch. I met a sweet, retired couple from Michigan and a nice group of guys making the rounds of local breweries for their bachelor party.

None of it helped change my mood.

When the taproom was quiet, I stepped into the small kitchen space adjacent to the bar. It had been there when I'd moved in. So far, I'd used it only for tinkering with smaller recipes I wasn't ready to brew at scale. It wasn't much bigger than the inside of a food truck, but my brother Finn, a classically trained chef, was looking for an occasional workspace. His main job at the moment was head chef at Heartstone Manor, our family home. He claimed he was happy feeding his family, glad to enjoy life with his new wife and son, away from the rat race of cooking in a high-pressure kitchen. But he'd been toying with the idea of doing some pop-ups here and there. He said he missed feeding people on a bigger scale, but he wasn't ready to start his own place.

I wasn't looking to turn Sawyers Bend Brewing into a restaurant, but I thought my little kitchen off the taproom might be the answer to Finn's itch to cook for the public and also level up the Brewery itself. I knew if word got out Finn was cooking, the place would be packed. I wasn't averse to the increase in sales that would lead to. I had bills to pay, and this felt like a win-win. Matthew had hated the idea. I think he'd worried Finn would take over his territory.

Making a note that the small kitchen needed a thorough cleaning before Finn could use it, I got back to my to-do list. Work had always been my cure for everything that ailed. But by the time Cammie showed up, I was a ball of nerves, jumping every time the door opened. I thought once the confrontation with Matthew was over, my anxiety would dissipate. I'd done the hard thing. What was there to be nervous about?

Instead, it only got worse. I drove home to Heartstone Manor, wishing that my father hadn't left behind a complicated will that had forced me to move back into the Manor if I wanted to keep my business. I loved my family—a surprise after so many years of keeping them at a distance—but I missed the days when I'd occupied the tiny living quarters adjacent to the brewery. The rooms had been tacked on as an afterthought. Drafty in the winter and hot in the summer, they were spare and tiny, but they'd been mine.

"I just need a good night's sleep," I said aloud as I drove through the iron gates to the Manor, waving at the security camera tracking my arrival. "I'll shake off the day and start fresh tomorrow."

I WOKE EARLY, SKIPPING BREAKFAST TO HEAD BACK to the brewery, eager to take back the reins of my business. Sleep had helped, but I was still feeling off.

Pulling my car into my usual parking space at the side of the building, I sat for a second, something tugging at me. Something hadn't been right about the brewery, but I couldn't pin down what it was. Getting out of the car, I locked the door, and instead of heading to the big metal door into the brewery, I walked to the front, scanning the building for whatever had tweaked me as I'd driven in. The small parking lot was empty, as it should have been at this hour, the pumpkin display I'd arranged still beside the door to the taproom. The open door to the taproom.

I reached out to push it all the way open and stopped cold—my hand dropping to my side.

Cammie wouldn't have forgotten to close and lock the door. She never did. And she and I were the only two with the keys to the new locks I'd had installed yesterday.

Which meant that no matter how much I needed to see what was waiting inside, I wasn't going in by myself. I was headstrong, not stupid.

I pulled my phone from my pocket, scrolled through the contacts, and hit the one I was looking for.

ARE YOU READY FOR AVERY & WEST'S STORY?

Visit IvyLayne.com/RecklessHeart

to see what happens next!

Never Miss a New Release:

Join Ivy's Reader's Group

@ ivylayne.com/readers

&

Get two books for free!

About Ivy Layne

Ivy Layne has had her nose stuck in a book since she first learned to decipher the English language. Sometime in her early teens, she stumbled across her first Romance, and the die was cast. Though she pretended to pay attention to her creative writing professors, she dreamed of writing steamy romance instead of literary fiction. These days, she's neck deep in alpha heroes and the smart, sexy women who love them.

Married to her very own alpha hero (who rubs her back after a long day of typing, but also leaves his socks on the floor). Ivy lives in the mountains of North Carolina where she and her other half are having a blast raising two energetic boys. Aside from her family, Ivy's greatest loves are coffee and chocolate, preferably together.

For More Information:
www.ivylayne.com
books@ivylayne.com
Facebook.com/AuthorIvyLayne
Instagram.com/authorivylayne/

Also by Ivy Layne

Don't Miss Out on New Releases, Exclusive Giveaways, and More!!

Join Ivy's Readers Group @ ivylayne.com/readers

THE HEARTS OF SAWYERS BEND

Stolen Heart

Sweet Heart

Scheming Heart

Rebel Heart

Wicked Heart

Wild Heart

Broken Heart

Reckless Heart

THE UNTANGLED SERIES

Unraveled

Undone

Uncovered

THE WINTERS SAGA

The Billionaire's Secret Heart (Novella)

The Billionaire's Secret Love (Novella)

The Billionaire's Pet

The Billionaire's Promise

The Rebel Billionaire

The Billionaire's Secret Kiss (Novella)

The Billionaire's Angel

Engaging the Billionaire

Compromising the Billionaire

The Counterfeit Billionaire

THE BILLIONAIRE CLUB

The Wedding Rescue

The Courtship Maneuver

The Temptation Trap

Made in the USA
Monee, IL
13 January 2025

76760395R00213